MW01037673

THE

UNANNOUNCED

CHRISTMAS

VISITOR

An award-winning novel by

Patrick Higgins

THE UNANNOUNCED CHRISTMAS VISITOR

COPYRIGHT © 2014 FOR HIS GLORY PRODUCTION COMPANY

**2018 READERS' CHOICE GOLD MEDAL
AWARD WINNER IN CHRISTIAN FICTION**

**2016 IPA GOLD MEDAL AWARD WINNER
(INTERNATIONAL PUBLISHER AWARDS)**

All rights reserved under International and Pan-American copyright conventions. No part of this book may be reproduced, stored in a retrieval system, or transmitted in any form, electronic, mechanical, or other means, now known or hereafter, without written permission of the author. Address all inquiries to the author.

All scripture quotations are taken from the Holy Bible, English Standard Version (ESV) © 2001 by Crossway Bibles, a publishing ministry of Good News Publishers.
Library of Congress
Cataloging in Publication Data
ISBN 978-0-9658978-0-8

Published by:
www.ForHisGloryProductionCompany.com

Publisher's note: This is a work of fiction. All names, characters, organizations, and incidents portrayed in this novel are the product of the author's imagination or are used fictitiously. Any resemblance to actual persons, living or dead, events or locales is entirely coincidental.

Manufactured in the United States of America.

This story was inspired in part by the Christian feeding ministry
Jesus Loves You, Love Him Back
based in Orlando, Florida.

This book is dedicated to the founder of this magnificent Christ-centered outreach group, who just happens to be my twin brother, Michael Higgins. When I see how mightily God is using him, I can only rejoice. I pray that our Heavenly Father will keep opening doors for him that no man can shut, despite whatever forces may come against him. With God's continued blessing, the positive impact his feeding ministry will have on the Sunshine State, and beyond, will only increase.

I also need to express my heartfelt thanks and gratitude to the late Bhrett Black, for all he did over the years for *Jesus Loves You, Love Him Back,* most of which was done out of the spotlight.

It was both refreshing and inspiring to witness his many selfless acts of charity and kindness when the ministry needed it most. I miss you, brother, and look forward to seeing you again on the other side, the Good side.

There are many soldiers involved with this growing organization, from the many humble volunteers who come to feed, to the praise and worship leaders from various churches in the community to the pastors sharing God's Word before meals are served. Many of these volunteers I do not know.

Nevertheless, I feel the need to mention some I do know for what they do each week to help move this ministry forward. I will list them in alphabetical order: Kevin Atchoo, Raul and Celimar Freijo, Dave Hook, Kevin Kozial, David and Rose McNeilly, Joshua Mendez, Gilbert Montez, Jeff and Renee Parker, Roger and Cathy Throneburg, Richard and Noah Viera, Michael Ward and Steve Westcomb.

To the parents who bring their children to these weekly feedings—Gilbert Montez topping this list—may God continue to richly bless you all for it. What awesome life-lessons they are learning by simply observing and participating! God is using this humble setting to better prepare and equip your children to be the next generation of mighty warriors for His glory.

After receiving their 501c3 early in 2014, they now feed the homeless once a month in Jacksonville, Daytona Beach, Cocoa Beach,Tampa, St. Petersburg, Sarasota and Miami Florida. They have also done feedings in Philadelphia, PA., New York City, New Orleans, LA. Nashville, TN. Chicago, IL., Las Vegas, NV, Los Angeles, CA., Cancun, Mexico, various locations in Brazil and the Philippines.

To donate money, clothing or anything worthy of resale:
www.JesusLovesYouLoveHimBack.org

3

1

ANYWHERE USA - PRESENT DAY - 3 WEEKS BEFORE CHRISTMAS

"WHO'S THAT MAN?" LYDIA Jensen whispered softly to her husband.

"What man?" John Jensen replied, half-heartedly. His face was glued to his phone screen, thumbs ramming keys, firing off text messages to whomever. He was too focused, as always, skimming through dozens of unread messages from earlier in the week to pry his squinty eyes away from his mobile device for even a second.

"That man over there," Lydia said, pointing in the man's direction off to her right.

The Jensens were seated in the seventh row of a nearly full church, close to the middle of the assembly. They were the very same seats they'd occupied the past 17 years since they first started dating.

"And how many times must I remind you that church is *never* the place to reply back to text messages!" Lydia's voice was no louder than a whisper, yet it carried the force of a shout.

John rolled his eyes and continued scrolling. *You're not my mother!*

Even with his mobile device turned away from her, Lydia could see his phone screen reflecting off his eyeglasses. "John?!"

"Okay, okay, you win," he barked under his breath. It was loud enough for Lydia's closest friend at church, Ann Chen, to hear. The woman of Asian descent pretended not to be listening. Her husband, Jack Chen, would join them after he and the other deacons collected the offering.

John angrily turned off his phone and stuffed it inside his pants pocket. Glancing up, he noticed the unsightly specimen his wife was referring to. He was an elderly gentleman, perhaps 80 or 90, hidden beneath an oversized, worn out, charcoal gray trench coat that reached all the way down to his ankles.

A thick maroon and gray scarf circled his neck. Both ends draped down the front of his coat. Underneath the wool coat was a light gray hoodie. The hair on his head was long and wiry just like his beard. Both were silver-gray in color. Both were unkempt.

Walking at a snail's pace, the old man was being escorted from where he was briefly seated in the front row to the back of the assembly, by two church ushers. One of them, Guillermo Vargas, was a longtime friend of the Jensens.

Dressed in a neatly pressed, olive-colored suit and bright red tie, Vargas towered over the old man. He shook his head in disgust to everyone with whom he made eye contact, as if he'd just caught a thief and was about to hand him over to the authorities.

"I don't know," John Jensen said to his wife. "Looks like a vagrant to me. Perhaps he's here to beg money for booze or drugs."

"I've never seen him before."

"Probably never see him again after today," John opined, dismissively.

Though his answers were short and to the point—judgmental even— Lydia was just glad to be communicating with her husband without arguing for a change. She was even more thankful that he came to church at all. Lately, Lydia attended church service alone each Sunday, while their two children, Matthew, age 10, and Grace, age 7, went to Sunday school.

But it wasn't just church that John seemed totally disinterested in these days. At 42 years of age, life in general had become mundane, boring even, to the extent that nothing motivated him, including the job he once loved so much. Overwhelming fatigue and depression had taken his soul hostage.

This downward spiral started roughly seven months ago, mercilessly changing John Jensen from a loving, churchgoing, devoted husband and father of two, into someone who was increasingly standoffish and argumentative. It was miraculous when a sourpuss expression didn't follow him around everywhere he went.

Pushing these troublesome thoughts from her mind, Lydia Jensen craned her neck back and focused her attention on the mysterious-looking elderly man being escorted to the rear of the church, to see what would happen next.

She wasn't the only one. It seemed half the congregation was doing the same thing; eyes narrowed, heads slanted, irritated glances displayed on so many faces.

Stopping at one of the back doors, the three men huddled together for a brief exchange of words. After that, the shriveled up old man took a seat in the last row, causing a family of four to angrily rise from their seats in search of a new place to sit.

5

Lydia observed as Guillermo mouthed the words, "Sorry" to them as they passed. The empathetic expression on his face was no match for the unbridled agitation on the faces glaring back at him.

When the two ushers exited through the back doors, the old man dropped his head and prayed, "Yahweh, Jehovah God, change the overall heart of this gathering place of believers to resemble the heart of Yeshua, rather than the unconverted world."

Lydia's eyes remained glued on him. She couldn't help but wonder if his overall appearance was the reason for his being humiliated the way he was, in front of so many. *What else could it possibly be? Did he reek of body odor?*

From what she could see, he hadn't been the slightest bit disrespectful to anyone. Aside from his ragged, worn-out clothing and unkempt appearance, he seemed completely harmless. *Yes, it must be because of his appearance.*

The back door opened, and Guillermo emerged with Betty Rainer. Her left arm was practically woven into the handsome Latino man's right arm. Lydia observed as they slowly proceeded down the empty aisle leading to the front of the assembly.

Betty's husband, Tom Rainer, followed closely behind smiling brightly, waving enthusiastically for all to see, determined to shake as many hands and hug as many friends as possible, before reaching his seat in the front row.

As always, Tom and Betty Rainer were impeccably dressed. Both in their 70's, the still-vibrant successful business owners were regarded as solid pillars not only in the church, but in the community as well. It was no big secret that they were the top financial contributors at the church. What should have been kept between them and God was no secret at all.

"Welcome back, John!" Tom Rainer took John Jensen's hand into his own.

"Thanks, Tom," John replied sheepishly, unable to maintain steady eye contact with him. "Nice to be back. Been busy lately."

"Understood." The look on Tom Rainer's face betrayed his one-word reply. But now wasn't the time to press the issue. He still had friends to greet.

The energetic senior gave Lydia Jensen a quick hug and picked up his pace to catch up to Guillermo and his wife.

Upon reaching the front row, the 28-year-old usher with broad muscular shoulders and slicked back, jet-black hair, gently kissed Betty's right cheek. The gesture caused even more pink to surface on her makeup-covered cheeks. Guillermo then squeezed Tom's right hand, cupping it with his left hand, before fading to the back of the house of worship.

The moment the Rainers were seated the service promptly began.

"Good morning, church family," the music leader declared robustly, nodding in the Rainers direction. "Would you please rise and join us in worshiping our Savior, the Lord Jesus Christ, through song and praise!"

Everyone rose as one as the twelve-member band quickly roared to life performing the song, *Your Grace is Enough.*

Hundreds of voices scattered throughout the sanctuary joined together in song, including Pastor Flores and his wife, Maria, who were both seated next to the Rainers.

This being Lydia's favorite part of the service, the confused wife and mother of two put aside her hurt feelings for the moment and sang with a voice that was glad.

John stood alongside his wife but refrained from singing. Eyes surveying the sanctuary, he felt entirely out of place being surrounded by what he had gradually come to believe were a bunch of weak-minded people who were too afraid to govern their own lives that they prayed to a God they couldn't even see, a God John was increasingly unsure even existed.

How could he fully accept that God really existed, when the messages preached at this place were diametrically opposed to what he was taught in college two decades ago, from professors whose minds were so much more advanced than his pastor's?

According to them, humanism, or better put, mankind without God, was the only hope humanity had of realizing their full potential. Because he was raised in a lukewarm Christian household, it didn't take long before the four years John spent seeking higher education started chiseling away at the already shaky spiritual foundation upon which he was raised.

The more his intelligence increased, the more his already weak faith in God decreased. Yet if anyone asked, he unhesitatingly declared that he was a Christ follower. "If You do exist," John whispered, almost sarcastically, "why do I feel so utterly empty inside?"

After two more songs were sung, associate pastor, Amrit Chattergee, read a few church announcements. After that, the man of Indian descent said, "Now, let's all stand and find someone near you. Help make them feel welcome in the house of the Lord."

7

As if on cue, the two-level assembly—capable of holding up to 3,000 people per service—sprang to life like an over-sized honeycomb being invaded by thousands of bees. Only instead of stinging one another, they shook hands and exchanged hugs.

Normally, Lydia would greet everyone within her reach during this time, but not now. She kept to herself. Eyes darting left and right, she was more interested in the old man seated in the back of the church to give anyone else her undivided attention.

Finally, she spotted him standing not too far from his seat, eagerly anticipating being greeted by someone, anyone. Some smiled and nodded at him, but no one dared shake the man's hand, let alone embrace him. If anything, they distanced themselves from him.

The faint smile on his face was one of the saddest Lydia had ever seen before. Though she did not know him, her heart ached for him.

"Now it's time to receive the offering," Amrit Chattergee declared, slowly regaining control. "I'll ask our ushers to get into place..."

Everyone found their seats. Pastor Chattergee prayed, thanking God for the offering they were about to receive. Then the band started playing, *Worthy is the Lamb*. Dozens of ushers got busy patrolling their designated areas, handing offering plates to fellow congregants, then collecting them a few moments later.

Lydia placed a check into the plate, passed it on to Ann Chen seated to her left, and resumed her spying on the back of the church.

From what she could see, the old man appeared to be counting loose change in his right hand. When the offering plate found its way to him, with a grateful expression on his face, he dumped all of it onto the plate.

Lydia was astounded. He looked honored just to have the privilege of giving back to God. *Talk about a cheerful giver!* she thought to herself, unable to mask her growing curiosity.

"How many times must I remind you to mind your own business at church," John whispered to his wife, scowl on face, striking back for her earlier comment about his checking text messages.

Lydia turned around and stiffened up. She wanted to counter but thought better of it. This wasn't the time or the place. Besides, she had long since grown weary of the daily fights with her husband of 13 years.

She was tired, drained.

Throughout the remainder of the service, Lydia fought strong urges to glance back one more time. Already on emotional overload, she managed to control herself. Her mind was too crammed with thoughts of her sagging marriage to give the old man her full attention.

Something had to give soon, before the dam burst wide open.

Once that happened, who knew what lay ahead?

Lydia dropped her head and said the same prayer she'd uttered for seven straight months. "Please, God, help me! I'm desperate for my marriage to be fixed. Intervene before it's too late. I'm open to anything at this point! This I ask in Jesus' name, Amen!"

With the Christmas season—the season of miracles—fast-approaching, that's exactly what Lydia Jensen needed; a miracle from God Almighty Himself.

If her Maker didn't intervene soon, Lydia feared her marriage would continue to free fall, which, in and of itself, was a frightening thought to conjure up.

How could it possibly get any worse?

2

"I'LL BE WAITING IN the car," John Jensen said stoically to Lydia, the moment the church service had ended. Lydia remained seated, as she recorded final thoughts from the sermon onto her listening guide. "Be there as soon as I can," came the reply. "Take your time." John rose from his seat, car keys in hand, looking for the quickest exit from which to leave. He was perfectly fine waiting in the car surfing the Internet until his wife returned with their two children. So long as they made it home before kickoff at 1 p.m., all was well with John's world. At least temporarily.

Lydia headed off in the opposite direction to fetch Matthew and Grace in the adjacent annex building. The aisle-way leading to the back of the sanctuary where the mysterious old man was seated, was full of anxious people trying to exit through one of the four back doors.

Desperate to see him one last time before he disappeared, Lydia was tempted to elbow her way through the crowd, but she refrained.

When she finally made it to the back of the congregation, to her great dismay, the old man was nowhere to be found. Her eyes swept from left to right frantically searching for him, but to no avail.

Lydia frowned. It's not that she had anything of importance to share with him. If anything, she just wanted to give him what she thought he deserved as a fellow Christ-follower, a proper greeting from someone at this place. What she really wanted was to hug the man, as a silent apology for the way so many had mistreated him. But it was too late. He was gone.

"Hey, Lydia."

"Hey, Guillermo."

"Great service, huh?"

"Yeah," Lydia answered, less enthusiastically than usual. Normally she would tell him how handsome he looked in his suit, but that was the last thing on her mind at present.

"You look like a woman on a mission."

"Time to get Matthew and Grace."

"Take your time," Guillermo said, glancing at his wristwatch. "It's probably a zoo up there."

It could wait no longer. "What was all that about earlier?"

"You mean with the homeless man?" Guillermo said.

"Yeah," Lydia said, matter-of-factly.

"Can you believe he actually tried sitting in the Rainers' seats?" Guillermo chuckled without humor. "The nerve of him!"

"So that's it, huh?" Suspicion dripped from Lydia's lips.

"Yup. Mike Hastings said he did the same thing in the first service."

"Wonder why he wanted to sit so close to the front?"

"Said he wanted to be as close to the pastor as possible."

"Sounds reasonable enough to me. Why didn't you let him, Guillermo? You saw how old he was."

"Come on Lydia! In the Rainers' seats? Are you serious?! You know we have an image to uphold."

"We do?"

"Could you imagine someone from our television audience seeing him sitting in the front row? Besides, he didn't exactly throw off a pleasing aroma, if you know what I mean."

"Are you saying you could smell him?"

"Actually, I'm not sure, but it looked like he smelled bad to me," Guillermo chuckled again, hoping to elicit laughter from Lydia this time.

It never came.

Guillermo shrugged his shoulders. "If I had to guess, I'd say he probably hasn't bathed in more than a month. The Rainers flat-out refused to enter the sanctuary until he was gone, or at the very least seated as far away from them as possible."

"You can't be serious?!"

"As a heart attack."

"I can't believe I'm hearing this."

"Come on, Lydia, think about it. We actually did the old man a favor."

"Oh, yeah, how's that?"

"We prevented him from looking like a lowly caterpillar gathered among Monarch butterflies, in front of a live television audience. So, in that sense, we saved him from further humiliation."

Lydia dropped her head in disgust. "I've never been more ashamed to be part of this church than right now!"

"I only did as I was instructed."

"From whom?" Lydia glared at Guillermo. She could feel the heat of anger rising-up inside. "Pastor Flores? Or the Rainers?"

"I'd rather not say," Guillermo replied, awkwardly.

11

Instead of retaliating, Lydia turned on her heels and stormed out of the main church building, without saying bye to Guillermo.

Before entering the annex building, Lydia became even more distraught seeing her image staring back at her in the glass doors in front of her. It literally caused her to stop dead in her tracks.

Gazing deeper into the squeaky-clean pane of glass, she silently gasped. Deep stress lines were cruelly stenciled onto her face, the obvious result of too many arguments with John of late.

And no amount of make-up could cover up the dark bags beneath her eyes, from too much crying. They kept resurfacing.

Lydia was painfully reminded again that she looked nothing like when she first got married to John 13 years ago. Not only was she losing ground in her marriage, she was losing the battle with the aging process, not to mention with gravity itself.

At 39, the half-Irish, half-German, slightly overweight mother of two was still shapely but, after giving birth twice, what once was firm had slightly weakened and loosened.

Even her face, though much fuller than it was a decade ago, was gradually losing its overall shape. Skin that once was silky smooth was starting to sag in some places, snaking all the way down to her neck.

Lydia wanted to cry. Even the wavy, long brown hair John fell in love with, and couldn't stop touching when they first met, was much darker these days. And shorter. And more brittle.

John, on the other hand, was still quite fit, and looked a couple years younger than his 42 years of age. Six feet tall, save for a slight potbelly due to the fact that he drank a beer or two each day after work—something he seldom did in the past—he still looked good.

Of Scandinavian descent, Norwegian to be precise, he had deep-set blue eyes, a prominent chin, and a head full of light brown hair. Even though his sideburns were slowly turning gray in color, if anything, it made him look even more distinguishing.

About the only lackluster quality to his overall appearance was that the man who once stood so tall, brimming with confidence, who lived life with unbridled passion, now slouched with great indiscipline.

This was something he never did in the past.

Other than that, John was aging so much more gracefully than she was. With her 40th birthday a little more than three months away, Lydia couldn't help but wonder if her unshapely body was the reason her husband no longer looked at her the way he once did. *Am I really that unsightly?*

Taking one last look at her reflection in the glass doors, she was struck with a troubling thought. *If I sat in the front row, would I also be considered by some as a lowly caterpillar gathered among Monarch butterflies?*

Lydia rode the elevator up to the second floor. She couldn't help but wonder for the millionth time if John had another woman. She quickly dismissed the thought, hoping John wasn't the cheating type.

What was it then? She had no idea what had caused her husband to all but disconnect from his family the way he had. All she knew was that it started in late Spring and had progressively worsened as the weeks passed.

Was John having a mid-life crisis? Whatever it was, he wasn't the same man to Lydia or the same father to Matthew and Grace he was just a few short months ago. *A few long months ago,* she corrected herself.

On those rare occasions when her husband wasn't in a foul mood, his mind was usually elsewhere. Unlike before. But what had caused the glaring disconnection? It was the million-dollar question...

Though the married couple always did their best to shield the children from the near-constant arguing, it was impossible at times since John was even snappy toward them of late.

Without even inquiring, Lydia knew Matthew and Grace had already seen and heard too much the past few months, to feel at peace at home.

How could they feel otherwise when the tension lately was both constant and palpable? She feared they, too, were preemptively bracing for the inevitable. She could see it in their overall demeanor. It's like they, too, were forced to walk on eggshells.

Once everyone's seat belts were securely fastened, John started the car and left for home. As usual, the mood was somber. Lydia knew it wouldn't improve all that much as the day dragged on. The good news was that she would have a three-hour reprieve once the football game started and John's eyes were glued to the TV, from start to finish.

But once they were gathered at the dinner table, the bickering would resume. As it was, they were still in mid-argument from the night before when John rolled over in bed and fell asleep, leaving Lydia all alone with her thoughts. And tears.

The arguing continued this morning until they left for church.

Lydia was so numb she couldn't even remember what had started this latest quarrel in the first place.

13

Yes, indeed, something had to give soon. Not only for John and Lydia, but for Matthew and Grace as well. Otherwise, they would keep drifting apart until there was nothing left to cling to.

Lydia blinked the thought away, not wanting to go there, even if only in thought…

3

ONE WEEK LATER - TWO WEEKS BEFORE CHRISTMAS

LYDIA JENSEN WAS SEATED in church waiting for the 10:45 service to begin. After another week of constant quarreling with her husband, the ever-desperate woman feared she might explode. Or implode. Whichever came first.

Drained of all emotion, she wondered if God was even listening to her constant cry for help. Either way, it was starting to devour her from within.

What came as no surprise was that John wasn't with her this time. He said he was too tired to go to church, that he worked long hours and wanted to stay in bed all day.

The last thing Lydia heard him grumpily say as she left the house with Matthew and Grace was, "I deserve this break! I need it!" Though greatly disappointed, his absence made for a peaceful ride to church.

Lydia knew how hard her husband worked. But as a stay-at-home Mom, she worked just as hard herself. Whereas John got to leave his workplace each day, Lydia didn't have that luxury. Home was her place of business, and business was open 24/7, 365 days a year at the Jensen residence.

Lydia pushed these unhealthy thoughts from her mind. With Matthew and Grace in Sunday school class, she was grateful for this quiet time. After the turbulent week she had, even ten minutes of peace and quiet was like gold in her hands.

With Christmas just two weeks away, next week would be even more hectic, making this the perfect opportunity to recharge her batteries.

"Let next week take care of itself," she told herself, as her eyes drank in the winter wonderland her church had been transformed into. It looked more like a concert hall than a sanctuary.

Thousands were expected to attend the five upcoming Christmas concerts, the last one ending on Christmas Eve.

Lydia could only marvel at how her church had grown so exponentially the past few years. Ten years ago, it was half this size. It was quickly becoming a mega-church.

Taking one last glance at the soothing lights on the two trees on stage behind the pulpit, Lydia opened the church bulletin and found the listening guide Pastor Flores included each week for his sermons. The message was aptly titled, "Being Thankful this Christmas Season."

Just as she was considering the title, out of the corner of her eye she spotted the same mysterious-looking man she saw the week before, wearing the same tattered gray wool coat, slowly, gingerly making his way to the front of the sanctuary.

Quickly gaining on him, a mere ten steps behind, were Guillermo and the same usher from the week before that Lydia knew only by face.

Before lowering himself into an open seat, the old man glanced back and saw them approaching. If he was surprised by their presence, he didn't show it.

Just like the Sunday before, the three men formed a small circle and spoke in hushed tones, before all three quietly and unceremoniously made their way to the back of the church.

Lydia was so busy this week arguing with her truant husband that she totally forgot about last week's unsettling incident. Once again, she wondered where this man came from. Was he really homeless? If so, where did he sleep at night? A homeless shelter? On the streets?

Craning her neck back, Lydia watched him settle into the same seat in the last row as last Sunday, without the slightest hint of a protest. Once the two ushers left, he dropped to his knees and lowered his head in prayer, his face disappearing behind a shock of long, wiry, silver-gray hair.

Lydia watched in silence, unable to pry her eyes off of him.

Suddenly, just like last week, Guillermo emerged through the door closest to him. Betty Rainer clung to the handsome Latino man's right arm looking prim and proper as always. Every hair was in place.

Tom burst through the doors a few steps behind his wife, waving to friends like he did each week, an infectious smile plastered on his face.

Then it happened: Lydia saw Betty glaring down at the homeless man seated in the last row. Her smile flickered, and her face quaked in anger the moment she saw him. It quickly returned to full beam upon turning her head away from the old man.

It only lasted a split second, but sometimes that's all it takes.

Lydia felt her pulse race in her ears. Unsure if anyone else saw the smug, "How dare you try sitting in our seats," scowl on Betty's face, Lydia knew she would never forget it as long as she lived.

16

Though brief, as far as Lydia was concerned, the endearing smile Betty Rainer was famous for in this place was forever tainted.

Thankfully, the old man in the back row was too busy praying to his Maker, to know he was the object of her wrath.

Upon reaching the front row, Guillermo gave the grinning senior her customary embrace, then shook Tom's hand before scurrying to the back of the assembly.

Once the Rainers were seated, the service promptly began.

Lydia was astounded. Even though she'd witnessed this same posturing every week, everything suddenly felt different. Betty's actions troubled her deeply. To see a woman whom she highly esteemed acting so un-Christlike before her very eyes was extremely unsettling.

Like everyone else, Lydia always looked up to the Rainers as two of her spiritual mentors, often referring to them as the finest Christian couple she knew. Whenever someone needed prayer, counseling or just friendly advice, Lydia never hesitated to send them to Tom and Betty.

They no longer seemed so perfect to her...

The nerve-shredding scowl on Betty's face changed everything. Everything Lydia had loved about them suddenly seemed jaded, perhaps scripted even. And for what? Because the old man wanted to be close to the pastor, and accidentally sat in their seats? Perhaps he was hard of hearing or visually impaired or didn't like an obstructed view...

Whatever the reason, ragged appearance or not, it was wrong of Tom and Betty Rainer, Guillermo or anyone else to treat this visitor to their church with such contempt. This wasn't what the Bible taught about treating others properly; especially fellow believers, as this man most certainly appeared to be. *Would Jesus treat him this way?*

No. If there was one thing Lydia Jensen knew, it's that her Savior was more interested in the condition of the heart and how His followers treated others, than how many Christian songs and Bible verses they could memorize.

But something else was gnawing away at Lydia's insides, something that had nothing to do with the old man seated in the last row. Why did the Rainers always wait until the very last minute to be ushered to their seats?

Lydia knew they arrived at church each week at 8 a.m., for morning coffee, before teaching one of the life group classes in the annex building. John and Lydia gratefully attended their class for two years before moving on to a new group.

17

Mostly due to sheer embarrassment, Lydia stopped going to life group class altogether, last August, after John started missing church so much. Bottom line: she didn't want to constantly subject herself to making excuses for her husband.

Like all other life groups at this church, classes ended at least 20 minutes before the late service began, giving each participant ample time to find their seats, including the Rainers.

So what took them so long? Lydia had a sinking premonition it was so everyone would notice them as they made their grand appearance each week. What else could it be? Did they think they were President and First Lady of this church, and now that they were finally seated the service could officially begin?

After so many years of friendship, Lydia felt guilty for allowing herself to think such suspicious thoughts about the two most popular people at this place of worship. But it was difficult thinking positive thoughts when it suddenly seemed more like a presentation to Lydia than a church service. Was their grand entry as important as the Message itself?

The very thought sickened her. Bowing her head, she prayed, "Father God, please forgive me for...," just as the church band started playing a familiar song most here knew, *Blessed be the Name of the Lord*, causing Lydia to lose focus.

Everyone rose from their seats as one and started singing, including Tom and Betty Rainer.

Lydia remained on her knees observing the aging couple. Hands raised high above their heads, they belted out the lyrics as if God Almighty Himself had suddenly materialized and was seated before them.

This was truly a snapshot moment. If anyone looked up the words, "Genuine Christians" in the dictionary, this sparkling image of Tom and Betty could be posted instead of words. At least that's how Lydia used to see them. She didn't know what to think about the Rainers now.

Were they really the perfect godly couple? Or was it nothing more than a mirage, a vain outward attraction from two people hiding their true inner selves and motives?

Lydia tried brushing these unhealthy thoughts aside, so she could focus on why she was here in the first place. Easily overcome by emotion when singing to the Sovereign God of the universe, it wasn't uncommon for others to catch her brushing back tears during this segment of the service.

Even if it made John uncomfortable at times—when he was here, that is—nothing could stop the raw emotion from rising to the surface, sometimes forcing Lydia to her knees.

But her mind was too cluttered, her heart too pained for that now.

When the band reached the chorus, the vast majority turned up the volume a few notches and shouted the lyrics, "You give and take away, You give and take away, My heart will choose to say, Lord blessed be Your name!"

Lydia rose from her knees and tried lending her voice to the singing, but no words came out of her mouth. Eyes sweeping over the assembly, she wondered how many of her fellow congregants came here more to be seen and heard, rather than out of pure spiritual conviction?

Could it be true that some, or even many, merely went through the motions of playing church, instead of coming for the sole purpose of earnestly seeking and worshiping their Creator?

Did some think it was a country club and this was the ideal time to socialize and catch up on gossip? Did they think they would receive extra credit for coming once a week, that it would guarantee their entry into Heaven, when their lives came to an end?

Feeling overwhelmed for all the wrong reasons, Lydia sat down again to collect herself. "Sorry, Lord, for ruining our date today, and for thinking bad thoughts about my fellow brothers and sisters in Christ."

Shame dripped from her soft voice. *Are they really my brothers and sisters in Christ?* Lydia could only wonder...

When they came to the chorus again, Lydia's eyes drifted back to the Rainers. She quickly looked away, unable to contain her growing disappointment.

Glancing to the back of the church, her head bobbed and weaved through the large gathering of believers, looking for the old man.

Spotting him, she wasn't surprised to see him standing in the aisle singing with everyone else. Eyes lifted skyward, joyous smile on his face, it was like he was totally disconnected from everyone else, as he praised God with everything that was in him.

Clearly, he had a passion for God no one else could duplicate.

What made this spectacle even more miraculous was, aside from his unbuttoned trench coat, gray hoodie, and layers of exposed mismatched clothing, this man apparently had nothing else.

Perhaps the good Lord decided to take everything away from him, as the song they were singing implied. Yet no one looked more at peace, more comfortable in the presence of God, than him.

It dawned on Lydia: what if God took everything away from the Rainers? How would they react? What about everyone else gathered? Would they still praise their Maker despite the great loss? Or would heartfelt praise and worship be replaced by anger, contempt and rebellion?

Lydia dared not venture a guess. She couldn't help but wonder again what everyone's true intentions were for coming to this place.

Was God pleased with the condition of each heart in this place of Christian fellowship? For so many years, Lydia Jensen thought the answer to that question was yes. At least for the vast majority.

Now she wasn't so sure...

Glancing back at the homeless man one last time, if anyone needed an object lesson depicting the title of today's sermon, "Being Thankful this Christmas Season", all they had to do was look at him.

Yet, for most, he was the very last person they wanted to see in this place. *Go figure...*

4

LYDIA JENSEN LEFT THE sanctuary feeling more like she was in a courtroom, seated among a bunch of judges, than fellow grace and spirit-filled Christ followers. Not everyone weighed in on the matter. In fairness, many seemed okay with his being there. But for those who did weigh in, though it was a silent rendering, the verdict was crystal clear: GUILTY!

The question was, guilty of what? It's not like the seemingly kind and gentle homeless man came to cause trouble with anyone. Nor was he there to beg, loiter or trespass. It was evident his sole purpose for coming was to worship his Maker, and perhaps make a new friend or two. He even gave an offering both times he visited their place of worship.

What right did any of them have to judge him based solely on his appearance? *How shallow!* All it took was a few brief observations of the man for Lydia to conclude that his heart was undoubtedly right with God.

Wasn't that the true mark of a genuine Christ follower?

Lydia thought so. *Why couldn't they see it too?*

Seeing Guillermo out of the corner of her eye, Lydia rushed off in the opposite direction. The last thing she wanted was another confrontation, especially with so many others around.

Best to just keep my mouth shut, she thought, leaving the sanctuary headed to the annex building to fetch her kids.

A few minutes later, with the children buckled into their seats, Lydia guided her vehicle to the nearest exit. Sunday was always her favorite day of the week. Spending quality time with her family after church was what she looked forward to more than anything else. But that hadn't happened in many months. At least not as a complete family.

What motivation was there for going home only to find her husband lying on the couch watching football, totally disconnected from the rest of the world? *Not much*, she quickly concluded. Instead of turning left onto Oak Street like she normally did, Lydia made a right.

"Where we going, Mom?" Matthew said, realizing his mother had turned the wrong way.

"I feel like going for a ride."

"But kickoff's at one," he said, sulking.

"I know, son. We still have time."

Matthew wanted to retaliate but thought better of it.

At the second stop light, Lydia turned right on Main Street. A half mile or so down the road, out of the corner of her eye, she spotted the elderly man walking on the sidewalk, breathing the labored breath of the elderly.

Lydia gasped, then pulled her vehicle into a vacant parking space and observed him from roughly 50 feet away.

"Why'd you pull over, Mom?" Matthew said.

"There he is!"

"Who, Mommy?" Grace asked.

"The homeless man who came to our church the past two weeks."

"Who?" Matthew was suddenly curious.

Lydia pointed in his direction, "That man over there, with the long gray hair and trench coat."

Matthew straightened up in his seat hoping to secure a better view outside the car front window. "The old man?"

"Yes."

"Do you see him, Grace?" Lydia asked.

"Uh-huh."

"It pains me to say this, children, but many at our church treated him very badly."

"Why?" Matthew asked.

"Because of the way he dresses..." Lydia was clearly disappointed.

"Really? So sad," Grace said, watching him limping along ever so gingerly.

Seeing her long-faced daughter pouting in the rear-view mirror, Lydia frowned. "I know, sweetie. It isn't right."

Grace was on the verge of tears. "He seems harmless."

"One thing I know is he truly loves Jesus."

"How could any Christian treat someone who loves Jesus so badly?" Matthew said, no longer concerned about the one o'clock kickoff.

Lydia sighed, "Doesn't make sense, I know."

Lydia pulled out of the parking space determined to inch as close to the homeless man as she could. She wanted to get a good look at him in the bright sunshine. When she was just a few feet behind him, the old man turned right and slipped into the city park, totally unaware that he was being followed. Sort of, anyway.

Lydia pulled over again and the three of them watched the old man amble toward what appeared to be a small community of homeless people bundled in shabby old clothing. Some had blankets draped over them for warmth. They circled the old man like a bunch of vultures, until he vanished from their sight.

The Jensens watched in silence to see what would happen next. But nothing happened; nothing exciting anyway.

The peaceful, downtrodden group of humanity slowly proceeded to the other side of the city park, before settling onto a bunch of well-worn blankets and sleeping bags spread about the dying grass. Save for a few brownish-green patches here and there, the lawn was steadily losing its battle against the progressively colder temperatures.

Not knowing what to say or do, Lydia started the car and drove off.

They arrived home just after one p.m. As usual, Freeway was waiting at the front door, tail wagging, excitement coursing through her eleven-year-old body. Though they were only gone for a few hours, to their pet dog, it was more like ten years.

Their pet cat Alex was nowhere to be seen. Perhaps he was upstairs in one of the bedrooms or hiding behind the couch. You never knew with him. Unlike Freeway, the aging feline was fiercely independent and oftentimes antisocial.

As was fully expected, John's near-lifeless carcass was planted on the couch. He was too mesmerized with the football game on TV to care who had just walked through the front door. A half-empty beer bottle was on the coffee table.

Like he did for each game, he wore gray sweatpants and his favorite player's jersey. There were no "hellos" or "how was church?", only silence. The only thing on John's mind was football.

Lydia went to the kitchen and took ground beef out of the refrigerator for homemade meatballs, which she planned to serve with pasta for dinner. She then prepared soup and sandwiches for lunch.

Matthew raced up the stairs and threw on his team jersey. At 5'0", the 10-year-old boy was tall for his age. His scrawny, twig-like arms dangled from the over-sized jersey that would probably still fit him next season. Matthew had innocent facial features—soft blue eyes, thick eyebrows, tiny freckles on his nose and cheeks, and a mouth full of braces.

Though still a few years away from reaching that transitional stage of physical and psychological human development known as adolescence, Matthew had already developed the habit of constantly checking his look in the mirror to make sure his shoulder-length, brown hair was messy enough to be considered "socially cool" by his friends.

Once adolescence kicked in, his hormones would erupt like a volcano, causing his voice to change practically overnight, and his body to sprout awkwardly in some places, until the rest of him caught up at a later time.

But for now, Matthew Jensen was still a Momma's boy.

Instead of watching the game with his father, like he did all last season, for the third straight week Matthew was granted permission by his mother to watch it at his friend Bryce's house.

At least there would be no arguing there...

Matthew opened the front door to leave. "What about lunch?"

"I'll eat there, Mom."

"Come straight home after the game."

"I will," he said.

"Bye Dad," Matthew said, leaving the house.

"Enjoy the game," John replied sarcastically, as if his son were a traitor for watching it elsewhere. But he also understood. *I wouldn't want to watch the game with me either!* he thought in disgust.

Lydia could only watch and wonder in silence. The anguish in her heart, having already reached mountainous proportions, was about to spew like lava shooting from a volcano.

Grace settled into her favorite chair near the fireplace hoping to finish the novel she'd been reading all week, a book that was recommended by her Sunday school teacher. Spunky by nature, for only being seven, the youngest member of the family was exceedingly bright. Blessed with her father's intelligence, she preferred reading children's stories to playing with dolls or engaging in online games with friends.

On the petite side, Grace Jensen had soft brown hair that almost reached her lower back. Her facial features were small, smooth and rounded. Her deep blue eyes were always active and alert, always probing. She had thick eyebrows like her brother, and tiny freckles on her small nose and cheeks.

The frigid home atmosphere the past few months had transformed Grace into a voracious reader. Whenever her parents argued, reading provided the perfect escape, by allowing her mind to travel to wherever the author was gracious enough to take her. By simply reading, Grace didn't need to take a train or plane or boat to reach these destinations.

All she had to do was keep turning the pages.

At 5 p.m. the Jensens were gathered together at the dinner table for spaghetti and meatballs.

"Can I say grace, Mommy?"

"Sure, you can, sweetie," Lydia said to Grace, with a faint smile. Whenever the youngest member of the family offered to pray aloud, there was something on her mind that everyone else needed to hear.

Grace lowered her head, "Lord, bless the food we're about to eat. More importantly, bless the homeless man from church and his friends at the park..." There was a sensitivity in her voice that touched Lydia deeply. "I hope they have enough food and plenty of blankets to keep them warm tonight. Please protect and keep them safe from harm, in Jesus' name I pray, Amen."

"Amen," everyone said, including John, even if in a near whisper.

Lydia was amazed that her daughter had prayed so heartily for the man she herself couldn't stop thinking about.

John, on the other hand, was greatly relieved not to be the object of his daughter's prayer this time. He was equally confused.

Stabbing a meatball with his fork, he said, "How do you know he lives in the park, honey?"

"We saw him there after church."

Shooting a quick glance at his wife, John said, "The city park?"

Lydia looked down at her plate. "Yes."

"What possessed you to take that way home? It isn't even on the way."

"I felt like taking a different way," Lydia replied stiffly, coolly. Frustration was evident in her tone.

After a five-second stare down, John backed off and focused his attention on his meal. He was already in a grouchy mood after his team lost on the final play of the game, and might miss the playoffs as a result. He didn't want this day to get any worse.

After dinner, the man of the house went upstairs to watch more football in bed, while Lydia and the children watched the movie *ELF* together in the living room.

During a commercial break, Lydia reached for the TV remote and flicked to the Weather Channel. The temperature had already dropped seven degrees since the first time she checked, and was still falling. A frost advisory was in effect for the region.

"It's getting cold out there," she whispered softly to no one in particular, unable to stop thinking about the homeless group at the city

25

park. The cold air she always loved this time of year for having a hot chocolaty quality you could almost taste, now concerned her deeply.

A pang of guilt twisted through her body. While the Jensens were safe and warm, the old man Lydia surmised to be 80-years-old—at least that old—apparently had no place to call home.

Tears flooded her eyes. *Is he safe? Will he survive the night?*

Complete stranger or not, Lydia had a sudden urge to drive to the city park and invite him to spend the night with them or, at the very least, take him to a homeless shelter. But she knew John would never agree to such a crazy notion.

After brushing her teeth, Lydia climbed into bed to find her husband sound asleep, leaving her all alone with her thoughts. And tears. Again.

The lonely wife grabbed her Bible off the small table beside the bed. Mostly due to overwhelming guilt from so much arguing with John, she opened it to the Book of James, chapter three.

For the third time this week, she read what the half-brother of Jesus wrote about taming the tongue. James called it "a restless evil, full of deadly poison." He went so far to warn his readers that every beast and bird, reptile and sea creature could be tamed, but not the tongue.

Admittedly, when Lydia first started reading this difficult chapter a few months ago, it was with her finger pointed more at her husband than at herself. In the back of her mind, she hoped by simply reading it John would receive James' message by osmosis and his tongue would be tamed, thus curing herself as well.

That all changed a few weeks back, when Pastor Flores preached an entire sermon from just one Bible verse, Romans 2:1, "Therefore you have no excuse, O man, every one of you who judges. For in passing judgment on another you condemn yourself, because you, the judge, practice the very same things."

It was a soul-penetrating message that convicted Lydia deep in her spirit. Especially when her pastor openly rebuked those who went to church with their fingers constantly pointed at other people.

"Those who do that need God's forgiveness more than those at the end of their pointed fingers," Pastor Flores said sternly that day.

Since that time, Lydia read James chapter three with her finger pointed at herself, and no one else. The only tongue she had the power to tame was her own. After reading those verses so many times the past few months, she practically had them memorized.

26

Verses 9 and 10, especially, always left her feeling guilt-ridden. Regarding the tongue James wrote, "With it we bless our Lord and Father, and with it we curse people who are made in the likeness of God. From the same mouth come blessing and cursing. My brothers, these things ought not be so."

The fact that James addressed his readers as "his brothers" in the text meant they were true followers of Jesus, making it all the more difficult to digest. *We really are a bunch of hypocrites!*

For whatever reason, Lydia's eyes were drawn to James, chapter two. The subtitle read, The Sin of Partiality. Verses 2-4 really got her attention.

She read, "For if a man wearing a gold ring and fine clothing comes into your assembly, and a poor man in shabby clothing also comes in, and if you pay attention to the one who wears the fine clothing and say, "You sit here in a good place," while you say to the poor man, "You stand over there," or, "Sit down at my feet," have you not then made distinctions among yourselves and become judges with evil thoughts?"

Lydia could only shake her head. Many at her church were guilty of this very thing. Her former heroes in the faith, the Rainers, topped the list.

"Why did you show me this passage, Lord?" Lydia whispered skyward. "And why did I take that way home from church today? Was I driving under Your influence without even knowing it? Do You want me to visit the old man walking to the city park?"

For whatever reason, Lydia felt the answer was yes.

"If that's what You want, Lord, I'll do it!"

Lydia placed her Bible on the table next to her side of the bed and turned off the light. It was settled then. After dropping the kids off at school in the morning, she would go to the city park and introduce herself to the man who kept invading her mind. *Hopefully he'll still be there*, she thought. She quickly realized how ridiculous her thought really was.

"Hopefully he won't be there," Lydia said under her breath, correcting herself. *Hopefully he found some place warm to stay...*

27

5

13 DAYS BEFORE CHRISTMAS

AFTER DROPPING MATTHEW AND Grace off at school, Lydia Jensen returned home to find Freeway waiting at the front door, yelping loudly, tail wagging, excitement coursing through her body.

"I think someone's ready for her walk!" Lydia knelt down to embrace her mixed-breed pet with golden-brown hair. "Okay, okay, let me get the leash."

Freeway's tail wagged all the more. After a ten-minute walk, Lydia checked to make sure Freeway and Alex had enough food and water. Satisfied that they did, she did a quick sweep of the house to make sure everything was in order.

Alex was curled up on his favorite throw pillow near the unlit fireplace, like a white ball of fur, purring away.

Freeway was at the front door, stretching her paws and yawning. Lydia was unable to hold Freeway's desperate stare. It dripped with sadness. Even after all these years, it was impossible to get used to.

"Sorry, Freeway. Be back later," she said, locking the front door behind her.

Lydia drove to the neighborhood McDonald's fast-food restaurant and was thankful to see only two cars in line at the drive-through. After being handed her food order, she practically raced crosstown to the city park.

Upon arriving, she saw dozens of homeless people roaming the streets weighted down by backpacks and blankets. Others sat on the outskirts of the park, cardboard signs in hand, silently begging for money, totally reliant on the charity of others but finding so little. Most drivers and pedestrians ignored them as if they were completely invisible. Other panhandlers played their worn-out guitars, showcasing their musical talents for all to hear, hoping to score enough cash to feed serious drug and alcohol addictions.

Lydia had to circle the 50-acre park twice before finding an empty parking space on a side street. Exiting the car, she stretched her arms high above her head, then grabbed the to-go bag from the front passenger seat, thankful it was still warm.

For whatever reason, Lydia sensed she would be perfectly safe in this man's presence. *Why am I so nervous then?*

With a rush of uneasiness pumping through her veins, Lydia Jensen lowered her head and ambled toward the gathering of people she saw the day before, in search of the man she came to meet.

She wondered how it was possible for anyone to still be sleeping, with the constant hustle and bustle of society moving so briskly all around them.

Those who were awake followed her every move with their eyes. Filthy backpacks were at their sides holding all their personal belongings. One woman who Lydia surmised to be in her 50's was confined to a wheelchair.

Blanket draped over her body for warmth, a few strands of gray hair had somehow escaped from underneath the old wool hat she wore. Her nose and cheeks were chapped and rosy red from the cold wind.

There was this faraway expression on her face as if the whole world had forgotten about her.

Lydia nodded at the Caucasian woman and smiled faintly but kept walking. A few moments later, she spotted the man she came to see buried beneath a dirty green blanket. His hair was a dead giveaway. He looked like a silver-haired turtle with its head popped out of its shell resting on its right shoulder. The bottoms of his trousers were tethered, and the leather on his old shoes was quite worn.

Is he sleeping? Lydia stood silent, motionless, feeling a little silly for being there. A few awkward moments passed before the old man with unkempt hair slowly lifted his head to see who or what had caused the sudden blockage of sun he had been drawing upon for warmth.

Squinting through old wrinkled eyes, he saw her. "Can I help you?"

Clearing her throat, Lydia said, "Good morning."

"Good morning," the old man said. His voice was low and mysterious, his face saggy and lined. But there was intrigue in those ever-curious, passion-filled brown eyes of his. "What brings you here on such a chilly day?"

Should I tell him? "Hmm. Uh, well, you."

"Me? Why me?" *Is she the one, Lord?* the old man thought.

"I brought you breakfast and hot coffee. Least I hope it's still hot." Lydia handed him the food and drink.

29

"That's very kind of you, ma'am," the homeless man replied gratefully, taking the bag from his visitor. His eyes smiled more than his lips. They comforted Lydia greatly.

"My name's Lydia. Lydia Jensen."

"Thank you for the food, Lydia. Your timing couldn't be more perfect. I was just saying to myself before you showed up that I felt hungry."

"It's my pleasure, sir," she said, not knowing what to call him.

"Sir? Do I look like someone of prominence to you?"

"No. I mean, not no but, hmm..." Lydia tensed up. "It's just that I was raised to respect my elders."

"Your parents taught you well, Lydia."

Nodding agreement, she said, "What shall I call you?"

"Call me Enoch."

"That's different."

Enoch smiled and left it at that.

Not knowing what else to say, Lydia returned an exhausted smile. "There are creamers and sugar packets in the bag for your coffee and plenty of ketchup packets for the home fries."

Enoch opened the bag. "I will be sure to use all those things. As you can imagine, nothing edible ever goes to waste here, including creamers and ketchup packets. Sometimes items most take for granted are our main source of nourishment for the day."

Lydia tried to conceal her astonishment. Having never experienced the sheer dreadfulness of homelessness a single day of her life, how could she possibly relate to that raw statement on any level?

At any rate, the constant turbulence racking her personal life seemed futile compared to what she was witnessing at this place. Lydia took a deep breath and relaxed a little more, realizing this was one of the most satisfying moments she'd had in quite some time.

Enoch opened the wrapper to find a sausage McMuffin stuffed inside, with melted cheese stuck to the wrapper.

"Looks delicious," he said, bowing his head to give thanks for the food.

Finished praying, Enoch grabbed the breakfast sandwich with both hands. His grime-stained fingers caused by living on the streets seeped into the still-warm muffin. He stuffed the sandwich into his mouth and let his teeth sink in.

"There's another one in the bag for you. Eat it now or later. It's up to you."

"Thanks for the kindness, Lydia." Taking another bite, the kind, homeless man swallowed and said, "Would it be okay if I give it to one of my friends?"

"Of course," Lydia replied, a pang of guilt rising-up for not bringing more food for the others. It wasn't even a thought.

There was a moment of silence as Enoch feasted on his breakfast sandwich. Stirring two creamers and two sugars into his coffee, he took a sip and smiled.

"Forgive me for saying this but after seeing you at my church the past two Sundays, my children and I were driving home after service yesterday and saw you walking down Main Street." Lydia sighed. "That's how I knew where to find you."

"I see."

"Please don't think I'm a dangerous person or a stalker or anything like that. I can assure you I'm not."

"That thought never crossed my mind," the old man said, searching his visitor's warm, friendly eyes. "How could I think that when you came here to bring me breakfast?"

Lydia looked relieved. "My daughter would be jealous if she knew I was here."

Enoch looked confused by her comment. "Why is that?"

"When we were thanking God for our dinner last night, Grace prayed for you. Not by name, of course, but as the home..." Lydia paused.

"It's okay. You can say it. The homeless man from church, right?"

"Well, yes. Sorry..." Lydia regretted mentioning this to him.

"Think nothing of it. After all, I *am* the homeless man from your church."

It was time to level with him. "This may sound a little strange to you but last night before going to sleep, I felt prompted in my spirit to come here and introduce myself to you."

"Doesn't sound strange at all. I'm glad you came. It's always nice to have company, especially from someone as kind as yourself." *Surely, she must be the one...*

"Thank you, Enoch."

Lydia let her gaze wander over the vast expanse of the park. The few businessmen and women seated on benches a hundred yards away eating their lunches was a far cry from how it used to be at this place. The cold temperatures had little to do with it.

31

A few years ago, this park was considered the crown jewel of the city; it was the place to go for families seeking outdoor recreation.

Lydia and Ann Chen used to bring their children once a week when their husbands were at work. Then the street people took over and scared most others away.

"Is this really your home?" Lydia blew into her glove-less hands to warm them.

"Now that you put it that way, yes. I guess you can say I'm emulating my Mentor."

"And who might that be?"

"Yeshua, of course!" Enoch brimmed with assurance.

"As in Jesus?"

"Yes."

Lydia smiled just enough to let him see it.

Enoch closed his eyes and, from memory, quoted scripture. Yeshua said, "'Foxes have dens and birds have nests, but the Son of Man has no place to lay his head.' That's from the Book of Matthew, chapter eight, verse twenty, in case you were wondering."

Nodding her appreciation Lydia said, "Mind if I ask how long you've lived here?"

Enoch took a long sip of his coffee, and let the steam pressing through the cup to warm his nose a bit. "Not too long."

"Are you from around here originally?"

"Truth be told, I'm just a temporary earth-dweller." Seeing how his comment caught Lydia off guard, he said, "Then again, aren't we all?"

"I suppose so." Lydia was totally captivated by this remarkable street person. The childlike manner in which he conducted himself, his unwavering faith in his Maker, his being grateful for even the smallest things without a trace of worry on his face, despite his present predicament, made Lydia marvel all the more. *Simply amazing!*

"Will you be here again tomorrow?"

Enoch studied his visitor over his coffee cup. His bushy eyebrows arched high above his eyes, as if to say, "Are you serious?"

"Of course, you will. Please forgive my insensitivity and stupidity." Lydia suddenly felt like a high school girl asking her teacher a bunch of childish questions. "Would it be okay if I stopped by again with more food?"

"I can assure you no one here would ever refuse a request like that," Enoch said, his eyes moving left and right.

Lydia got the point. "Shall I bring extras for everyone else?"

"There are many of us here."

There was a brief pause. "How many?"

"It varies each day."

"Thirty?"

"I think more than that."

"Forty?"

"Perhaps…" Enoch's words lacked conviction.

"Fifty?"

"That sounds about right. It's always best to have too much than not enough. Too much never goes to waste here."

"Would it be okay if I make sandwiches from home? Buying fast food for so many people can be quite expensive."

"Sounds perfect," the homeless man said, with a sparkle in his eye that almost required the use of sunglasses to deflect. The peaceful expression on his face betrayed his incredulous situation. He seemed like he didn't have a care in the world. "You have a kind heart, Lydia."

Blowing more warm air into her chilled hands, she said, "I'll try to come before noon."

Enoch nodded gratefully. "May God richly bless you for what you're doing."

"It's my pleasure. See you tomorrow then." Lydia bent down to hug the old man. The fact that he may not have showered in days never crossed her mind.

Enoch didn't thank her for the hug. There was no need to: what Lydia saw on his face was all the thanks she needed. She shared every emotion he just expressed.

Walking back to her car, she couldn't remember the last time she felt this satisfied. *Will it be better tomorrow after feeding 50 instead of just one?*

"We'll just have to wait and see," Lydia told herself, sliding behind the wheel of her car and putting the key into the ignition.

6

"WHAT'S WITH THE FIVE loaves of bread on the kitchen table?" John Jensen said, suppressing a yawn, lying in bed next to his wife.

Those were the first words the married couple had uttered to each other since their last scuffle at the dinner table, albeit a silent one.

It all started when Lydia included the homeless man in her prayer again, a man she identified this time as "Enoch".

John had interrupted, raising an eyebrow, giving his wife a sideways look. "Who?"

Lydia had countered saying, "Of course, John would have known this too, Lord, had he taken a greater interest in things other than himself, including going to church more often."

Even six hours later, she still felt bad for saying it in front of the children, and for judging her husband during prayer time. It was wrong of her.

"I need them for tomorrow," Lydia retorted clinically, a thick blanket covering her body all the way up to her neck.

For twelve straight years, Lydia took comfort knowing the man she married would kiss her each night before turning off the lights. Then he would hold her in the darkness until they both dozed off.

These days, cuddling was gradually replaced with a sizable gap between them large enough that Matthew and Grace could easily fill it. Feeling uncomfortable in her own bed, of all places, did nothing to help the escalating situation.

"School project?"

Lydia shook her head no, "I plan to feed lunch to fifty homeless people at the city park." Her tone was aiming for casual, but she missed the mark. Excitement dripped from her words.

"Come again?"

"I went to visit Enoch today," she confessed. "I brought him breakfast from McDonald's."

"Seems someone's been doing lots of things lately. Wonder what else you might be doing behind my back?"

"What do you mean by that?" Lydia tensed up.

"Just what I said."

34

"Don't start, John. I wouldn't have done it without your knowledge, but we never talk anymore. All we do is argue."

John snapped. "What possessed you to do such a thing?" His nostrils flared as he brushed off her accusation. "You know how dangerous it is in that part of town. That place is always in the news. Remember the murder last year?"

"I felt perfectly safe in his presence the whole time I was there."

"And just how long were you there, Lydia?"

"Not even an hour."

"And what kind of name is 'Enoch' anyway?"

"I don't know. All I know is he's a kind and gentle man. Godly too!"

"How can you say that, Lydia, when you don't even know him! Do you know how many homeless people are alcoholics, or drug addicts, or wanted for serious crimes?"

"No. Do you?"

"I'm sure a high percentage," John commented, blandly. "What if he's a serial killer?"

Lydia snorted laughter.

John went on, "I remember watching something on TV about serial killers. One was even known for always quoting Scripture."

"I can assure you that's not the case with this man. I would be shocked if Enoch ever drank a drop of alcohol in his life. And there's no way on earth he takes drugs."

"How can you be so sure?"

"He's too wise for that," Lydia said, without hesitation. "Nothing he ever does or says alarms me. I know it sounds crazy, but I felt this perfect peace while in his presence. It's like I've known him forever. Actually, it's more like he's known me all my life. It's hard to explain."

John shrugged his shoulders. "Even so, I'm not comfortable with you going there."

Lydia grew defensive. "Are you forbidding me from going?"

Her comment stopped John dead in his tracks. Searching his wife's face, something he hadn't done in a long time, there was a determination there that told him all he needed to know: she was doing this with or without his support.

John looked away, "I never said that."

"Good, because I'm going!" Lydia snapped. She felt her face warming starting at her cheeks. It quickly spread to her ears and forehead.

35

John closed his mouth before a new burst of anger could escape. The room grew icy cold and silent. It was late, and they were both tired. The last thing either wanted was another flare up.

Lydia was desperate to tell John how alive she felt for going there earlier, like normal husbands and wives did. But lately their relationship was anything but normal.

Besides, he wouldn't be interested anyway. Aside from watching football, she couldn't think of a single thing John was interested in these days. If she tried sharing these strong thoughts and emotions knotting up in her chest with him, he would roll his eyes and the conversation would come to an abrupt end.

Not wanting to further torture herself—as it was, Lydia was already on self-torture overload—she toned it down a few notches. "But don't worry, I'll be careful."

John rolled onto his side. "Great! Just what I need! Fifty more mouths to feed," he whispered to himself in a calm tirade. "As if I don't already have enough to worry about..."

"What?"

"Nothing," John snorted. Then, "It's not our fault they're homeless. I'm sure they did something really bad to end up there. Enoch too! Perhaps being homeless is God's way of punishing their reckless living!"

Though his words were unintelligible, Lydia had a pretty good idea what he was saying.

A few moments later John was sound asleep, leaving her all alone with her thoughts. And tears. Again.

Lydia reached for her Bible and opened to the Book of James, chapter 3, very much feeling like Bill Murray in the movie *Groundhog Day*. At least when it came to this part of the day.

Even if John was oftentimes the instigator of their arguments, Lydia was just as guilty herself for saying things to her husband, in anger, she knew she shouldn't say. All it did was further prove that her tongue was in no way better than his.

She read the first twelve verses of chapter 3, then closed her eyes and whispered this week's Bible memory verse, found in Proverbs 21:23: "Those who guard their mouths and their tongues keep themselves from calamity."

After that, Lydia flipped back to James chapter 2, and read verses 2-4 again. Had her homeless friend at the park worn fine clothing the past two weeks, instead of shabby garments, no one would have objected to his sitting up front.

But since he wasn't properly groomed, he was forced to the back of the church without a shred of compassion from anyone, despite that he was an elderly man.

Lydia placed her Bible on the table next to her bed. *That just ain't right! At the very least, what about respect for elders?*

"Stay warm tonight, Enoch," she whispered in the darkness. "May God bless and keep you from harm."

Lydia turned off the light and rolled onto her side facing away from John. She was anxious for the sun to rise, so she could see her new friend again…

7

12 DAYS BEFORE CHRISTMAS

THE NEXT DAY, LYDIA Jensen arrived at the city park at 11:37 a.m.

In the trunk of her car were two wooden produce crates she'd found in the garage. Each was stuffed with bags full of peanut butter and jelly sandwiches, cheese crackers and either an apple or an orange.

Each crate held 25 bags. One crate held the bags with apples in them; the other held the bags with the oranges. She also made sure to bring a case of bottled water and two cases of soft drinks.

After dropping the kids at school and taking Freeway on her morning walk, Lydia cranked up K-LOVE radio and spent two hours preparing the bagged lunches, enjoying every second of it.

The contemporary Christian music, mixed with Christmas music, blared through her radio speakers, stirring and enriching her soul to the point of weeping joyous tears at times.

She thought it ironic how some might think something so simple as making lunches for the homeless could breathe so much life into a person, but that's precisely how Lydia felt.

This new-found joy she'd tapped into was something that needed to be personally experienced in order to be fully understood.

"This is fun!" Lydia got out of her car, thankful for this brief reprieve from her ongoing marital problems. Whereas the last time she felt shy and nervous, she was more confident now. Leaving everything in the trunk of her car, she went in search of Enoch with the boundless energy of a teenager. A moment later, she was standing in his presence.

"Good morning, Lydia!"

"Good morning! I was wondering if someone could help unload the lunches in the trunk of my car."

Enoch's face lit up. "How many volunteers do you need?"

"Three should be enough," came the reply. With no green blanket covering him this time, Lydia got a close-up look at his gray wool coat. It was so worn that it almost looked moth-eaten.

The old man signaled for three of his fellow parkies for assistance. Troy, Dillon and Rocky—three wannabe grunge rocker hippies in their mid-20's—were more than willing to help, especially if it meant being fed a meal for their efforts.

The only time the three gifted musicians weren't seen jamming together was when they were sleeping or out panhandling for money.

All three had long brown, matted hair. Their bodies were heavily tattooed like many others at the park. But only their ink-stained hands and necks were visible this time of the year.

A few moments later, the two crates and three cases of beverages were placed on a patch of dying grass next to Enoch.

"What now?" Lydia was quite eager to start passing out lunch bags.

"First we must give thanks to God."

"Gather around everyone," a man named Leroy yelled in a deep, booming voice. "Enoch's about to pray."

Those interested in giving thanks formed one big circle and held hands. To Lydia's left was Enoch. To her right was the woman she saw the day before confined to a wheelchair.

"Father God, El Shaddai, Jehovah Jireh," Enoch began, "we give thanks to Thee this day for the food You have provided for us. May it nourish us and give us strength for today. Bless your servant, Lydia, for being obedient to Your call. Meet her needs this day, and the needs of each of us here, in the mighty name of Yeshua of Nazareth I pray, Amen."

"Amen," came the grateful reply from all who joined in the prayer.

Blackened by the grime of the streets, Tiwanna and Wanda—fellow parkies and good friends since childhood—started passing out lunch bags. The two African-American women in their early 30's hadn't felt the warmth of a home in many years.

Tiwanna was short and stocky with short cropped hair. Wanda was lanky and thin. At 5'6", she was four inches taller than Tiwanna, but looked seven inches taller with her hair rising three inches above her scalp.

Leroy was tall and broad-chested, standing 6'4", with a crown of thick, tightly coiled slowly graying hair. He wore a worn-out green army coat, the only thing left from his service in the Vietnam war.

The dirt- and grease-stained Vietnam Veteran baseball cap he wore did nothing to tame his Afro. Hair shot out in all directions.

At 53, the burly black man's face was weathered and beaten down by so many failures over the decades. He was quite menacing to those who didn't know him. But to those who did, aside from Enoch, Leroy was the kindest, gentlest person at the park, serving as chief protector to many at this homeless community.

Leroy handed out drinks with his friend, Pedro. On the thin side, the 36-year old, 5'7" Hispanic man had already lost 80 pounds in the three years he was homeless. Pedro's face was thin. The hair on his head was black. His most distinguishing feature was the salt and pepper goatee circling his mouth.

Since becoming brothers in Christ a few months back, Pedro and Leroy were practically inseparable. They often called each other, "Brothers not from another mother but from the same Father."

It didn't take long before 47 of the 50 bags were gone.

Looking at Lydia, Tiwanna said, "You want one?"

"No thanks. I'm sure someone will eat it."

"You know das right," Tiwanna said, matter-of-factly.

"Hope you enjoy your lunches."

"Oh, we will," Wanda said softly, shyly, speaking on behalf of everyone else. "Beats dumpster diving any day of the week!"

Not knowing what to say, Lydia sighed and left it at that.

A moment of silence ensued as this bundled-up eclectic group of mixed ethnicity sat on blankets on the brownish tundra eating their lunches. Even in the bright sunshine, a cool steady wind made the forty-five-degree temperature feel more like thirty-five.

Most appeared to be sober and coherent for the time being. Those still drunk or high on drugs kept to themselves. They displayed the pale, translucent skin and jerky manner of those whose bodies and minds had been substance-abused to the point of no return. It looked as if sound reason had left them long ago.

Deemed worthless by society, it was easy to understand why many of them looked so eaten by fear and anxiety. Peering into their eyes hollow entities stared back, desperate and powerless. Their bodies wilted like dying flowers, suffering various stages of degeneration.

Though saddened for their current lot in life, Lydia still managed to drink it all in. Her eyes feasted on them as they feasted on their lunches. What most went out of their way to avoid was something she now saw as a beautiful sight. Her heart melted inside her chest in a good way and bad.

Eyes finally resting upon Enoch, the old man motioned for her to join him, to which Lydia didn't object.

Taking a seat on his grass-stained blanket, she said, "I can't tell you how good I feel right now."

"That's because you're doing a good thing. Most people do nice things hoping for the applause of others. But the select few do it more for the smile of God than anything else. I can assure you that your generosity has put a smile on our Maker's face. How could you not feel good under such conditions?"

"It truly is my pleasure."

"Yahweh already knows that, Lydia. That's why He prompted you in the first place."

It's like he's one of God's personal representatives here on Earth, she thought, not knowing how right she was.

"But you see, dear Lydia, though thankful for the food and drink, these things are not what my fellow parkies, as many call us, need most."

"What is it then?"

"In a word, hope!"

Knowing Enoch was about to get "deep" again, those interested gathered around their spiritual mentor and grew silent.

Those not interested, including those professing faith in other gods, migrated away from him.

Those who were still high on drugs or suffering from hangovers, after a night of too much drinking, rolled onto their sides and covered their heads. The last thing they wanted was to be preached at.

Included in this group were Troy, Dillon and Rocky. Though the three stoned-out musicians considered Enoch to be the coolest old man they knew, they wanted nothing to do with his religion.

Of the 20 or so who were interested, most were churchgoers in the past but never found Jesus there. It took meeting Enoch to finally open their spiritual eyes and experience what abundant living was all about.

They went from attending church service once a week, at most, to having church seven days a week in this humble homeless community.

Having finally hit rock bottom, they clung to Enoch's messages of hope for dear life and were slowly but surely being transformed from the inside out. Some had completely turned their lives around and were no longer homeless.

But since this was the only church that felt authentic to them, they came back to the park each chance they got, to hear Enoch's soul-stirring messages. They also came to encourage their still-homeless friends to remain strong, and even took them into their rooms and apartments whenever possible.

Enoch was invited on several occasions, but the old man politely refused. He was a Mission waiting to happen and, therefore, needed to stay put until God commanded him otherwise.

"What kind of hope are you referring to, Enoch?" Lydia asked.

"Not just hope for today, but eternal hope."

"Doesn't everybody need that?"

"Yes, but I'll come back to that." Pausing a moment to make sure everyone within the sound of his voice was listening, Enoch went on, "As I'm sure you know, Lydia, the definition of hope is having a feeling of expectation and trusting that things will ultimately turn out for the best."

Lydia nodded agreement.

"The definition of hopeless, on the other hand, is having no expectation of anything good happening now or at any point in the future. Hopelessness represents desperate, depressed souls who firmly believe their situations can never be changed for the better. With no remedy to cure whatever it is they have given up on, they are reduced to feeling that they are beyond hope or optimism."

As Enoch spoke, Lydia glanced at the many faces staring back at her eating their lunches in total silence. What she saw beyond the dirty, grimy faces of those listening to the old man were contented souls, despite their dire surroundings.

At the top of the list were Leroy, Pedro and Tiwanna.

Consequently, the overall demeanor of those not interested in Enoch's message provided the perfect object lesson for his explanation of hopelessness.

Eyeballing Lydia carefully, Enoch explained, "Whether one wears tailored apparel or beggar's garments matters not. Hopelessness is an internal debilitation. Certainly not a healthy mindset for anyone to harbor. Wouldn't you agree?"

"Yes," Lydia said softly, almost guiltily.

"Because of society's overall negative view toward homelessness, many think we are beyond hope, that we have sinned all our days of grace away, and that the food and clothing they give us is more than enough to sustain us. Having met our basic survival needs for that day, they get to go home feeling good about themselves.

"Naturally, we're grateful for the food and clothing. But what we really want is for others to make us feel like human beings instead of pitied charity cases only. Contrary to what many believe, society hasn't grown more tolerant over the years.

"Human causes come and go. But since the dawn of mankind, homeless people have always been the subject of universal intolerance. We are treated by the majority as sub-human. This has never changed."

Enoch paused to take another small bite of his sandwich. Swallowing, he said, "Sadly, regarding this matter, there isn't much difference between Christians and the unconverted world."

Seeing Lydia's eyes widen, the old man knew his comment had landed hard.

"Many followers of Yeshua can be tolerant of so many things, yet when a fellow brother or sister struggles financially or worse, ends up homeless, that person tends to be treated as if they had lost their way in society or they were living in great sin.

"Granted, sometimes that is the case. Homeless or not, after receiving God's salvation, believers still fall into sin at times. When this happens, it is necessary for Yahweh to discipline His children. No discipline seems pleasant at the time, but later on it produces a harvest of righteousness and peace for those who have been subjected to the sternness of God.

"But with sanctification being a lifelong process, sin isn't the only reason for trials touching a believer's life. Yahweh sometimes allows trials to test His children, like when He told Abraham to sacrifice his own son as a burnt offering to Him."

Pausing a moment to look at everyone, Enoch said, "Could you imagine God telling you to do something so unthinkable?"

Many shook their heads in bewilderment.

"Wanting to be obedient to his Maker, Abraham woke early the next morning and loaded his donkey, taking two of his servants and his son, Isaac, with him. On the third day they reached the place God had told him about. Abraham built an altar and arranged the wood on it. He bound his son, Isaac, and laid him on top of the wood.

"Just as Abraham was about to slay his son with the knife in his hand, the angel of the Lord called out to him from heaven saying, 'Do not lay a hand on the boy. Do not do anything to him. Now I know that you fear God, because you have not withheld from me your son, your only son.' Seeing a ram caught in a thicket, Abraham took the ram and offered it up as a burnt offering instead of his son, Isaac.

"Another reason Yahweh allows trials is to realign a life and point that person in the right direction. The Apostle Paul was a good example of this. While on the road to Damascus to persecute and imprison Christians, Paul,

43

then Saul, suddenly saw a light from heaven flashing all around him. He fell to the ground and heard a voice say to him, 'Saul, Saul, why do you persecute me?'

"'Who are you, Lord?'" Saul asked.

"'I am Jesus, whom you are persecuting,' came the reply. 'Now get up and go into the city, and you will be told what you must do.' The men traveling with Saul stood there speechless; they heard the sound but did not see anyone. Saul got up from the ground, but when he opened his eyes he could see nothing. So they led him by the hand into Damascus. For three days he was blind, and did not eat or drink anything.

"Then Ananias the disciple went to the house where Saul was staying. Placing his hands on him, he told Saul that Jesus sent him so that he may see again and be filled with the Holy Spirit. Immediately, something like scales fell from Saul's eyes and he could see. He got up and was baptized, and after taking some food he regained his strength.

"He changed his name to Paul and began preaching in the synagogues, boldly declaring that Jesus really was the Son of God. Suddenly, many Jews conspired to kill Paul. By changing sides, the hunter suddenly became the hunted...

"Sometimes Yahweh allows the most unpleasant trials to occur in the lives of His best servants, like when Joseph was sold into slavery by his own brothers. Yet in the end, after suffering countless indignities, including false imprisonment, Yahweh used it all for good by choosing Joseph to save His own people from severe famine.

"The point to consider, Lydia, is this: when things go well, and all seems perfect in the world, many of God's children tend to stray off track. Whether it is disciplinary, to test one's faith, or to realign a life, trials test the faith of believers better than anything else. Once they have passed the test, they are seen for what they really are, Yahweh's mercies in disguise."

"Preach on, Pastor!" someone shouted.

"When it comes to the trial of being homeless, however, from a human viewpoint there isn't much mercy to go around. Sure, many caring individuals like yourself come here to feed us, but they quickly leave, making us feel worthy of their food but not their time," Enoch explained.

"To feel like a total outcast from society is a heavy burden for anyone to carry. I can assure you that no sandwich or blanket can take that dreadful feeling away. What most people here need is something they can sink their teeth into in the form of hope."

Enoch took a sip of water, "When visitors go out of their way to spend quality time with us like you are now, with no fanfare, that's when they see it."

"See what?"

"That you care enough to treat us like friends or even as members of your own family. The best form of love anyone can show a homeless person is the gift of time. It makes us feel like equal parts of society again, even if only temporarily. And that, my dear Lydia, is called hope.

"And when you do it all in the name of Yeshua, and others see Him working in and through you, that's how Yahweh becomes more visible to the unconverted world. Once others become convinced that you are different from the rest, many will want whatever you have that makes you so different."

"Amen!" came the reply from some, Leroy's being the loudest. His deep, booming voice practically shook the atmosphere, startling Lydia. She was so absorbed by Enoch's many nuggets of wisdom that she nearly forgot she was encircled by a bunch of homeless people.

Enoch went on, "Let me end by saying this, from an eternal standpoint, just like it only takes one dedicated follower of Yeshua to restore a church, the same is true that one genuine person can help restore hope in fifty street people, better than fifty who come here just to feed us and leave."

"True that," Tiwanna shouted.

"But just like a boiling pot of water gradually cools off after the flame has been extinguished, hope can be extinguished just as quickly, if too much time passes in between visits.

"Of course, while Yahweh does all the choosing, He uses humans to carry out His purposes. In that light, consistency will be key to eventually winning souls to Yeshua with your new Mission."

Mission? Lydia was too blown away by this humble man of God to utter a reply. *Does he know my deepest thoughts?* As far-fetched as it seemed, Lydia couldn't place it outside the realm of possibility.

Lydia checked her cell phone for the time: 2:19 p.m. *Time to go.* "Time sure flies when you're having fun!"

"Thanks for stopping by and feeding us, Lydia," Suzie said gratefully.

"Thank you, Lydia," Leroy said.

"Thank you," said Pedro.

"Thanks, kind lady," said Dillon, one of the grunge rockers.

And on and on it went.

"The way I feel, I should be thanking you," Lydia admitted. Before leaving, she made sure to hug everyone in the circle, including the woman in the wheelchair, named Suzie.

Enoch observed in silence. *Perhaps she's not the one?* Her life was too on track to be the one God sent him to rescue. But Enoch felt in his spirit Lydia was somehow connected to his reason for being there.

8

"I HAD THE MOST incredible day, kids," Lydia said, at the dinner table. Her eyes locked on John to see if he would show any interest in the conversation. As always, his head was down, more focused on the plate of food in front of him than anything else. Was he even listening?

Grace picked at the food on her plate. "What did you do, Mommy?"

"I fed lunch to fifty homeless folks."

"The group we saw at the park?"

"Yes. I must say it was one of the most satisfying experiences of my life."

"That was nice of you." Grace was happy to see her mother's face aglow again after so many months in hiding.

"I'm proud of you, Mom." Matthew was unable to mask his surprise; not that his mother went to the city park, but that she went alone. It was so unlike her.

"I spent two and a half hours there and met many nice people."

"What kind of people?" Grace asked.

"All sorts, honey. There was even a woman in a wheelchair, named Suzie. They were some of the humblest people I've ever met."

"Of course, they're humble, Lydia," John grunted sarcastically, "they're homeless!"

Lydia ignored her husband's snide remark, "Anyway, as they ate their lunches, Enoch preached a sermon on hope verses hopelessness. It was as good as any church sermon I've ever heard. It's like I went to church without even knowing it. It was a church without walls."

"Can I meet Enoch, Mom?" Grace said.

"I don't see why not, sweetie." Lydia shot another quick glance at John. "As a matter of fact, I plan to feed them again on Saturday..."

John raised an eyebrow but remained silent.

"Would you two like to join me?"

A moment of uneasiness ensued when John mumbled something that only he understood.

"I'd love to, Mommy," Grace said, despite her father's incoherent protest.

47

"Me too," said Matthew.

John stopped chewing the food in his mouth and glared at Lydia. Whether he was mad at his wife for not asking him first, or hurt, Lydia couldn't tell. "You can't be serious?!" His eyes narrowed, "I don't think some at our church would approve of your potentially placing our children in harm's way, by bringing them to a hostile environment like that."

"Then according to Proverbs fourteen, verse thirty-one, which states, 'Whoever oppresses the poor shows contempt for their Maker, but whoever is kind to the needy honors God,' they're not real Christians. Or at the very least, they're being disobedient to God. If we respond to others based solely on outward appearance, haven't we entirely missed the point of the Gospel?"

"That's all well and good, *dear*," John replied, the word "dear" coming out of his mouth a little too harshly, "but just because you fed them doesn't mean you know them." John looked up at the ceiling and shook his head. "Now she wants to bring the children!"

Lydia grunted frustration and lowered her head in disbelief.

The children clammed up, silently fearful of another outburst between their two earthly protectors.

Finally, Lydia said, "Do you really think I would willingly expose our children to a harmful situation? Give me some credit, John. If I had even the slightest inkling that it would be too dangerous, I'd never think to bring them."

A wave of sadness tightened her throat and burned her eyes. "I'll admit on the surface some of them looked potentially dangerous. Others were passed out on the grass, either drunk or high on drugs. A few moped around angrily as if the world owed them something. They even seemed ungrateful for the food they were given.

"But my goal wasn't to receive praise. I felt blessed just to be able to give them food, even if some may not have appreciated it. If my actions reached just one person, that's all that matters."

"Did they smell?" Matthew asked inquisitively.

"Yes, honey, some smelled like they hadn't bathed in weeks. The stench took some getting used to, but I kept telling myself that if I lived on the streets, I would reek of body odor too." Lydia's brow furrowed, "Remarkably, Enoch didn't smell at all."

After a few uneasy moments, John looked up from his plate and the married couple locked eyes. Lydia was desperate to catch a glimpse of the passionate, fun-loving man she married way back when. She knew he was in there somewhere. At least she hoped he was.

"Wanna know what I couldn't stop thinking about driving home?"

With his hands, John motioned for his wife to continue.

"Some of the things you told me long ago that I still remember to this day."

"Yeah, like what?" came the reply. John seemed totally disinterested.

"Didn't you once say we're surrounded by danger at every turn, but we need to press on with whatever we feel called to do in life, despite the potential danger?"

John bristled in silent annoyance. He clenched his hands nervously, not knowing what to say.

"Aren't you the one who said we've become a generation of self-centered wimps? In fact, I believe you said we're the worst to ever inhabit this nation." When John remained silent, Lydia pressed on. "To refresh your memory, you said our greatest societal setbacks have more to do with the human spirit than anything else, including technology. Do you even know how deeply your words touched me back then?"

John shifted his body in the chair, "That was a long time ago, Lydia!"

"You once told me if a family had a few small leaks in their roof a century ago, they would praise God that it was only a few. But in today's world, once a small leak has been discovered, the first thought for many is to contact an attorney."

"We all change." Clearly, John wasn't enjoying this stroll down Memory Lane.

"Yes, John, we do, but your intelligence and relentless spirit are two of the things I fell in love with. You once said society as a whole was trying to create this perfect environment that will never work. I still remember how you compared the human spirit to the perfect temperature, which you said was seventy-two degrees. Do you remember?"

When John remained silent, Lydia kept going. "You said if they ever achieve this seventy-two-degree society, heat and air conditioning would no longer be necessary. You said it would feel good at first, perhaps a month or two, but without a constant influx of air—whether hot or cold—this new society would eventually stagnate.

"You then compared that anecdote to the human spirit. 'Without a constant flux of air, hot or cold,' you had said, 'good times or bad, our souls would eventually stagnate.' I still remember all these things as if it were yesterday." Lydia bit her lower lip. "Sorry for saying this in front of the children, but you went from being bold and daring to this?"

John lowered his head knowing he couldn't defend himself. How could he when his wife was using his own words against him?

"For the first time in a long time, my spirit feels fully alive. I'll admit I may have ventured into potentially hostile territory, but it was for a good cause. And even though it was only my second time there, I believe if someone tried to harm me, I had the full protection of many."

Glancing at Matthew and Grace, she said, "This may sound crazy, but I think I feel called to do this. Who knows, perhaps it's my life mission. Only God knows what lies ahead."

Returning her gaze back to John, "And yes, this is something I'd be proud to expose our children to. Potentially dangerous or not, it may be life-changing for them as well. I'd love for you to come, too, but I know you'd never agree to it."

John didn't answer, but Lydia saw the deflated expression on his face. He wanted to say, "Why bother, when everything seems so meaningless." He refrained. But that's exactly how he felt.

9

SATURDAY MORNING - 8 DAYS BEFORE CHRISTMAS

AFTER BREAKFAST, THE KIDS helped Lydia clear the table and load the dishwasher. John plopped down on the living room couch, looking for something to watch on TV. Anything to escape his present reality.

Placing a plastic tablecloth on the kitchen table, Lydia designated three manning stations; one for herself, one for Matthew, and one for Grace. She turned on K-LOVE radio. The Christmas song *While You Were Sleeping,* by Casting Crowns, was playing.

Lydia said to her children, "Let's get busy."

Matthew and Lydia opened jars of peanut butter and jelly and started making sandwiches. Using purple and pink Sharpie markers, Grace drew hearts on the fronts and backs of each brown paper bag to be handed out later. It was an idea the youngster conjured up all by herself.

Lydia marveled at her daughter's creativity.

Once Grace was finished, she helped make sandwiches. While she wasn't nearly as fast as her older brother, she was careful to make sure each sandwich looked perfect, as if preparing them for a mayor or senator or governor.

The female voice on the radio said, "Here's 'Do Something' by Matthew West".

Lydia had heard this song many times, but this was the first time she really listened to the lyrics. One part, especially, made her ears perk up like a puppy dog's.

"People living in poverty
Children sold into slavery
The thought disgusted me
So, I shook my fist at Heaven
Said, "God, why don't You do something?"
He said, "I did, I created you..."

51

"We are doing something! Right, children?" Lydia declared triumphantly.

Matthew and Grace both smiled, grateful to see their mother so happy again.

One down, one to go, Matthew thought, referring to his father.

Using her mobile device, Lydia took a short break from sandwich-making to take pictures and a short video of her two children.

She uploaded them to Facebook with the caption, "Preparing to feed the homeless."

Before she could even sign out of Facebook, she received five likes.

"Wow, that was fast!" Lydia smiled.

As much as she enjoyed making sandwiches alone the other day, this was infinitely better. To see the joy on her kids' faces as they prepared food for 50 complete strangers was too marvelous to put into words.

After the sandwiches were made, they stuffed homemade Christmas cookies in plastic sandwich bags—three per bag—and placed them inside brown paper bags with a bag of potato chips.

For the first time in a very long time, the Jensen household was alive with activity. Not counting the near-lifeless slouch lying on the living room couch, totally oblivious to his surroundings, an air of joyousness permeated every inch of the residence.

What the three of them didn't know was beneath John's downtrodden exterior, the head of the household felt like he was dying a slow, painful death. Actually, it was as if John Jensen had died seven months ago; only he hadn't been buried yet. The happiness his wife and kids had rediscovered only served to punctuate the dreariness all the more.

Normally his favorite time of year, even decorating the house for Christmas was burdensome this year. He reluctantly went through the motions, doing his best to mask how terrible he felt. But it was impossible with the same debilitating question that had dominated his thinking the past seven months always resurfacing: *What's the point?*

John wanted to be passionate about life again. He really did. But how could he when nothing made sense anymore?

Grace stared her father in the eyes. When he looked away, she kissed him on the forehead. "Bye, Daddy. Wish you were coming with us."

"Enjoy yourselves." When his family drove away, John covered his face and wept softly on the couch. Overwhelming depression took root in his soul. He wanted to curl into a fetal position and slowly fade away until he eventually disappeared. *What's wrong with me?*

LYDIA AND THE CHILDREN arrived at the park just before noon. Lydia was surprised to see Leroy standing in the street holding a parking space just for them. Wearing the same worn-out Vietnam green army coat he wore the other day, the giant homeless man looked more like a sentry guarding this spot for a commanding officer, than for a mother and her two children.

Lydia looked in her rear-view mirror and saw Matthew and Grace both stiffen up, suddenly fearful.

Leroy waved to Lydia.

Lydia waved back. "Don't be afraid kids. That's Leroy. He may look rough and tough on the surface, but beneath it all he's a giant teddy bear. Definitely one of the kindest men you'll ever meet."

Matthew and Grace waved back cautiously. This would take some getting used to.

The Jensens climbed out of the vehicle.

Craning his neck back toward the park, Leroy whistled loudly for assistance. Within seconds, two other homeless men approached to help carry the crates.

"Good afternoon, Lydia," both men said in unison.

"Good afternoon, gentlemen," came the reply. Lydia recognized their faces but didn't know their names.

"Your kids?" Leroy asked.

Lydia nodded yes. "This is Matthew and Grace."

"Nice to meet you, children."

"You too," they said in unison.

"We may need a few more helpers," said Lydia. "We brought a hundred meals instead of fifty. This way, you'll have food for dinner tonight, too."

Leroy's face lit up like a Christmas tree displaying a thousand lights. "Yes, ma'am," the giant of a man shouted, signaling for more helpers.

Troy, Dillon and Rocky came and grabbed the remaining crates from the trunk of Lydia's vehicle. Troy and Dillon both had serious heroin addictions. Rocky suffered from severe alcoholism.

The three grunge rockers desperately needed Jesus for deliverance.

"Follow us," Pedro said.

The Jensens followed Leroy and his four helpers into the park.

53

Hardened by life on the streets, most softened instantly at the sight of the two children.

"Hope you're all hun..." the mother of two said, quickly stopping. *Of course, they're hungry, dummy!*

Matthew and Grace were astonished to see their mother, the OCD clean-freak as their father often referred to her, greeting each person with a warm embrace.

Speaking loud enough for everyone to hear, Lydia said, "I'd like you all to meet my two children. This is my handsome son, Matthew, and this is my precious daughter, Grace."

"Hi, Matthew. Hi Grace," many voices shouted at the same time.

Matthew waved back shyly.

Grace ducked her head at the sudden burst of attention.

The first person they recognized, other than Enoch, was the woman waving to them in a wheelchair. Thanks to their mother, they knew her name was Suzie.

"Gather 'round, y'all," Leroy yelled, "Enoch's about to pray!"

Everyone interested held hands.

Once Enoch was finished, Lydia asked, "Would it be okay if my children and I served you? It was Matthew's idea." Lydia rubbed her son's head, with a proud expression on her face that could only come from a loving parent.

"Very kind of you, young man," Leroy said to Matthew, with a nod of approval and admiration.

Matthew's cheeks turned various stages of pink. "Just sit and relax, we'll do the rest."

"As you wish," Enoch said, smiling proudly.

A few moments later everyone was eating their lunches.

"How long have you been homeless?" Grace asked Suzie.

"Eight years..." came the reply, "...and counting."

"Why don't you have a home to live in?"

"Can't afford it," Suzie said flatly.

"Do you have children?"

"Yes. A son and a daughter. My son's a doctor and my daughter's married to one."

"Why can't you live with them?"

"And disgrace the family by having an alcoholic living among them?" Suzie grumbled. She took a deep breath and exhaled. "Sorry for my outburst, children."

54

"But you're handicapped," Grace said softly mostly to herself, unable to mask her surprise. It was the very last thing she expected to hear.

Suzie lowered her head in shame.

Pedro chimed in, "But praise God you haven't had a drop to drink in more than a month. We're all so proud of you, Suzie." The day she quit drinking was the day Pedro became her accountability partner.

"Yes, Amen," Suzie replied, humbly. "After many years of heavy drinking, I'm finally on my way to sobriety. But only because I'm trusting in God for my complete deliverance this time."

"Amen," came the reply of many.

"You see, dear Grace," Enoch said, "everyone here has a story to tell. Many have made bad decisions that put them here. While it's true that drug and alcohol addiction are the chief causes of homelessness, not everyone here battles those addictions. Nor do we all have criminal records.

"If you spend enough time in any homeless setting, you will find most used to be responsible citizens until something happened that caused their lives to spiral downward, ultimately taking the wind out of their sails. No one living on the streets ever planned on being homeless."

Turning to Pedro, Matthew said, "What made you homeless?"

"Drugs and alcohol mostly," Pedro admitted. "Cost me everything I owned, including my wife and daughter."

"How old's your daughter?" Matthew said, maintaining eye contact. His query was a compassionate one.

"Eleven. About your age, right?"

"Yes. I'm ten. What's her name?"

"Erica."

"Nice name. When was the last time you saw her?"

The homeless man lowered his head sadly. "Six years ago. But that doesn't mean I don't love my daughter. I love her with all my heart and think of her every day."

Eyes pleading for understanding, Pedro went on, "I didn't leave her. I would never leave my own child. She was taken from me."

He looked away momentarily before making eye contact again. "The day my ex-wife got a restraining order against me was the day I completely shut down. I cried myself to sleep for weeks on end. My drug use grew worse until I lost everything and found myself living on the streets.

"I don't blame my ex that I'm homeless. But I do blame her for taking my daughter away from me. Even with my past addictions, Erica was always safe with me. I would never do anything to harm any child let alone my own daughter. I believe the same is true with most parents who are denied access to their children.

"What right does any parent have to keep a child from seeing a loving father? I hate to think how many good fathers out there have been barred from seeing their children, for reasons that have nothing to do with the child's overall protection. Aside from excessive neglect or child abuse, anyone who keeps a child from a loving parent will have to answer to God for it."

Everyone grew silent, unwilling to be the next to speak.

Wiping tears from his eyes with dirty hands, Pedro continued, "But praise God for using that man," he said, pointing to Enoch, "to bring me into the Light. I was living in complete darkness, battling serious addiction and constant regret, until he showed up.

"Enoch reminds me all the time that God is in the restoration business. He always encourages me to remain patient and redeem this time by drawing closer to God, until He restores things between me and my daughter, in His perfect timing."

"Amen," said Suzie, shaking her hands skyward in victory for her accountability partner to see.

"All I can say is a few months ago, I was blind," Pedro said, his black eyes radiant after being washed by his own tears, "but now I see. God has completely delivered me from drugs and alcohol. Just started a new job last week washing dishes at a restaurant down the street. I get my first paycheck next week."

Gazing at some memory in mid-air, hopeful expression on his face, he said, "Soon I'll have a place to call my own again. Once that happens, I'll petition the court to drop the restraining order, so Erica and I can be together again."

"Very good, Pedro," Matthew said, thoughtfully.

"Enoch's been a Godsend to us all. A real angel," Tiwanna said, not knowing how precise she was on both counts. "Thanks to him, many who used to be full-blown alcoholics and drug addicts are clean and sober now, myself included!"

Tiwanna smiled gratefully, revealing several missing teeth. "Many of us even have jobs now. Those of us who can't find work collect bottles and cans and take them to recycling centers for cash. Enoch helped us regain a sense of self-worth again."

"Glory to God," the Hispanic man said, humbly.

THE UNANNOUNCED CHRISTMAS VISITOR

"But the most important thing to happen since Enoch's arrival," Leroy said, taking control of the conversation, "is that dozens of us are now children of the Most High God. I'm eternally grateful to be one of them."

Everyone in the circle started clapping.

Lydia had never attended a *Celebrate Recovery* meeting at her church, which basically was the Christian's version of *Alcoholics Anonymous* (AA) or *Narcotics Anonymous* (NA). She suddenly felt like she was smack dab in the middle of one.

"You see, Matthew," Leroy continued, "Jesus didn't come into the world for those who *think* they are well. He came for those who *admit* they are sick. Too many people think they're near-perfect when, truth is, we're all broken—homeless or not! We all have weaknesses and we all fall short of the glory of God, in so many ways. We're all sick and need a Doctor. And that Doctor is Jesus.

"It pains me to say this, but every time I read Matthew chapter seven, verses three through five, I can't help but think of the many churchgoers in the world. Jesus said, 'Why do you look at the speck of sawdust in your brother's eye and pay no attention to the plank in your own eye? How can you say to your brother, 'Let me take the speck out of your eye,' when all the time there is a plank in your own eye? You hypocrite, first take the plank out of your own eye, and then you will see clearly to remove the speck from your brother's eye,'"

Matthew was impressed how Leroy had quoted it from memory.

Leroy continued, "Simple truth is many who call themselves Christians are just as sick as those who've yet to be converted. Many have done everything there is to do in church but be converted. If you ask them, they'll deny they're sick and might even become furious with you. But that doesn't make it any less true."

My disciples are really getting it! Enoch silently praised God for using these humble, broken servants to teach His Word so beautifully.

"I thought church wasn't until tomorrow," Matthew said, sort of jokingly. Then again, Sunday school class never impacted him quite the way these kind people did. It was immeasurable.

Enoch smiled as only he could. "Yes, Matthew, many people will attend church tomorrow. And that's a good thing, to be sure. But for those who truly belong to Yeshua, let this day always serve to remind you that true church doesn't only take place inside buildings. Nor is it meant to take place only once a week. The three of you proved that much today."

Matthew grinned. The corners of his mouth quirked upward, showing a mouth full of braces for all to see. The young boy was never more grateful for having been exposed to this new world, a world he sort of knew existed, but was a million miles away from the life he knew.

He already looked forward to doing it again. Hopefully soon.

Grace was thinking similar thoughts.

At 3 p.m. the Jensens returned home to find John asleep on the couch.

After cleaning the kitchen and showering, Lydia opened her Facebook account and nearly gasped seeing more than 100 likes and 37 comments to her post, and still counting.

Many who seldom, if ever, replied to her posts in the past wrote the nicest, most heartfelt comments. Some even offered to volunteer if she decided to do it again.

Matthew and Grace stood behind their mother, who was seated at the living room table. The kids listened with great interest as Lydia read each comment aloud.

Gathering her children in her arms, Lydia couldn't ignore the satisfied expressions on their faces. Not that she was looking for compensation for what she did at the city park, but if she were, no other form of payment could top what she saw on her kids' faces. It was priceless.

10

THE NEXT DAY - 7 DAYS BEFORE CHRISTMAS

"CAN WE SAY HELLO to Enoch before Sunday school?"

"Sure," Lydia said to Matthew, locking the car doors electronically, "but we need to hurry. There will be plenty of time after church service."

"Can I be the one to invite him to lunch?" Grace asked, walking hand in hand through the church parking lot with her mother.

"Sure, sweetie. Just make it quick. We're running late."

They entered through the back door of the sanctuary. Matthew spotted Enoch sitting in the last row of seats. He wasn't alone this time. Leroy and Pedro were with him. It was difficult at first recognizing Leroy with his long Afro tamed for the occasion. Tiwanna spent three hours braiding his hair so he would look more presentable.

Matthew and Grace raced toward them, bypassing all the clean cut polished members of this sizable congregation. Matthew fist-bumped the three men without the slightest concern of what anyone might be thinking.

Grace said hello by waving her hand wildly, excitedly. "Would you care to join us for lunch after service?"

"That's a very kind offer, Grace," Pedro said.

"We'd love for you to join us!" The enthusiasm in Matthew's voice was evident.

Enoch glanced up at Lydia. She nodded yes. Settling his eyes on Matthew and Grace, he said, "We will join you, children."

"Great!" Grace said, smiling.

Lydia looked at her phone screen. They were cutting it close. "Say bye for now kids. Can't be late for Sunday school class."

Grace hugged the three men, thus marking the first hug Enoch ever received at this place of worship.

"Enjoy Sunday school class," Leroy said.

"Thanks," the two children said at the same time.

Matthew fist-bumped all three men again before leaving, suddenly aware of the great attention they were receiving from so many others.

Lydia noticed too. She wondered if they also saw the anger slowly building on her face. "Be right back." She made sure to say it loud enough for their many onlookers to hear.

A few minutes later, Lydia rejoined them. Having attended this church for so many years, this was the first time she noticed how dark it was in the back rows. *Talk about being banished to the darkest recesses of the sanctuary!*

"I was wondering, gentlemen, if you'd like to sit closer to the front?" Enoch stiffened up, "Well..."

Lydia didn't let him finish, "With me. It may not be the front row, but it's a whole lot closer than here."

"Are you sure?"

"There's nothing I'd like more." The genuineness in her voice, the sparkle in her eye and luminous smile on her lips, told them all they needed to know. She really wanted this.

"It would be our honor to join you, Lydia," Enoch said.

The three men rose from their seats to the usual irritated, contorted faces glaring back at them. They may have looked entirely out of place to the many gathered, but they certainly weren't out of touch. In fact, no one was more in touch with their Maker than they were.

As they moseyed down the aisle, the look on Lydia's face gave the impression that she was in the presence of true greatness, not three homeless men, befuddling her onlookers all the more.

Lydia almost smiled. "Good morning, Ann!" she said rather cheerfully to her friend, upon reaching the seventh row.

"Good morn....," Ann Chen stopped in mid-sentence. Eyes shifting to the three men with Lydia, her mouth was agape. She easily recognized the old man from the past two weeks, but she didn't know who the other two men were.

"I'd like you to meet my three friends, Enoch, Leroy, and Pedro."

"Nice to meet you, gentlemen." Ann studied their faces cautiously, carefully. She was aware of Lydia's ongoing marital problems and wondered if her good friend was suffering a mental breakdown of sorts, and this was her way of compensating for John's not being here.

"Nice to meet you too," Leroy said, on behalf of the three of them.

Sizing the three men up in her mind and deeming them harmless, even if untidy, Ann took a deep breath and relaxed. That is, until she noticed many staring at them. Shy by nature, she always shrank when garnering the attention of others.

Some churchgoers seemed perfectly fine with their being there. The youth, especially, were more curious than anyone else. Many managed to somehow look comfortable and uncomfortable at the same time.

But the ones who made Ann's skin crawl the most glared angrily at them with no compassion whatsoever, as if their precious space had just been violated.

Ignoring it all, the three men knelt together to pray to their Maker.

Lydia wasted no time joining them. Before bowing her head, she took one last look around. Judging by what she saw on some faces, one might think she was harboring three dangerous fugitives. Her chest heaved, and her heart burned within her.

Why don't you all focus on removing the planks from your own eyes, before worrying about the specks in my friends' eyes! Lydia thought angrily, remembering what Leroy had said at the park. She wanted to say, "Are *we* the reason you came to church? If not, please stop staring at us!"

She thought better of it. *Two wrongs don't make a right!*

It was as if the Book of James, chapter 2, was materializing before her very eyes. Even if only in thought, her fellow congregants were dishonoring her three friends solely because of the way they were dressed. If they wore gold rings and fine clothing, they would be most welcome here. *Isn't this what loving the least of these was all about?*

Lydia couldn't help but feel like she was gathered among a bunch of hypocrites instead of fellow churchgoers. To prevent anger from rising up, she blocked it out of her mind, so she could worship her King, in peace, with her three brothers in Christ.

Shortly before the service started, Betty Rainer made her grand entrance into the sanctuary. She walked down the aisle, arm in arm with Guillermo as always, her husband Tom in tow, waving and smiling to everyone with whom she made eye contact.

When Betty saw Lydia kneeling next to her three unsightly guests, she quickly turned her head. Her face didn't quake with anger this time, but the fact that she totally ignored Lydia because of the company she was keeping, exposed even more of the senior's ugly, ungodly character.

Guillermo didn't even bother looking. His head remained forward the whole time.

The moment the Rainers finished their grandstanding, Guillermo hustled to the back of the sanctuary and the service promptly began.

61

Finally seeing this well-oiled presentation for what it was, Lydia was able to block the elderly couple out of her mind, along with all the other nonsense that should never find its way into a church, and worship her Creator with her three brothers in Christ.

When it came time to receive the offering, associate pastor Amrit Chattergee prayed before the ushers, already in place, began patrolling their designated areas collecting tithes and offerings.

A female voice started softly singing a capella, "*O come let us adore Him, O come let us adore Him, O come let us adore Him, Christ the Lord.*"

Lydia received the offering plate from Ann Chen, gave her tithe, and passed it to Enoch seated to her left. She observed in utter amazement as her three friends reached deep into their pockets for loose change and a dollar bill or two, placing everything they had onto the collection plate.

The expressions on their faces made it look as if they were being handed money instead of giving it away. What made it even more remarkable was that they gave every-last cent they had to a church that treated them like vagrants at best.

Lydia thought, *We're treated like family here, yet we struggle at times to give 10 percent back to God. And even that causes arguments at times!*

The very thought of it saddened her.

The young woman with angelic voice repeated the chorus, *O come let us adore Him*, this time with the aid of musical instruments. Many scattered throughout the assembly rose from their seats and joined in.

Then more people stood. Before you knew it, the vast-majority were standing, hands lifted high above their heads, lending their voices to the choir, singing joyfully, including Lydia.

Ann Chen rose from her seat the moment her husband Jack returned from collecting the offering. As the married couple praised God together in song, Lydia couldn't discern Jack's true thoughts regarding the three homeless men seated a few spaces away from him. If anything, it looked as if he was trying to ignore that they were even there.

Enoch, Leroy and Pedro weren't standing. All three had their faces pressed down on the seats they were seated on a few moments ago.

The way they bowed in reverence to the Glorious One, completely lost in His presence, penetrated Lydia's weary heart, soul and spirit, all the way down to her bones.

The song's chorus, "*O come let us adore Him, O come let us adore Him, O come let us adore Him, Christ the Lord,*" was repeated many times before the song ended. Enoch, Leroy and Pedro remained on their faces the entire time.

In a way, Lydia felt like she was in the presence of the three wise men of the Bible. Only they were three wise homeless men from the neighborhood. But who else in this place adored Jesus, as the song being sung boldly declared, to the point of falling prostrate before Him in worship? The answer was no one. It made it even more difficult to accept that these caring, humble, selfless men were the objects of scorn from so many filling the sanctuary.

This was the most peaceful Lydia had felt in this place in many weeks. It suddenly felt like church again. *Finally!*

11

THE MOMENT THE SERVICE ended the Chens rose from their seats, gathered their belongings, and quickly left without saying bye to anyone. Lydia winced. *Hmm, that's a first.* Erasing the thought from her mind, she turned to her three guests, "Be right back, gentlemen. It shouldn't take long to get Matthew and Grace."

"Take all the time you need."

"Why don't we meet back at my car?"

"Sure," Enoch replied, speaking on behalf of the three of them.

Since Leroy already knew what her car looked like, Lydia handed her keys to him and pointed them in the general vicinity of where it was parked. *If John only knew I just gave my car keys to three homeless men, he'd have a heart attack!*

Lydia chuckled at the thought.

When she arrived on the second floor of the adjacent annex building, Ann Chen was already there waiting for her son, Edward.

Eyeballing Ann, Lydia said, "You and Jack left so quickly after service. I never even got to say bye to you."

Ann was unable to hold Lydia's gaze, "You were busy with your friends. We didn't want to disturb you."

A likely excuse, Lydia thought. She quickly reconsidered. Perhaps if Ann brought three homeless people to church, she might feel uneasy at first herself. At the very least, she would need time to adjust. "So, what do you think of them?"

"They seem nice," Ann said.

"What about Jack?"

Ann shrugged awkwardly, unable to contain her uneasiness. "He didn't say."

"I don't know about you, but I never saw anyone worship like them. It's like they were able to retreat into their own little worlds and connect ever so deeply to their Maker. Hope I can learn to worship like that someday."

"I admit it was impressive," Ann said, relieved to see Edward approaching. Matthew and Grace were right behind him. Ann did a quick check to make sure her son had all his belongings. Satisfied that he did, she said, "See you next week, Lydia. Don't want to keep Jack waiting."

"I understand," came the reply. "Will I see you at Christmas Eve service?"

"Lord willing, right?"

Lydia nodded yes. Watching Ann and Edward leave the room, she didn't know how to gauge her friend's overall reaction. She just hoped the uneasiness on Ann's part had more to do with the unwanted attention she received from so many during the service, than from the three men seated in her company.

"CHILDREN, WOULD YOU LIKE to know why I brought Leroy and Pedro with me today?" Enoch said, in between bites of food.

"Sure," Matthew and Grace said in unison.

"Because of the three of you."

"Why us?" Grace asked nonchalantly, fairly certain she already knew the answer. One did not need to be a grownup to see what was going on.

"I came to your church looking to fellowship with those who are supposed to be my own kind. But I must say, after seeing thousands who proclaim to be followers of Yeshua for two straight weeks, if church is the place to go to find Christians at their best, I would hate to see many outside the church."

Enoch observed Matthew nodding his head sadly.

"Until today, I felt more like a nobody at your church than I ever did at the city park. Many who feed us at the park aren't even followers of Yeshua, yet they show us more genuine kindness and compassion than many who worship at your church and call themselves Christians."

Grace dropped her head in shame, unable to believe what she was hearing.

"Don't get me wrong; not everyone went out of their way to avoid me. Some welcomed me verbally. Others nodded and smiled. But no one extended a hand in friendship. If anything, most inched away from me, as if they might catch a deadly disease by touching me."

Lydia remained silent, but the look on her face said it all: she was never more ashamed of her church.

Enoch paused to wipe his mouth with a napkin. "When I left church last Sunday, I had no intention of ever coming back. Your mother changed everything, when she visited me at the park the next day, to apologize for the way some at her church had treated me. She even brought me food. I knew she was genuine the instant I met her. She further proved it the next day when she returned to the park to feed my friends. Not only did she feed us, she spent time with us.

Enoch leaned up in his seat, "When she came back a third time with you and Grace, we got to see the Spirit of God put on full display. So, in that sense, Matthew, seeing Yahweh working through the three of you so beautifully, is what ultimately prevented us from visiting another church today."

Lydia and Grace wiped tears from their eyes.

Matthew managed to hold back his tears, and drilled down deeper, "How can you know if a church is good or not?"

Enoch took a sip of water. "By her fruit, Matthew."

Leroy and Pedro both nodded agreement.

"The true character of any church is put on full display when faced with difficult or awkward situations. It doesn't always take a major crisis to test the mettle of a body of believers. It could be something as simple as a homeless person looking for a place to worship with fellow brothers and sisters in Christ. In that sense, your church failed the test."

Matthew sighed, "How can this be fixed?"

The way he asked caused Enoch to smile. "By going back to the basics. Do you know what Yeshua said was the greatest commandment?"

When Matthew didn't answer, Enoch recited Matthew 22:37-38. "'Jesus replied: 'Love the Lord your God with all your heart and with all your soul and with all your mind. This is the first and greatest commandment.'"

"And the second is love your neighbor like yourself, right?"

"Precisely, Lydia! This includes homeless people too. Messiah said that all the Law and the Prophets hang on these two commandments." Enoch searched Lydia's face. "Which brings me back to your church..."

Lydia braced herself, "Yeah?"

"In truth, there's much to like about it. Despite that I've been greatly mistreated there, I believe many are sincere in their faith. The extensive outreach your church does in the local community, not to mention with various missions abroad is commendable."

Finally, Lydia thought, *something to hang my hat on.*

"Another thing I like is that your church represents so many different ethnicities. Walking through the aisles of your church is like wading through a bouquet of colorful humanity. It's refreshing seeing people of all skin colors worshiping under the same roof, just like Yahweh had intended it."

Enoch sighed. "But from a sociological standpoint, some at your church have forgotten that we're commanded to treat *all* who walk through the doors with true Christian love, not just some."

"What about Pastor Flores?"

"I believe he is a true child of God. He always stays true to the Holy Scriptures. But because your church is so big, much of what happens between himself and people like us often goes unnoticed."

Lydia sighed. "Sorry for the way some have treated you." The positive walls she'd built up about the church she loved so much kept crumbling all around her. She almost didn't want to eat her lunch.

"Don't feel bad, Lydia. It happens everywhere I go. So, in that sense, I got exactly what I expected."

Part of Lydia wanted to ask if he thought his overall appearance had anything to do with it. She refrained. Besides, she already knew what his reply would be, "Should that matter?" *No, it shouldn't,* Lydia thought to herself, especially in the house of God. *Apparently, it still does...*

A pang of guilt snaked through her.

A few moments of silence ensued as everyone ate their meals. When Enoch was finished, he crisscrossed his knife and fork over his plate and sat back. Glancing to his right the old man's expression changed. He shook his head in disappointment.

Following his eyes, Lydia saw a family of six dining two tables away from them. It didn't take long to see what had upset Enoch so much. Both parents had their mobile devices turned on as their three children played games online using netbooks. They were completely swallowed up in their own little worlds—playing games, texting, surfing the internet, whatever—to know or care what was happening around them.

The youngest member, no older than four, had her netbook propped up on the table in front of her. With one hand, she slowly chewed on a French fry. With her free hand, she pushed buttons on the touch screen, totally disconnected from everyone else.

Meanwhile, the grandmother, who didn't have a mobile device, looked entirely lost and out of place. There was no communication among them, none whatsoever. With the loneliest expression Lydia could ever remember seeing, the grandmother looked as if she were a stranger in a strange land, like she didn't matter to those with whom she was dining.

Her face said it all...

Lydia glanced away, unable to stomach this microcosmic glimpse of the gradual deterioration of the American family. Then again, she didn't need to see this pitiful object lesson to be reminded of it. All she had to do was examine her own marriage; it was crumbling before her very eyes.

"Certainly not a comforting thought", Lydia told herself under her breath, paying the check.

Lydia dropped her three homeless friends back at the city park. Part of her wanted to stay there with them. She dreaded the thought of going home to her husband. Just thinking about it zapped the positive energy from her body, replacing it with the same sense of anguish and dread that had followed her around for too long. Seeing her kids' reflections in the rearview mirror she knew they, too, were battling similar thoughts.

"Lord, give us the strength!" she prayed.

12

THE NEXT DAY - 6 DAYS BEFORE CHRISTMAS

JOHN JENSEN WAS SITTING at his desk at work, staring at the walls, nervously awaiting this unscheduled meeting with his boss. The day had already started badly after being stuck in traffic for nearly 30 minutes, while on the way to the office.

It got worse when he spilled hot coffee on his suit pants after jamming on the breaks a little too hard, to avoid hitting the car in front of him. He had a slight burn mark on his right thigh to prove it.

Now soon-to-be meeting with his boss, John sensed his day was about to get a whole lot worse. Then again, from a production standpoint, the web designer/IT technician was shocked his boss had waited this long. The past few months had shown a steady decline on his part. This was the day his boss finally decided to confront him. Enough was enough!

Already on edge, to make things even worse, Lydia informed him on his way out the door this morning that she invited her new friend, Enoch, to the house for dinner. *The hits just keep on coming!* John thought, as his boss entered inside his office, a determined look on his face.

Or was it disappointment?

Either way, John feared the outcome.

Taking a few moments to peruse John's production charts, his boss placed his tablet on his employee's desk. He removed his glasses and slowly massaged the bridge of his nose. "These numbers are pathetic, John! What happened to my once star employee? Not only is the number of new clients you bring in-house on the sharp decline, some have decided to take their business elsewhere, claiming they never hear from you anymore. When was the last time you visited our clients at their place of business to give them the personal touch you were known for in the past?"

When John didn't answer, his boss answered for him, "I'll tell you when. Seven months ago! No wonder they're looking elsewhere for service. Can't say I blame them. It's like you no longer care." Shifting his weight in his seat, he said, "You were always on airplanes in the past. Now it's like you're going through the motions just to collect a paycheck. This

69

is unacceptable, John! Do you realize your Christmas bonus this year will be one-tenth of what it was last year?"

John pressed his lips together. He didn't need to do much calculating to figure that 10 percent of $7,500—his bonus last year—came to $750. *Not even half my mortgage payment!*

A new wave of worry crept onto his face...

"Your once-boundless passion and energy has faded to the point of near robotism. I don't need robots! I need leaders!" his boss yelled. "I want you to take a few days off. In fact, take the rest of the year off. Consider it an extended paid vacation. Come back only when the John Jensen I've known all those years resurfaces!"

All John could do was listen, then apologize. *Hopefully a few days off will help me. Something better help soon!*

John left the building and sat in his car parked in his reserved employee parking space, feeling all alone in the world. Nausea swam through his body at the thought of his minuscule bonus check. *How will I tell Lydia I won't be working for the remainder of the year?*

His thoughts quickly shifted to Enoch. The last thing John needed now was to have a complete stranger over to his house for dinner, a homeless man at that! Could he be trusted in their home? John didn't know.

With that in mind, he decided to make two stops before going home. Stop number one was at the Taco Bell down the street from his office. Stop number two was the city park.

John found an open parking space and gently guided his vehicle into position. He grabbed the fast food bags and went in search of the homeless man who had completely captivated his wife and two children the past few days.

While Lydia and the kids came to this place out of the goodness of their hearts, John was there to feel the old man out, to see if it would be safe to invite him to his home. If not, he would do all he could to dissuade him from coming.

John ambled toward a sizable group of homeless people scattered on the brownish park grass. Some were sitting. Others were passed out, completely motionless, as if just sucker-punched in the face by Mike Tyson.

Dodging a few bundled-up souls, the sharp-dressed man wearing suit and tie practically stumbled onto Enoch. Because the old man had a gray hoodie pulled over his head for added warmth, John wasn't able to identify him by his long silver-gray hair.

But he easily recognized the green blanket Grace told him about the other day. *Grace was right; it really is in dire need of washing!*

"Good afternoon," John said, a nervous tension in his voice.

Enoch looked up. "Good afternoon to you, too, sir," the kind old man replied warmly, despite his frigid cold body.

"Hungry?"

"A little, I suppose."

"There are thirty tacos in these bags. Feel free to pass them out to your friends if you like."

"That's very kind of you, sir."

"Name's John, Enoch." John extended his right hand. "John Jensen."

Meeting his hand halfway, Enoch said, "I wasn't expecting to see you until later at your house."

"I wanted to meet you without my wife and kids around, so I decided to come alone. Hope you don't mind."

"Not at all," Enoch replied. "You are blessed with a lovely wife and two remarkable children. All three have wonderful servant's hearts."

"Thank you." John's reply was even, clinical.

"Care to sit down?"

Hmm, John thought, suddenly wishing he wasn't wearing work clothes. Then again, his pants were already coffee-stained from earlier. "Sure, why not?"

Enoch spread his well-worn blanket out to make room for his visitor. Using his left hand, he motioned for John to take a seat.

"Actually, there are thirty-two tacos. All I want are two. Do whatever you want with the rest." After just being laid off from work, and learning that his Christmas bonus would be substantially less this year, this new uncertain climate made purchasing 32 tacos suddenly seem as if John had just purchased an expensive vehicle that he knew he couldn't afford.

Enoch removed a taco from one of the bags. After briefly introducing John to Leroy and Pedro, he handed the bags to them. Leroy reached into one of the bags and pulled out a taco and passed it on.

Pedro did the same.

After all the tacos were distributed, Enoch turned around to find John's teeth clamped onto one of them. Without saying a word, the homeless man bowed his head and prayed aloud thanking his Maker for the food.

Enoch opened his eyes to find John frozen, as if on ice, mouth closed, partially eaten taco in his hand, with an expression on his face that begged forgiveness.

"It's okay, John. Don't feel bad."

"It was selfish of me to eat without first thanking God," John remarked, unsure if he meant it or not.

"When someone doesn't know from where their next meal will come, or when, he tends to be extremely grateful for everything he eats."

"Amen to that, preacher," Pedro shouted.

John was rendered speechless.

Enoch took a bite of his taco. Part of it fell back into the wrapper. "Compared to some of the food we get here, this is like manna from Heaven."

"What exactly is manna?" John knew it was mentioned somewhere in the Bible.

"According to the Book of Psalms, it's the grain of Heaven, the bread of the angels."

"Really?"

"Feel free to check it for yourself when you get home, in chapter seventy-eight, verses twenty-four and twenty-five."

The way Enoch explained it, with such absolute certainty, made John believe this man had once tasted this so-called "manna". Looking into his eyes, eyes that were fully aglow, John felt shame for prejudging him at church.

"Does anyone ever feed you spoiled food here?"

"Occasionally, yes. At least when it comes to the expiration dates. Then again, massive hunger greatly improves the taste of everything." The old man smiled. Even amid this humble wall-less, roofless community, it was no more trouble for Enoch to joke than for a bird to sing.

"I'll take your word for it," John said, his eyes darting left and right, regretting his ill-timed remark.

The two men sat in silence and consumed their meals.

Finally, John said, "Can I ask you something?"

"Sure, John, anything."

"What made you become homeless?"

"Ah, the number one question." Enoch steadied his gaze on John. "I may be homeless, but praise God my house is still in order," the old man said, gesturing to his body with his two hands. "How about your house, John? Is it in order?"

72

John gulped hard. In a near whisper, he asked, "To which house are you referring?"

"You tell me." *Is he the one, Lord?* the old man thought, knowing his Maker wouldn't reveal him or her until the time of His choosing. His orders from above were specific: *Wait and always be ready.*

John cleared his throat. "Well, if you mean my body, after all, I'm aware that the Bible calls our bodies temples, I do a pretty good job taking care of it. For the most part, I watch what I eat and exercise fairly regularly. Until lately, that is…"

The look on Enoch's face said it all. In a softer tone, he said, "If you could look in the mirror and, instead of seeing your true reflection, see how your wife and children observe you, would you like what you saw staring back at you?"

"No," John replied, without hesitation.

Enoch remained silent, unwilling to be the next to speak.

John took a few deep exasperated breaths and exhaled. *Is this man a shrink or something?* Whoever he was, John felt comfortable enough to take the next step, even with so many others eavesdropping on them. "If, by house, you mean at home, well..." He wondered if Lydia had already spilled the beans to this wise old man. "...lately things haven't been so rosy with me and Lydia."

"I see. Care to share why?"

"I'll admit it's mostly my fault. I feel like I'm in an endless rut."

"Why do you feel that way?"

"There's this constant pressure to keep pushing hard to earn a good wage so I can support my family. It's been a real struggle lately. Even without the constant financial pressures," John confessed, without revealing what happened at work earlier, "nothing seems real to me anymore. Nothing makes sense like it used to. Life has become a demoralizing rotating cycle. I feel so burnt out."

"I understand your concern, John," Enoch said. "But you need to know everything you do in life produces a wage of some sort, whether good or bad. For instance, raising your children properly produces a good wage in the form of a thriving legacy. The kind things you do for others, like bringing us food, produces a good wage in that you get to feel good about yourself.

"On the other hand," the old man said, growing more serious, "the bad wages of working too much is separation from your family. I'm sure your wife and kids would gladly trade any additional wages you may earn in the future, just to spend more time with you."

Enoch paused and waited until John's eyes had fully settled onto his, then went on, "But the worst kind of wage comes from the sins we commit in life. Romans chapter six, verse twenty-three clearly states that "the wages of sin is death."

"Amen to that," Leroy declared, still chewing the taco in his mouth.

John let Enoch's words register, then sighed. "I suppose you're right. It's just that everything seems meaningless these days. My marriage. Family life. My job. Even going to church. I mean, what's the point? I feel like I've reached the breaking point. Part of me wants to give up."

"As in ending the precious life God gave to you?"

John clammed up. He suddenly felt foolish for sharing his innermost thoughts with a man he just met, especially surrounded by a bunch of homeless people. But he couldn't help but feel drawn to Enoch.

The old man closed his eyes and, from memory, recited, "'Meaningless! Meaningless! says the Teacher. Utterly meaningless. Everything is meaningless. What do people gain from all their labors at which they toil under the sun? Generations come and generations go, but the earth remains forever.

"The sun rises and the sun sets, and hurries back to where it rises. The wind blows to the south and turns to the north; round and round it goes, ever returning on its course. All streams flow into the sea, yet the sea is never full. To the place the streams come from, there they return again.'"

Enoch reached for a breath and continued, "'All things are wearisome, more than one can say. The eye never has enough of seeing, nor the ear its fill of hearing. What has been will be again, what has been done will be done again; there is nothing new under the sun.

"Is there anything of which one can say, 'Look! This is something new'? It was here already, long ago; it was here before our time. No one remembers the former generations, and even those yet to come will not be remembered by those who follow them.'" Enoch opened his eyes.

Finally, someone who understands me, John thought. *Perhaps he is a shrink!* "Sounds familiar. Shakespeare?"

"No. King Solomon, son of King David. The wisest man who ever lived."

"Really?" John replied, feeling a little foolish.

"Yes, from the Old Testament, in the first chapter of the Book of Ecclesiastes, verses two through eleven."

John sighed. "Pretty much sums me up."

"You are not alone in this matter, John. Everyone arrives at this crucial point in life, including King Solomon. He applied his mind to study all that was done under the sun. Having seen all things, he concluded that all of them were meaningless, a chasing after the wind. I challenge you to read the Book of Ecclesiastes. It might help with your present dilemma."

"I'm just scratching the surface," John thought to say, but refrained. "Are you a prophet or something?"

"Let's just say I am here to do the will of God."

"Fair enough." *Who is this man?* Everything about him was shrouded in mystery.

There was a long pause as both men surveyed the landscape. John stared at a man sleeping on the grass a few feet away from him. He was bundled up from head to toe. "Must get cold here at night..."

"Quite cold."

John winced. *What right do I have to complain about anything?* He pointed a finger at a man buried beneath a blanket ten-feet away. He was shivering uncontrollably. "What's his problem?"

"Heroin addict. Like many here, he receives government assistance on the first of each month. Some use the money to stay at cheap hotels until the money runs out, and they are forced back on the streets until the next allotment arrives. The majority, however, spend whatever they have on drugs and alcohol, including him.

"The first half of the month he is high as a kite on heroin. Once the money runs out, he suffers from violent withdraw attacks. He shakes uncontrollably for days on end before finally drying out. Then the first of the month comes and the same thing happens all over again."

John shook his head in bewilderment, "I see."

There was another pause. Then, "So, did I pass your test so far?"

"What test?" John asked.

"Oh, nothing, I just hope you feel comfortable enough to still want me as your dinner guest."

"Okay, I'll admit my main reason for coming here was to feel you out a bit, to make sure you were harmless."

"And what have you concluded?"

"I can see why my family likes you so much. And, yes, I still want you to come for dinner."

"Thank you, kind sir."

75

"What time is Lydia planning to pick you up?"

"Four o'clock."

"Would you like to come a little earlier? I mean, why make her drive when I'm already here, right?"

"Makes sense to me."

"Why don't you gather up all your belongings, so we can wash them back at the house."

"Since I don't have much, would it be possible to bring some of my friends' things? They would be most grateful. Despite what some might think, many of us clean ourselves each day in the park bathroom. The problem is that we're forced to put the same dirty clothes back on our just-washed bodies, making it nearly impossible to rid ourselves of that unpleasant odor I'm sure you can easily detect."

John glanced at the impoverished lot of humanity before him. For the most part, distant eyes stared back. "Sure, why not?"

"Thank you, kind sir."

"Shall we?"

13

LYDIA WAS ON THE couch folding laundry when the front door opened. To her great surprise, Enoch suddenly appeared in the doorway.

Freeway sprung to her feet, then froze. Ears propped up, head turned sideways, the look on her face was, *who is this strange visitor to my domain?*

Matthew and Grace were seated at the kitchen table doing their homework. Both heard the front door open and knew it was their father. After the way he'd misbehaved the past few months, running into Daddy's arms was gradually replaced with, "Hi Dad," or "How was work?"

Nothing more.

John walked through the door loaded down with filthy backpacks and duffel bags full of dirty laundry.

Seeing her master, Freeway raced to greet him. Of late, the mixed-breed canine was the only family member happy to see him come home from work each day. Tail wagging a mile a minute, her attention was divided—half on John, the other half investigating this new stranger using the old sniff maneuver.

Satisfied that he was a "friendly" Freeway welcomed Enoch warmly without the slightest concern for his ragged appearance.

"I wasn't expecting you until later," Lydia said cordially, rising from the couch to greet her dinner guest.

"Nice to see you again, Lydia," Enoch said, in a voice that was unmistakably his, diverting Matthew's and Grace's attention to the living room.

"Enoch!" Grace exclaimed, racing from the kitchen to greet him.

Matthew followed close behind his sister. "Hi Enoch!"

"Hi Daddy." Grace embraced her father.

"Hi Dad," said Matthew. He was merely going through the motions.

Lydia glanced to John. "No work today?"

"I left early." John's brow was wrinkled from too much worrying.

Lydia wanted to further inquire, but something told her not to. Not now, anyway. "I hope you like roast beef, broccoli, glazed carrots and mashed potatoes," she said to Enoch.

"Sounds delicious."

"The roast beef's still in the oven and won't be done for an hour or so."

"I am fine for now. John was kind enough to bring tacos to the park for me and the others."

Lydia shot a sideways look at her husband. She arched an eyebrow, unable to mask her shock. "He did, did he?"

"That'll give us plenty of time to start the laundry," John remarked, diverting the unwanted attention leveled upon him, from his wife. "Please make yourself comfortable."

"Thank you, John." Enoch said, taking a seat on the couch.

"Take everything to the laundry room," Lydia told John. "I'll do the rest."

"There's more in the trunk," John said to Matthew. "Can you help me, son?"

Matthew's eyes lit up. "Sure!" He was just thankful to be doing something with his father again; even if it involved carrying dirty laundry.

"Would you like to shower before dinner?" Lydia asked Enoch.

"I would like that very much."

"This way I can wash the clothes you're wearing. In the meantime, I'll get you a clean change of clothing, washcloth and a towel."

"Thank you, Lydia," the old man said.

John and Matthew returned a moment later, arms wide open, hugging a bunch of filthy blankets. The nasty stench attacked their nostrils, making them woozy to the point of gagging a few times.

Though unpleasant, the two Jensen males toughed-it-out all the way to the laundry room, where they dropped everything onto the floor.

After his bath, Enoch rejoined the family wearing one of John's sweat suits that had grown too tight on him. What was too tight for John was quite the opposite for Enoch. Two of him could have easily fit inside.

Grace wasted no time. "Can I brush your hair?"

Enoch peeked to see if either parent objected. Seeing that they didn't, he said, "Sure you may, Grace."

"It will be better if you sit on the floor, so I can reach your head."

"As you wish," came the reply.

As the old man gingerly lowered himself onto the carpeted floor, Grace positioned herself on the couch behind him. Freeway inched up as close to her new friend as she could. Tail wagging briskly, the mixed breed dog persisted until her wish was granted.

Using his left hand, Enoch stroked Freeway's back until she finally had enough and rolled over, prompting Enoch to rub her belly.

With so many knots in his long hair, Grace was extra gentle. "You should use conditioner next time."

Enoch erupted in a volcano of laughter. "I'll try to keep that in mind."

Even with no place to live, John marveled at how the old man had a laughter reminiscent of a child who hadn't yet realized the world wasn't simply fun and games. He seemed wise in all matters where wisdom was needed, yet ignorant of the unnecessary things that most deemed vital.

Nice man or not, his childlike aura rubbed John the wrong way.

Lydia wondered how long it had been since his hair had been so clean. She dared not ask him.

It took some doing, but the seven-year-old was finally able to loosen all the kinks in Enoch's hair.

"Thank you, dear Grace."

"My pleasure," she said sincerely.

With their homework finished, the washer working overtime removing vicious stains and odors from backpacks, clothing and blankets, Enoch's hair brushed to near perfection, and the roast beef fully cooked, Lydia called everyone to the dinner table.

"Everything looks delicious," Enoch said gratefully.

"Would you be kind enough to bless the food?"

The old man nodded, and everyone held hands. After praying, everyone dug in.

Now safely back on his home turf John no longer felt vulnerable like he did at the city park, with so many unfortunates constantly eyeballing him. With each bite of food he took, his apathy and skepticism toward life and religion slowly returned.

It was time to put the knowledge he spent four years and six figures to obtain in college to good use. What better way than a healthy debate?

"I must say, your faith in God is remarkable," the man of the house said to his lowly dinner guest, rather stiffly. "It's hard for me to comprehend you having nothing, yet praying to your Maker as if you were perfectly contented in this world."

Lydia lowered her head hoping her husband wouldn't go off on one of his tirades in front of this kind old man.

"Well, John," Enoch answered, "my unshakable faith in Yahweh is nothing for which I can take credit. Faith is a gift God freely gives to all

79

who belong to Him. Without faith, it's impossible to please God. One must believe in faith, live by faith and walk by faith. According to Ephesians six, verse sixteen, faith is part of the armor of God, the shield with which we protect ourselves from the flaming arrows of the evil one. So, in that sense, it is essential in our daily walk with the Creator."

Smug look on his face, John looked like a reporter zeroed in on his target waiting for the perfect time to pounce on him, thus discrediting him. "Didn't Jesus say only those with childlike faith will inherit the Kingdom of God?"

Before Enoch could reply, John shook his head. "That statement's always bothered me. I mean, aren't children supposed to be vulnerable and easily led astray, thinking up the silliest things? Quite frankly, reverting back to that way of thinking insults the intelligence of so many, myself included."

"Actually, the Bible never exhorts us to have childlike faith. Nor does it tell us to believe as children believe. As you rightly said, children are easily fooled and led astray. They tend to accept things unquestioningly, often missing truth while being drawn to man-created myths and fantasies. We need to look no further than this so-called Santa Claus many in the world embrace this time of year, to the point of worship, I might add.

"It takes great faith for anyone to believe that an old man dressed in a red suit could travel the entire world in a single day, leaving gifts under millions of Christmas trees for countless children, his mode of transportation a sleigh flown by animals who cannot even fly. Yet, most children exposed to the Santa Claus myth believe and embrace it wholeheartedly. Their faith is commendable, even if misguided.

"Often misunderstood is Matthew eighteen, verses two through four, where Yeshua said we must become as little children. Said Messiah, 'Truly, I say to you, unless you turn and become like children, you will never enter the kingdom of heaven.' Verse four states, 'Whoever humbles himself like this child is the greatest in the kingdom of heaven.' It's clear in verse four that Yeshua was not referring to faith here, but rather humility."

Enoch paused to take a sip of water. "The point to consider, John, is unless one is humble like a child to receive the Gospel message, which leads to conversion and is the very essence of being born again, I might add, he cannot enter the kingdom of Heaven. But it would be foolish for anyone to think Yahweh wants us to remain as children. Scripture exhorts us to mature in the faith and knowledge of Christ.

"First Corinthians chapter fourteen, verse twenty makes it clear, 'Brothers, do not be children in your thinking. Be infants in evil, but in your thinking be mature.' Those who do not mature are in danger of being tossed to and fro by the waves and carried about by every wind of doctrine, by human cunning, by craftiness in deceitful schemes."

"Well that's a relief," John said, almost mockingly, stiffening up in his chair. *He sure knows his Bible. I'll give him that.*

Lydia silently prayed that John would remain calm. At least he wasn't drinking beer now.

"I hear what you're saying, but it's hard for me to have faith at times with so many atrocities being committed by those who proclaim to represent God's Kingdom here on earth. I can't tell you how many stories I've heard over the years of pastors swindling money from churches, priests sexually molesting young children and a myriad of other great evils."

Fully mindful of John's "everything is meaningless" mindset, Enoch let him continue.

"And don't even get me started with those so-called evangelists, on TV and on the internet, seducing so many by promising them endless material blessings in return for sowing into their ministries. Do they think they're gods? They're not givers, they're takers. They sicken me."

Stabbing his fork in the roast beef on his plate, John said, "To be honest the whole tithing thing doesn't sit well with me. I mean, where does all that money go? I could go on and on..."

He took a moment to swallow the food in his mouth. "With so much hypocrisy in the church, no wonder so many are turned off to religion and want nothing to do with Christianity. It's hard knowing who to trust or who is genuine anymore. No wonder some say Christians are the chief cause of the spread of atheism in the world. Is it true?"

"I do not know if that is true or not," the old man said, "but I do agree it's high time for the church to get her House in order. Many who proclaim to be followers of Yeshua are doing a very poor job of showing it.

"Just like sitting in an airplane does not make one a pilot and sitting in a bus does not make one a bus driver, sitting in a church does not automatically make one a Christian. Nor does standing behind a pulpit preaching each week. Many may call themselves preachers, but not all are true men of God.

"Truth is, people attend church and profess faith in Yeshua for all sorts of reasons. Some do it to gain the acceptance of others, or to capture the heart of someone they like. Others go to church to further their business and political careers.

"Others go to keep from being lonely. Going there gives them a sense of belonging. Many parents go to provide structure for their children, nothing more. These reasons do not make anyone a true child of God."

Eyeballing John, Enoch said, "It is only the repentant soul that God will accept, the heart that is broken, not the mouth that professes faith then defies it by their actions. Nor is it the head that is bowed remorsefully in church for all to see. Even Judas Iscariot showed remorse after betraying Messiah. But let me assure you, John, remorse and true repentance are two very different things.

"Scripture is clear that the time will come and, in fact, is here when certain men and women whose condemnation was written about long ago have secretly slipped in among us. These false teachers have abandoned the faith and no longer put up with sound doctrine. They have changed the grace of God into a license for immorality, following deceiving spirits and things taught by demons.

"Since Satan disguises himself as an angel of light, it should come as no surprise that many of his servants do the same by disguising themselves as servants of righteousness. Tragically, so many churches are being inundated by these godless individuals whose consciences have been seared as with hot irons. Disguising themselves as apostles of Yeshua, they have turned away from the truth and say whatever their itching ears want to hear, greedily exploiting many with stories they have made up."

Enoch took a moment to put the last fork full of mashed potatoes in his mouth and swallowed. "The gospel they preach comes straight from the pits of hell. They are not serving God; they serve Satan."

"I couldn't agree with you more," John said. Funnily enough, he wanted to shout, "Amen!", but refrained.

"But you see, John, this is precisely why Messiah never commanded us to imitate or follow any man, only Him. As you rightly said, with so many atrocities being committed by those proclaiming to represent God's Kingdom, we must test everything we hear and compare it to the infallible Word of God, always holding on to what is good…

"In the end, only those who dwell in the Scriptures and live their lives according to them can lead lives worthy of the Gospel, and be effective in discipling others."

Enoch paused and studied John's face very closely. "All pretenders, the ones you alluded to, will have to answer to God someday for their great sin and deception. The judgment they receive for their vile actions will be rightly deserved."

John leaned back in his chair and stretched his hands above his head.

Enoch knew he'd made his point, "Let me end this discussion by saying that even if an angel from Heaven should preach to you a gospel contrary to the one the Apostle Paul preached, let him be accursed."

John flinched. The way his dinner guest said it caused chills to shoot up and down his spine. *Who is this man?*

Seeing that her husband was unable to speak, Lydia said, "How's apple pie a la mode sound?"

Enoch grinned, "Sounds delightful!"

14

AFTER THE DISHES WERE washed, Matthew and Grace watched TV in the living room, leaving the adults alone so they could continue their discussion.

Stirring whipped cream into his hot chocolate with a spoon—Enoch's new favorite drink—he said to John, "Care to further elaborate on your overall disdain toward tithing?"

John grimaced. "After many years of close observation, I've concluded that the main function of the church is to raise money. Everything else seems secondary at best, including helping those in need. Even before the sermon starts, they take up a collection. You know, sort of like prepaying for a presentation."

Enoch rested his hands in his lap. He wasn't at all surprised to hear John saying this. "Second Corinthians chapter nine, verse seven states that each must give as he has decided in his heart, not reluctantly or under compulsion, for God loves a cheerful giver.

"In that light, John, it all comes down to one's attitude toward giving, and knowing Who is in charge of their finances."

No doubt you have a very good attitude, Lydia thought, reflecting on how honored Enoch looked both times she saw him giving at her church. "Sorry for sounding insensitive," she interjected, "but since we're on the topic of tithing, I was wondering where you got the money you placed in the offering plate?"

"People give us money on occasion at the park," Enoch replied evenly, "which we use for food. Whatever is leftover at the end of the week, we give back to God. Not only that, some at the park who now have jobs set aside 10 percent of their earnings each week, which we give to the church on their behalf."

"That's very noble of you, but wouldn't it be better to keep it for a rainy day, as the expression goes? I'm sure God would understand in your case. Besides, why give money to those who treat you so badly?"

"I didn't give to your church, Lydia, but to Yahweh. He never fails to meet my daily needs, so why should I fail Him?"

Closing his eyes, from memory, Enoch recited Matthew chapter six, verses nineteen through twenty-one, "'Do not store up for yourselves treasures on earth, where moths and vermin destroy, and where thieves break in and steal. But store up for yourselves treasures in heaven, where moths and vermin do not destroy, and where thieves do not break in and steal. For where your treasure is, there your heart will be also.'"

John protested more, "With all due respect, I'm sure whatever amount you gave wouldn't be considered a 'treasure' by anyone's standard."

"Fair point you make. But are you familiar with the story of the poor widow Yeshua spoke of who gave everything she had?"

John pulled at his chin with two fingers, searching his memory.

Lydia saved him, "Two coins, right?"

"Precisely, Lydia. Yeshua watched as many rich people put in large sums that day. But the poor widow gave all she had. Yeshua told His disciples that she put in more than all those who contributed to the offering box. For they all contributed out of their abundance, but she out of her poverty put in everything she had to live on."

"Doesn't that further my point?" John said. "I mean, it sounds cruel and even heartless to take everything from someone who has nothing."

"Yahweh only requires ten percent. That should be the bare minimum. The money goes toward meeting the needs of the church and advancing the Great Commission. And for that, Jehovah Jireh promises to meet all your needs. He makes it clear in Proverbs three, verses nine and ten, 'Honor the Lord with your wealth and with the firstfruits of all your produce; then your barns will be filled with plenty, and your vats will be bursting with wine.' Did you notice this relates to food and drink, and not luxury vehicles and mansions?"

"Yeah, but taking everything from those who already have nothing? Sounds like legal extortion to me. In your case, perhaps you should purchase food with what little you have."

"I assure you, John, no one extorted me. Nothing was taken from me, only given. It's not the amount one gives but that he gives that matters most to Yahweh. When it comes to tithing, there are three types of givers in the Body of Christ. Those who give horizontally. Those who give inwardly. And those who give vertically.

"Those who give horizontally represent the stingiest, most tightfisted group, if you will. They are also the most skeptical givers in the church. They always wonder where their money will go and who will benefit from it. I like to call them the 'checks and balances' givers.

"Their mindset is more steadied on the fact that we live in a society full of complete distrust, where giving demands constant monitoring. Instead of realizing it's all God's anyway, their approach to giving is more worldly than anything else, because it completely nullifies giving for the sole sake of giving. Hence, the negative mindset and constant skepticism.

"Those who give inwardly are often generous but for all the wrong reasons. With many strings attached to their tithing, these people are the most self-centered givers. Their chief motivation is 'What's in it for me'?

"Many come from the kinds of churches we discussed earlier. This unholy way of giving is fueled by one of the most misunderstood passages in the written pages of God's Holy Word.

"In John fourteen, verse fourteen Yeshua states, 'You may ask me for anything in my name, and I will do it.' Though it is true that Messiah said if we ask for anything in His name, it will be given, many fail to realize this powerful declaration is only true if it lines up with God's perfect will for their lives.

"John fifteen, verses seven and eight confirms this. Yeshua said, 'If you remain in me and my words remain in you, ask whatever you wish, and it will be given you. This is to my Father's glory, that you bear much fruit, showing yourselves to be my disciples.'

"Instead of teaching those to whom they will most certainly be accountable about giving for the sole privilege of honoring God, many who call themselves servants of the Most High—pastors, priests, ministers, evangelists, rabbis, apostles and bishops—have successfully brainwashed countless multitudes into this self-centered way of tithing, by promising a constant flow of physical and material blessings in return for sowing so generously into their ministries.

"The end result is that many from these congregations give with the full expectation that God must honor His part of the deal, by giving them the desires of their hearts. Most are too caught up in the glitz and glamour of this fallen world to even know that the things for which they pray would do more harm than good if Yahweh ever granted such outlandish requests.

"I use the word 'grant' because so many prayer requests offered up these days more resemble a child's wish list at Christmastime than anything else. Instead of trusting that the all-knowing sovereign Creator of the universe already knows exactly what they need, many perceive Him as a genie in a bottle, lying in wait, ready to grant every material wish their greedy hearts desire. They fail to realize God's greatest blessings have nothing to do with material things."

John crossed his right leg over his left and relaxed all the more. *This is getting interesting!*

Enoch shook his head. "The God I serve is not some subservient invisible genie waiting to grant every last wish of those belonging to Him. If He were, nothing good would come from it. Could you imagine what would happen if Yahweh granted the wildest wishes of everyone praying to Him, simply because they asked for it in Jesus' name?

"Would it be wise, for instance, John, for God to grant heroin to a drug addict, simply because he gave at church then earnestly asked for the drug in Jesus' name? Or whiskey to an alcoholic? Or money to someone who had a serious gambling addiction?"

"Of course not."

"If Matthew asked you for a loaded shotgun so he could go outside and play with his friends, would you allow such an outrageous request?"

"No chance!"

"As your child's guardian, it would be foolish to even consider something so dangerous, right?"

John and Lydia both nodded yes.

"Despite how many times Matthew pleaded with you to finally give in, the answer would remain unchanged, right?"

"That goes without saying," John said.

Enoch pressed on, "How can those praying to Yahweh for all sorts of material things know those things aren't viewed by Him as loaded shotguns which, if received, would do great harm to them and potentially to others? How do they know the big house or fancy car they think they desperately need and constantly pray for, isn't seen by God as heroin to a drug addict or whiskey to an alcoholic?"

"You make a very good point." John felt like he was back in college under the tutelage of some well-renowned professor. All that was missing was a pad of paper and pen to take notes. At least that's how it was when he was still in college before the dawn of the internet revolution.

"In this 'prosperity-driven' society which has ensnared so many churchgoers, it's easy to see why you think the church is all about money, John. It's gotten so bad that some so-called pastors have become so blinded to the truth, they even instruct their followers not to pray, 'Thy will be done,' when praying to God, because it displays a watered-down faith, which ultimately limits Yahweh's power in their lives.

Enoch sighed. "Imagine that? Whether they do it knowingly or unknowingly, they end up praying, 'My will be done', instead of 'Thy will.' Talk about arrogance and self-centeredness!

"If praying, 'Thy will be done' displays a lack of faith in any way, that would make Yeshua guilty of being weak Himself. After all, that was Messiah's prayer shortly before being crucified on a cross two thousand years ago. Our Savior could have had legions of angels, each legion representing six-thousand, come to His immediate rescue.

"But knowing what needed to be done, He humbly prayed, 'Father, if you are willing, take this cup from me; yet not my will, but yours be done.'

"Talk about selflessness! Talk about love! It is foolish for any fair-minded believer to expect God to grant their every-last wish like a bunch of spoiled children in a candy store, simply because they give at church and ask for it all in Jesus' name.

"I wonder if those teaching such nonsense realize what would happen to their churches if God acquiesced to their self-absorbed prayer requests and blessed each member with great riches."

John leaned up further in his seat, anxious to hear what the old man would say next.

"No doubt many changes would occur." Enoch steadied his gaze on John. "Perhaps ten percent would continue walking down God's righteous path. But what about the rest? Suddenly debt free, many would take extended vacations, not only geographically, but also from their Heavenly Father.

"Having so much money at their disposal might even serve to turn part time habits into full blown addictions. Much like the prodigal son, many would fall into great sin as a result of suddenly being 'blessed' with financial riches. The ultimate casualty would be that the church would eventually collapse. Truth is, Yahweh always answers prayer, but oftentimes the answer is no. And for good reason."

Enoch shook his head, "Those who propagate this unbiblical type of giving grossly misrepresent Yahweh's sacred worship for their own personal gain, and rightly provoke God to anger.

"Conversely, many who sit under their leadership are just as guilty themselves, for wanting the same things their leaders possess in great quantities. These worldly carnal desires of the heart do not please God and have nothing at all to do with the true Christian walk."

John and Lydia shook their heads in astonishment. Lydia said, "How can Christians read the very same Bible, yet see things so differently?"

"It's easy for anyone to obtain knowledge of the mysteries of the Gospel, Lydia. All they have to do is open God's Word and read it. The problem for so many is that they are constantly learning but never arriving at the Truth. They end up sounding like solid believers, even quoting Scripture after Scripture, but that doesn't make anyone a true child of God. The blessing is not only in the knowing, but also in the doing."

Enoch placed his empty cup on the coffee table. "Which leads me to the third group of givers, those who give vertically. By far, they are the most blessed of God. To them, giving back to Yahweh is more of a pleasure than a command. The moment money comes into their hands their first thought is to set aside at least ten percent for God.

"I guess you could say they get as excited about serving Yahweh with their finances as many do singing songs to Him. While it's true vertical givers also pray for material things, huge mansions, luxury airplanes and great riches never come to mind.

"Mindful that God's greatest blessings are not monetary or material in nature, what they ask for most is for more wisdom to know God's will for their lives, for more of His peace that surpasses all understanding when storm clouds appear, and for more of the fullness of His joy whenever they do kind things for others."

"What if their funds end up being misused?" John asked studiously, trying one last time to punch a hole in Enoch's defenses.

"It is never good when money that was intended for Yahweh is misused by some. Sure, it stings at first, but vertical givers ultimately focus more on the fact that God will still bless their faithfulness and obedience to Him, while holding all who misappropriate what rightly belongs to Him accountable for it."

"I see. What about those who don't tithe?"

"According to Malachi three, verses eight and nine, they are robbing God, plain and simple. Read it for yourself sometime, John."

Enoch sighed, "I'm afraid this is happening with greater frequency these days. A true measuring stick of just how far the church has fallen is that only a tiny fraction of young adult Christians tithe regularly to the churches in which they are members.

"Aside from the entitlement mindset many youngsters now possess, I believe the other reason they do not tithe regularly, if at all, is that their churchgoing parents no longer tithe regularly. The trickle-down effect has been nothing short of disastrous...

"I can assure you it's not because these youngsters are unwilling to give. How can that be when so many generously donate to various charities that capture their attention? Not only do they give financially, many also volunteer their time to these organizations."

"Could that be considered tithing?" Lydia asked.

"No. Never," Enoch stated, without hesitation. "Despite how good a cause or charity may be, children need to be taught at an early age that Yahweh should never come second in anything, including their finances. Because money is so closely related to the desire for material things, many fall into the trap of thinking their finances should be kept separate from their spiritual lives, when nothing could be further from the truth.

"Since Yahweh is in everything, the more consciously one relates to Him in all things, instead of just some, the closer their walk will be with the Almighty. Returning one-tenth back to Him before doing anything else clearly demonstrates who is in charge of one's finances.

"And speaking of tithing, it should always go to your church. Anything above your tithe is considered an offering and does not necessarily have to go to your church. Nor does it need to be monetary."

Enoch glanced at Lydia. "Sometimes an offering of time is more effective than giving a few dollars to a good cause."

Lydia smiled and lowered her head humbly, knowing her service at the park was what prompted her dinner guest to say that.

"But even voluntary work is on the sharp decline these days. The simple truth is that it's not old age that slows most Christians down, it's comfort. Many churchgoers will freely give money for good causes, especially here in America. But very few will step outside their comfort zones and volunteer their time in the trenches with those who truly have nothing.

"As the vast-majority in the world suffer, many American Christians get to climb into warm, comfortable beds each night, in the complete safety of their homes, with full bellies and all their bills paid."

Enoch shook his head. "How could this ever be considered sacrificial giving, when they are merely giving out of their abundance?

"True vertical givers, on the other hand, always look for ways to please their Maker over and above their tithing, by making themselves available whenever and wherever they are needed.

"Whether it be monetarily or with their time matters not. To them, giving flows from a heart that has no need to be recognized, from a heart that sacrifices without bitterness or resentment.

"Receiving something in return is never their chief motivation for giving. The most important thing is that God knows and that He is pleased by their obedience to His command."

John shrugged his shoulders. Try as he might, his intelligence was no match for Enoch's wisdom. The old man answered each protest in a way that made it impossible to refute anything he said.

Instead of staunchly defending the church like John had sort of expected him to, his dinner guest did the exact opposite. If anything, he held the church in contempt on so many levels.

It made John want to delve into God's Word all the more.

15

WITH THE LAST OF the laundry washed and folded, Lydia placed everything into extra-large hefty trash bags. It would be up to them to sort it all out back at the park. She ended up washing everything twice after still smelling a faint odor after the first cycle. Thankfully the second cycle took most of it away.

Using an electric carving knife, Lydia sliced the leftover roast beef from dinner extra thin. She placed it inside an aluminum serving tray she retrieved from the kitchen cupboard, and covered the meat with piping hot brown gravy.

Meanwhile, Grace filled four empty jugs with hot water and placed 50 packets of instant hot chocolate mix and 50 Styrofoam cups inside a plastic Walmart bag for Enoch to take back to the park with him.

When Lydia went shopping for dinner earlier, she wasn't shopping only for five; she had many others in mind. Hence, the extra hot chocolate packets.

When John and Matthew returned from carrying the last load to the car, Lydia, Grace and Enoch were standing at the front door.

"Thanks for coming, Enoch." Grace hugged the old man. "You made my whole night."

"I should be thanking you, dear Grace. I had a lovely time. It was just what I needed."

"It was our pleasure, Enoch," Lydia said. "Please be careful out there." In order to keep from losing it, she shifted her attention to John, "Can you purchase a few loaves of bread on the way, so they can have hot roast beef sandwiches at the park?"

A lump formed in John's throat. Lydia still had no idea his bonus check would be substantially less this year. His thinking was diverted when he glanced at his daughter. What he saw on Grace's face tore him up inside.

Always the caring one, without inquiring, John knew what was on his daughter's mind: "Why are we making this old man go back to the cold park? Why can't he sleep here?"

"Yes, of course," John replied to his wife.

"Can I go for the ride, Dad?" Matthew said.

"Not tonight, son." John almost said, "It's cold outside," but thought better of it. "You have school in the morning."

"Okay." Matthew fist-bumped Enoch. "Stay safe."

"Don't worry, Matthew, I'll be just fine," Enoch insisted.

"Wait!" The youngest member of the Jensen family dashed up the stairs to her room. A moment later Grace was back. "Please take this."

"What is it?" Enoch said.

"It's my favorite blanket in the whole wide world. Hope it will keep you warm tonight."

"That's so nice of you, Grace, but I already have a blanket."

"Please take it," she pleaded. Her lower lip started quivering. "I want you to have it." Clearly, this was her way of apologizing to him, for her parents sending him back to the city park on a frigid cold night.

"Thank you, Grace. I'm deeply touched by your kind gesture."

Grace sniffled, then gave Enoch another prolonged hug.

Lydia looked away, unable to stop tears from swelling her eyes.

Matthew lowered his head and remained silent. He, too, was on the verge of tears due, to his kid sister's selfless act of goodwill.

At that, John and Enoch left for the city park.

Lydia and her two children glanced out the front window. Their sad, gloomy faces were illuminated by hundreds of bright Christmas lights covering the wooden window frame.

The old man glanced back one last time and waved, then slowly and gingerly lowered himself into the warm vehicle. The last thing the three Jensens saw was his cold breath floating skyward.

Once the car was out of sight, without saying a word to anyone, Grace burst out in tears and raced up to her bedroom, burying her face in a pillow. "It's not fair," she screamed.

Lydia and Matthew easily heard her loud sobs coming down the stairs.

For Lydia, her daughter's tears made her feel even more guilty for not inviting Enoch to spend the night with them. Guilt flooded her heart and soul. This was so hard.

Meanwhile, John stopped at a local convenience store and purchased five loaves of bread. They arrived at the city park soon after. At this late hour, there were plenty of parking spaces available.

John left the engine running, allowing Enoch to soak up as much heat as possible, before returning to the cold park. This would be the last real warmth the old man would experience this night.

A brief moment of silence ensued before John finally said, "Why is it you seem like you're from a different planet or something?"

Chuckling at his "different planet" comment, Enoch probed, "What exactly do you mean?"

John's brow furrowed, "I've never met anyone quite like you before. It's like you've materialized from the pages of the Bible, or at the very least, come from a different generation than ours. A better one, I might add."

"Perhaps I just have a different perspective than most others." Enoch adjusted his body to face John, "At any rate, there is only one generation that matters, John. And we needn't look back in time to find it, only forward.

"For those belonging to Yeshua, the greatest generation is yet to come. It's an eternal generation where we will all live together in perfect peace and harmony someday. Can any other generation since the dawn of mankind make such a claim?"

John didn't answer. There was no need to debate the old man any further. He was too wise. John took a deep breath and exhaled in defeat.

Staring out the windshield he confessed, "I haven't told Lydia yet, but I was sort of laid off from work today. My boss told me to take the rest of the year off and get my act together or else. A week before Christmas. Talk about the worst possible time."

"Care to share why?"

"For all the reasons I've already shared with you. It's hard to stay motivated when even the job I once loved so much, and was so good at, now seems so meaningless. It's like my whole life's unraveling before my very eyes."

"The man who develops a proper belief about God is suddenly relieved of each and every temporal problem he has."

"You score very high in that category, Enoch. But not me. I'm a bundle of nerves."

Seeing worry building in his eyes, Enoch said, "Those who rest in the promise that God really does take care of those who belong to Him, despite what happens each day, are the ones who leave all of the consequences to Him."

Rest in the promise, John thought, liking the sound of it, even if he couldn't relate to that statement on any level.

"I certainly will be praying for your work situation, John. But mostly I will pray that Yahweh will remove the 'everything is meaningless' spirit you now possess, supernaturally replacing it with a complete renewing of your mind."

John lowered his head. "Thanks."

"It was responsible of you to meet me here before inviting me into your home. It shows how much you care for the overall protection of your family."

"Of course. That goes without saying."

"Remember what I said about your wife and children having servant's hearts?"

"Yeah."

With the kindest eyes John had ever seen staring back at him, the old man said, "I believe you embody that same willingness to serve others. I'm living proof of it. You have been most generous to me."

"Thanks, Enoch. After the day I had, I needed to hear that."

Enoch opened the passenger front door and slowly climbed out of the vehicle. "Thanks again for a lovely evening with your family."

I should be thanking you, John thought to say, but didn't. "Let's do it again soon." His soul was stirring inside like never before.

"If it is God's will that we meet again, John, nothing can prevent it from happening," Enoch declared, with a certainty that was downright comforting.

Who is this man? "Would you like me to carry the food and duffel bags for you?"

Using his left arm to rest on the car exterior, the old man leaned down so John could see his face. "It wouldn't be wise leaving your car unattended at this place. Wait here. I'll send some of my fellow parkies to collect everything."

"As you wish. Please be careful."

"Thanks for the concern, John, but Yahweh will protect me. He always does," the old man said, his breath clouding the frigid night air.

Just seeing it caused more guilt to explode inside of John.

"May the Sovereign God of the universe bless and keep your family this night." Enoch smiled, then turned and walked toward the dimly lit park, clouds of smoke following each exhale, until the old man vanished into the darkness.

In no time, four homeless men arrived. John got out of the car and opened the trunk, then blew into his glove-less hands.

"Thank you for doing this, kind sir," said one man, grabbing the tin full of leftover food, grateful it was still warm. The container warmed his hands better than the threadbare gloves he was wearing.

Taking a whiff, he grinned, "Smells delicious! Could use a hot meal right about now."

"May God bless you for this," said another man, plucking two garbage bags full of clean clothing from the trunk. Another man grabbed two more garbage bags and two gallons of hot water. Another man grabbed the last bag of clean clothing and the two remaining gallons of hot water.

"My pleasure, fellas," John said, meaning it.

He watched the four men walking away. The mist of their collective exhales rose in the frigid night air, as if coming from four chimneys. A moment later they disappeared into the night.

John got back in his car. The heat felt good on his face. Though only outside in the cold elements for a minute or so, his hands and face were already cold. *How much worse for everyone at the park?*

John blinked the thought away and peered out into the darkness that had enveloped the city park one last time, then put the car in drive and drove off for the warmth and safety of his home.

His mind tortured him every mile of the way...

Locking the front door behind him, John went upstairs.

Peeking in on Grace, the disappointment he felt for leaving Enoch at the cold city park worsened. His heart burned within him, seeing a white piece of paper taped to the mirror above her dresser.

Scribbled in red crayon were the words:

Home = hope :) :) :)
Homeless = hopeless :(:(:(
Stay warm Enoch
I love you
Grace

John was never more thankful that his daughter was sleeping. He couldn't stop the tears from cascading down his still-icy cheeks.

For the first time in a long time, they weren't selfish tears, but tears for someone other than himself.

"What have I done?" the remorseful man whispered softly, lowering his head in shame. *What kind of example have I just set for my children?*

Have all my good deeds today been washed away by this one selfish act of unkindness?

It would be a long and difficult night for John Jensen.

Come daybreak, it would be even more difficult looking his children in the eye, especially Grace…

16

5 DAYS BEFORE CHRISTMAS

AFTER A FITFUL NIGHT of constant tossing and turning in bed, John Jensen finally decided at 4 a.m. that sleep would not come this night. His neck was stiff and his right shoulder sore from lying on his pillow the wrong way.

But the physical pain he felt paled in comparison to the guilt he still felt knowing he should have invited Enoch to stay at his house last night, but didn't. He felt like the worst person on the planet.

Normally a workday, John didn't know what to do with himself. The breadwinner of the house was too jittery to remain in a warm comfy bed any longer. He lowered his feet onto the plush carpeted floor, settled into his slippers beside the bed, stretched tight limbs, felt a creak and then a pop in his left shoulder, then ventured downstairs to the kitchen, without waking Lydia.

John flicked the switch on the coffeemaker. In just seconds, his nostrils were treated to the scent of fresh coffee brewing.

For the first time in many months, he appreciated that his wife prepared the coffeemaker each night before going to bed. All he had to do was turn it on each morning. *When was the last time I thanked her?*

This gave him something else to feel guilty about.

John took one last whiff and went to his office and opened his Bible to Ecclesiastes, which he found after Proverbs in the Old Testament. He went back to the kitchen and filled a cup full of coffee, which he took black, then sat at his desk and didn't stop reading until he finished all twelve chapters.

Much of it was repetitive reading, like an endless cycle, but perhaps that was the point, he reasoned. Still, it was a difficult read for him. Very difficult. *Talk about looking into a mirror!*

Flipping back and forth, John reread key points he highlighted using a yellow marker the first time through. Yellow was everywhere!

But instead of cheering him up, as he'd hoped it would, it only served to amplify the hopelessness he felt all this time. After a few moments of quiet reflection, he had more questions than answers.

THE UNANNOUNCED CHRISTMAS VISITOR

It was 5:30 a.m. John went upstairs and got dressed then tiptoed out of the bedroom, careful not to wake Lydia.

He quietly descended the stairs and went out to his car. The cold wind slapped his face repeatedly. Perhaps it was God's way of punishing him for what he did last night. *What I didn't do rather,* he thought, hurrying to his car. *How could I do such a thing?*

A few moments later, John Jensen was back at the city park, just as the sky slowly brightened and changed colors, filling the atmosphere with radiant light.

John went off in the direction of the homeless community, a remorseful spirit leading the way. What he was about to do needed to be done. At the very least, it would give him the chance to right a wrong and, in so doing, garner the forgiveness of his family.

Many of the 40 or so homeless people were still sleeping, bundled up from head to toe with everything they owned.

John noticed a woman pointing him out to another homeless woman lying next to her. She whispered something in her ear.

As John got closer, Tiwanna smiled brightly. "Thanks for the food and clean clothing," she said gratefully.

"My pleasure."

Hearing John's voice roused Enoch from his sleep. "Greetings John!" the old man said, slowly sitting up.

"Good morning, Enoch."

Enoch was buried beneath his thick green blanket. When John saw a fragment of his daughter's pink *Hello Kitty* blanket protruding from Enoch's threadbare attire, covering his face up to his eyes, it took all his strength to not start bawling in front of everyone.

"Welcome back to my lovely domain," Enoch declared cheerfully, lowering Grace's blanket. His winter breath fogged the early morning air. His body may have been frigid but certainly not his attitude.

If he was upset about last night, there wasn't a trace of it anywhere on his face or in his demeanor. If anything, he looked happy to see John again.

I would have been furious, John thought, shaking his head in disbelief. "My reason for coming here is twofold. First, I've come to ask for your forgiveness."

"Forgiveness for what?"

99

"For not inviting you to stay in my home last night." John said it soft enough so only Enoch could hear him. "I tossed and turned all night thinking about you."

"There's no need to ask my forgiveness, John. You did more than you said you would. Not only did you feed me a nutritious meal, everyone was grateful for the food and clean clothes.

"The women, especially, couldn't fill their senses enough of the fresh scent on their just-washed clothing. I believe the aroma alone helped them forget about the frigid temperatures for a while."

"Think nothing of it. It was our pleasure."

Seeing the pain in his eyes, Enoch said, "You are under no obligation to house me, John."

John sighed. "That may be so, but it was still wrong of me to do such a thing."

"Well, then, if it's my forgiveness you seek, I forgive you, John."

"I've also come to invite you back to the house. For as long as you want this time."

Enoch raised an eyebrow, then studied John's face very carefully. *Surely, he must be the one...*The old man suddenly felt God nudging him inside, confirming that John Jensen was indeed his Mission on Earth. *Thy will be done, Lord...*

"Yes, I will come with you, John."

"By the way, who can I give this to?" John pulled a $50 bill from his wallet and handed it to Enoch.

"What shall it be used for?"

"Perhaps hot coffee to warm everyone a bit. Hope it's enough for everyone. Sorry I can't give more." *I can't even afford this!*

"No need to apologize, John. They will be most appreciative of your kind generosity." Enoch handed the money to Tiwanna. "Please see that it is wisely spent."

Tiwanna beamed, "Absolutely! Very kind of you, John."

"It's my pleasure..."

Mindful of John's financial woes, Enoch saw the same worry surface in his eyes he saw the night before. "You will never lose anything you give away in love, John. But the things you keep all to yourself, those things you will surely lose."

How does he always do that? "Shall we?"

"Just give me a few minutes to say bye to everyone."

"Take all the time you need. I'll take your things to the car."

John gathered Enoch's belongings and placed them in the trunk of his car, wondering if he was doing the right thing by inviting a complete-stranger into his home, without first conducting a full background check on him.

He quickly dismissed all suspicions. If anyone was safe, it was Enoch!

For the first time in a long time, John felt this surge of peace knowing how happy his family would be seeing him again, especially knowing he was welcome to stay with them as long as he wanted this time.

For grace, it would be like receiving an early Christmas present.

What John didn't know was that he would be greatly challenged in the coming days, by the old man slowly making his way to the vehicle.

"You'll be greatly missed," Leroy said to Enoch, with a sinking feeling that his mentor's days on the streets had just come to an end. Part of him wanted to beg him not to go.

Pedro, Tiwanna, Wanda and Suzie also sensed Enoch's days with them were over. They, too, selfishly wanted him to remain with them, but knew he was a Mission waiting to happen all this time.

The fact that Enoch accepted John's kind offer, after politely refusing all others, spoke volumes. Was John his Mission?

The collective mindset among them was that he was.

"Visit us often," Tiwanna said softly, watching her spiritual mentor lower himself inside the car. Tears trickled down her frosty cheeks, one after the next.

When John and Enoch pulled away, all eyes were drawn to Leroy.

Without even asking, Leroy knew they would now look to him as the new spiritual leader at the city park.

Leroy gulped hard and left it at that...

17

AT 6:45 A.M. THE front door opened.

"We're home!" John announced, almost proudly.

We? Lydia was in the kitchen preparing breakfast. She lowered the heat on the stove and went to the living room to see John and Enoch standing at the front door.

A smile crossed Lydia's face, "Welcome back! We're just about to have breakfast. How does cream of wheat and homemade biscuits sound?"

"Sounds delicious!"

"Good. It'll be ready in just a few minutes."

Looking at John, she said, "No work today?"

"I'm off until after the new year."

"When were you going to tell me?"

"I'll explain later, okay?"

Explain? Hmmm. With Enoch around, Lydia refrained from probing any deeper.

"I'll get your things from the trunk," John said to Enoch. "Make yourself comfortable."

"Thank you, John."

"I can't tell you how happy Grace will be to see you."

Just as Lydia said it, Matthew and Grace came racing down the stairs in their pajamas. Their hair was still messy.

"Good morning, children. Your father was kind enough to invite me to stay with you for a while."

"Really?" Lydia's face lit up. She couldn't believe what she'd just heard. Whatever had gotten into her husband, it was refreshing.

"Yippie," Grace shouted teary-eyed. She embraced Enoch and clung to his body like a second skin. "I'm so glad you're back."

"And don't worry, I didn't forget your blanket."

Matthew was so overjoyed that the fist-bump he always gave to Enoch was exchanged for a hug. "Welcome back," the young boy said.

"Grace, why don't you show Enoch to his room."

"My room, Mommy?"

"Yes."

Grace's face lit up. "Oh, goodie."

"If you're tired and want to take a nap, feel free."

"I had plenty of rest last night, Lydia. But it sure would be nice to soak my weary bones in a hot bathtub after breakfast."

"Feel free to do as you wish. Our house is your house. We're just honored to have you here."

After breakfast, as the children got dressed for school, Enoch soaked in the tub for a half-hour before rejoining the Jensens in the living room.

"Mommy, can I brush Enoch's hair before going to school?"

Lydia looked at the clock hanging on the wall. "We still have time."

Just like last time, the old man gingerly lowered himself onto the carpeted floor, as Grace positioned herself behind him. And just like last time, Freeway inched up as close to her new best friend as she possibly could, tail wagging nonstop until Enoch finally caved in and stroked her golden-brown hair.

After a while Freeway rolled over, prompting the old man that she was ready to have her belly rubbed next.

As for Alex, the jury was still out as to whether or not he liked Enoch.

With much less knots in his long hair, the brush Grace used flowed evenly through Enoch's hair with little resistance.

To Lydia's great surprise, John offered to take the kids to school. She watched out the front window until they were out of sight, then joined Enoch on the living room couch.

The song *We Three Kings* was playing softly in the background.

"Doesn't the tree look beautiful?"

"It sure does," said Enoch. "I never thought twinkling lights could be so soothing to the eyes."

Lydia chuckled. "When was the last time you had a Christmas tree of your own?" She wanted to ask him earlier but not in front of the children, just in case. She didn't want to potentially embarrass him.

"Never had one before," Enoch said, matter-of-factly.

Lydia wanted to ask why but thought better of it. Besides, they only had so much time before John returned from the supermarket. There were more important issues to discuss.

They sat in silence a few moments basking in the festive holiday ambiance, before Lydia spoke, "I must say, having you here is such a blessing. John hasn't looked so alive in a very long time. But if you weren't here..." She stopped. There was a distant gaze in her eyes.

"What changes have you noticed in your husband?"

"Aside from the fact that we never talk anymore, except, of course, when we're arguing, for starters, he's been drinking a lot lately. Usually one or two beers a day. I'm not saying he's an alcoholic, but one or two a day can easily turn into three or four, if he doesn't snap out of it soon."

Lydia twirled her hair with her right pointer finger and continued, "Even when he drank beer on occasion in the past, it was never done in front of the children. Now he doesn't seem to care."

"And this all started seven months ago?"

"Yes. Give or take."

"Can you explain why?"

"Perhaps he's having a mid-life crisis."

"And what do you think constitutes a mid-life crisis?"

"I'm not sure, actually."

"Anything else, Lydia?"

"The only two things he's interested in these days are watching football on TV and doing who knows what on his cell phone. Aside from that, he shows no interest in anything else. Especially me..."

Lydia felt her heart palpitating. "Even if I bread-crumbed a path for him to get to me, he wouldn't take the first step. To the best of my knowledge, I don't think he visits pornography sites. I just hope he hasn't found another woman..." Her voice trailed off.

"Anything else?" the old man said very calmly, evenly, like a psychiatrist questioning a patient.

"John used to be so confident and full of life, ready to tackle any challenge that came his way. Everything was an adventure to him. And he always did his best to involve me and the kids. Now it's as if he's isolated himself from us."

"Let me start by saying I agree John doesn't have a problem with alcohol. At least not yet. I'm afraid his condition is far worse than that."

"Worse?"

Enoch nodded yes. "What makes his downward spiral so difficult to detect is that it has little to do with the things that destroy so many marriages—things like drugs, alcohol, adultery, pornography or gambling.

"While those things have little to do with what ails your husband, at least for now, what John suffers from is the chief cause of all those things. The world may call it a 'mid-life crisis', but I wouldn't call it that."

"What is it then?"

"From an eternal standpoint, John suffers from having no sense of belonging."

104

"What exactly do you mean?"

Enoch explained, "The reason he stopped caring so much and going to church is that nothing makes sense to him anymore. Most of his cynicism stems from not knowing who he is or why he's even on this planet. What does it profit a man to pursue something that no longer makes sense to him, and leads to nowhere in his mind?"

"Guess I see your point."

"Are you familiar with the Book of Ecclesiastes?"

"Somewhat."

"I challenged your husband to read it."

Lydia raised an eyebrow, "Really? And?"

"Time will tell. But even if he doesn't, I suggest you read it for yourself. I believe it will give you further insight into your husband's debilitating condition."

"I'll do anything."

"Good, because as the stable one in your relationship, you have an important role to play."

"What type of role?"

"To still love your husband despite himself, just like Yahweh loves you despite yourself."

Lydia sighed, "Of course, I still love John. But I'm just so tired of being the only one trying."

"Yahweh knows what you're going through, Lydia. He also knows how difficult it is when one spouse carries most of the load. I can assure you that He feels your pain."

Lydia looked down at her feet, "I admit sometimes I just want to give up. The kids sure would be better off not seeing us fighting all the time."

"That certainly is true. But do you think Matthew and Grace would be better off if their parents were no more? Imagine sitting them both down and explaining that you and John were going to divorce."

Tears rushed to Lydia's eyes. "That thought never crossed my mind."

"Good. Yahweh is ever mindful of the promise you both made to love each other in good times and in bad. While it's normal for you to not feel tender or sympathetic toward John right now, or eager to please him as his wife, if you continue showing him acts of love despite your present lack of feeling, at some point it may serve to bring him back to his senses."

"I hope so," Lydia said, softly, sadly.

105

"Your husband is severely depressed, Lydia. Therefore, he's incapable of seeing things rationally right now. If you develop the same destructive attitudes he has, your marriage will really be in trouble, much like a boat lost at sea without a compass or an anchor.

"So, in that regard, you must remain strong for the both of you, and always trust that Yahweh is walking with you every step of the way."

Enoch let his words hang thick in the air a few moments. "By loving John during this difficult time, you're really loving God. I assure you that your faithfulness to the covenant of marriage Yahweh has set forth will not go unrewarded."

Lydia remained silent, pondering what Enoch had just said.

He went on, "You must constantly remind yourself that John's toxic attitude of late has nothing to do with you and the children, and everything to do with himself. This should help you better cope with the situation. Another thing you can cling to is that he still loves you."

"How can you tell? I see no evidence."

"By his overall willingness to want to protect you and the children, despite that everything seems meaningless to him. The reason he visited me at the park in the first place, was that he wanted to make sure I was harmless enough to have in your house." Enoch leaned up in his chair, "He also wanted to make you and the children happy."

Seeing Lydia wasn't convinced, he said, "Granted, these examples are mere shadows of the love he once showered upon you in great quantities. Even so, these are the things you must focus on when looking for reasons to stay connected to John during this difficult time.

"Instead of getting overly emotional thinking about how things used to be, start looking for small but steady steps in the right direction. Count each one a minor victory. Can you do that?"

Lydia took a deep breath and exhaled, "I'll do my best."

"Indeed, this is a time of testing in your marriage. I'll even go so far to say this is where most marriages are either galvanized or destroyed. But take comfort knowing that the ones that survive after being severely tested, often end up being the most rewarding in the end."

Lydia looked down at the floor. The thought of her marriage being further tested crushed her in the deepest chambers of her heart.

Enoch said, "Are you familiar with Romans eight, twenty-eight?"

Lydia's face lit up, "It's one of my favorite Bible verses. 'And we know that in all things God works for the good of those who love him, who have been called according to his purpose.'"

106

THE UNANNOUNCED CHRISTMAS VISITOR

Nodding yes, Enoch expounded on it, "Despite how badly people mess things up, Jehovah Jireh is still sovereign and in complete control of all things. We can never forget that His ways are so much higher and wiser than our ways.

"If He works all, not some, things for the good of those who love him, which you certainly do, and for those who are called according to His purpose, which you certainly are, you must cling to the promise that Yahweh is allowing these things to occur to re-position everyone to where they need to be, according to His purpose for each of your lives."

Lydia sniffled, "Just like you said at the park the other day, right?"

"Precisely. So, with that in mind, think of this very trying time in your life as an opportunity for future positive change. To do your part, avoid focusing on the pain and your changing emotions. Also, it might be good to avoid discussing topics that will arm you both for battle."

Enoch gazed deeply into Lydia's eyes, "Most of all, keep praying without ceasing for Yahweh's divine intervention. I assure you He is listening to your many cries for help."

The way he said it made Lydia flinch. *It's almost as if he...hmm.*

Enoch noticed and leaned all the way back in his seat, "In the meantime, let's see if we can't get you both reading God's Word together, even if John doesn't know it for the time being. Assuming he is reading Ecclesiastes, you should read it too."

"I'll read it tonight before going to sleep."

"One more thing you must do."

"What's that?"

"Keep yourself and the children busy so John and I can spend lots of time alone."

"No problem," came the reply, without hesitation.

Freeway heard the car pulling into the driveway and dashed to the front door, so she could shower her master with unconditional love the moment she saw him.

Enoch leaned up in the chair again, "Who says dogs can't teach us valuable lessons? See how Freeway loves unconditionally in good times and in bad?"

Lydia nodded.

"That's precisely how Yahweh loves all who belong to Him, despite that we constantly let Him down. If a dog can do it, shouldn't we also?"

Lydia got the message loud and clear.

BEFORE CALLING IT A night, for the first time in many months, the Jensens dropped to their knees on the living room floor, as Enoch led them all in prayer.

The old man earnestly prayed for each of them by name, thanking Yahweh for meeting their needs this day, and asking the Most High to draw them closer to Him a little more each day. He then prayed the same thing for his friends at the city park.

Once he was finished, Lydia marched the kids upstairs to get them ready for bed. After brushing their teeth, Matthew climbed up onto the top bunk, giving his kid sister his favorite bed on the bottom.

Lydia tucked her children in, lit a few candles and soaked in a hot bathtub in the master bedroom, and started reading Ecclesiastes.

John retreated to his study, completely unaware that his wife was reading the very same thing he was about to read for the second time since he woke this morning.

Stretched out on Grace's bed, Enoch was grateful for the warmth of a heated house and a soft mattress to sleep on. It felt good on his back.

As he did each night before sleeping, Enoch spent an hour or so in prayer, worshiping his Creator, longing to be with Him again.

After that, he was completely still before the Lord awaiting his next instructions.

A few moments later, Yahweh told His servant what his next steps should be. "As you say, Lord," Enoch said, rolling onto his side and falling asleep.

18

4 DAYS BEFORE CHRISTMAS

AT 7 A.M. THE JENSENS were seated at the breakfast table. Grace sat next to Enoch. She was delighted to see him when she woke this morning.

After breakfast, for the second straight day, John offered to take the children to school. Lydia appreciated the gesture but, honoring Enoch's wishes, she insisted on taking them this time.

After that, she would find something to do until lunchtime.

Once they were gone, John wasted no time. "I read the Book of Ecclesiastes just as you'd suggested. Twice, in fact."

"And what have you concluded?" Enoch already knew John had read it, after Yahweh revealed it to him the night before.

"Honestly, it made me realize just how depressed I really am."

"Like I told you when we first met, John," Enoch reiterated, "you are not alone in this matter. Many feel depressed after reading Ecclesiastes. At least initially. The reason is that Solomon uses the absurdities of life to point to its ultimate meaning."

Meaning of life? "Perhaps I should read it a third time."

"You are now at the proverbial crossroads in life."

"Is it a good place to be?"

"That depends on you. As surely as a child is born and lives and breathes on this planet, he or she will one day wonder who they are and why they are here. Until one finds their true purpose in life and, more importantly, what will become of them in the life to come, they'll never experience true, sustainable peace. Nor will they find peace with God.

"In your case, John, it's not that the world around you has changed. You have. At least your perspective on life has. Things that used to add deep meaning to your life no longer do, because you finally got to see it all for what it really is, a chasing after the wind.

"Though penned three thousand years ago, Ecclesiastes still has a contemporary flare. Wouldn't you agree?"

John nodded yes.

"If anyone was qualified to write that book, it was King Solomon. In the forty years he was King of Israel, there wasn't much he didn't see or do. He undertook great projects. He owned many herds. Built majestic houses. Planted sprawling vineyards.

"He amassed great riches, denying himself nothing. No one lived life more lavishly or to the fullest, than Israel's third king. He even had the distinct honor of building the Temple of God.

"You may find it interesting that the word 'Ecclesiastes' means, 'Teacher' or 'Preacher'. You may also find it interesting that 'Solomon' means 'peaceable'. Perhaps Solomon chose 'Teacher' or 'Preacher' over his own name because His life was anything but peaceable at that time.

"Anyway, after many years of willful disobedience to his Maker, the repentant king reflected back on his many great accomplishments. Grandiose as they were, they weren't enough to sustain his happiness.

"Not only were they unquenchable, they proved to be nothing more than a chasing after the wind, bringing Solomon to the place where he felt completely empty inside."

"Interesting..."

"Have you ever read about the life of King Solomon in the Bible?"

John lowered his head, "I'm afraid I haven't read much of the Old Testament."

"Allow me to give you a brief history lesson. As the son of King David, Solomon was poised for true greatness, despite that his upbringing was rather dysfunctional. Sadly, his father wasn't the best of role models.

"Not only was he too soft when it came to disciplining his children, they were raised in an environment dominated by polygamy and the many evils accompanying it. These things contributed to Solomon's poor decision-making capabilities over time.

"Yet, when he sat on the throne his father had occupied for forty years as Israel's next king, Solomon prayed for wisdom above all other things. Hearing his prayer, Yahweh blessed him with wisdom and great riches, both of which were legendary in the ancient world.

"Construction of the Temple of the Lord began in the fourth year of his reign. Solomon made sure every detail was carried out to perfection, according to the exact specifications handed down to him from his father.

"Seven years later, it was finished. The king assembled the elders and all the heads of the tribes of Israel before him in Jerusalem, as the priests and Levites brought the ark of the covenant of the Lord and all the holy vessels that were in the tent to the Temple.

"Only the priests were permitted to bring the ark to its place in the inner sanctuary, in the Most Holy Place, where it rested underneath the wings of the cherubim.

"When the priests came out of the Holy Place a cloud, representing the Shekinah glory of the Lord, filled the house of the Lord. It was so overpowering that the priests weren't able to perform their services.

"After a while, Solomon stood before the altar in the presence of all the assembly of Israel and spread out his hands toward heaven, praising the Most High God of Israel with all that was in him, deeply humbled for having been chosen to build a place in which his Maker would dwell forever.

"When he finished praying, he consecrated the middle of the court so offerings could be made to the Lord. So many sheep and oxen were sacrificed that day that they couldn't be counted. Israel's king held a feast before the Lord for seven days, before sending the people home on the eighth day.

"As you can see, John, he was very much in the will of God during this time. After spending the first twenty years of his reign achieving many great and wonderful things, the Lord appeared to Solomon a second time, confirming that He had indeed heard his prayer and had consecrated the house his servant had built, by putting His name there forever.

"But the Lord warned Solomon that if he and his children turned aside from following Him, and didn't keep His commandments and statutes, but served other gods, He would remove Israel from the land He gave them, and the house He consecrated for His name would be cast out of His sight, and would become a heap of ruins."

Enoch shook his head, "Tragically, that's precisely what happened. After building something so magnificent for his Creator, Solomon slowly but steadily fell away from God and into great sin. He even did the very thing Yahweh had commanded the Israelites not to do—intermarry with foreign women. Yahweh, being a jealous God, knew this would cause His chosen people to pledge their loyalty to other false gods.

"Israel's king willfully disobeyed and married seven hundred foreign princesses. Can you imagine that? And even that wasn't enough to satisfy Solomon. The proof was that he also had three hundred concubines.

"If you think having one wife can be difficult at times, imagine seven hundred?" Enoch laughed, trying to lighten the mood.

John smiled wearily. *I can't even satisfy one wife these days...*

111

"And just as Yahweh had warned, when Solomon was old his wives had indeed turned his heart toward other gods. The backslidden king even built altars, so they could bring offerings and sacrifice to their gods.

"The Lord was rightly angry and raised up adversaries against him. The most formidable was a young man named Jeroboam, a man Solomon had put in charge over all the forced labor of the house of Joseph.

"One day when Jeroboam went out of Jerusalem the prophet Ahijah found him on the road. The two were alone in the open country. Dressed in a new garment, Ahijah tore it into twelve pieces, telling Jeroboam to take ten pieces for himself, signifying the ten tribes of Israel that God would tear from the hand of Solomon and give to him.

"But for the sake of his father, David, Yahweh did not do this in Solomon's lifetime. It happened during the reign of his son, Rehoboam. But Yahweh didn't take the entire kingdom away from Solomon. He left one tribe for the sake of His servant, David, and for the sake of Jerusalem.

"When Solomon got word of this, he tried to kill Jeroboam. But he escaped to Egypt and stayed there until Solomon's death. He was succeeded by his son, Rehoboam. And just as prophesied, Jeroboam and the northern people rebelled, forming ten northern tribes.

"King Jeroboam ended up reigning over the northern kingdoms for twenty-two years. He did more evil than all who lived before him, making for himself other gods and idols made of metal. This aroused Yahweh's anger against him.

"When Jeroboam's son became ill, the king sent his wife to visit the prophet, Ahijah, whose sight was gone because of his age. Jeroboam told his wife to disguise herself so the prophet wouldn't recognize her. But the Lord warned Ahijah what was happening.

"When she arrived, the prophet wasted no time exposing her as Jeroboam's wife. Not only did he prophesy that her son would die once she set foot back in her home city, he had even more dire news for her husband.

"Imagine how she must have felt going back home and telling her husband that the same prophet who rightly said God would give him ten tribes, now said the Most High would remove him as king because of his evil ways, and that every last male would be cut off—slave or free.

"All this while mourning the death of her son who, just as prophesied, died the moment she stepped over the threshold of the house."

Enoch paused when he heard Lydia pull into the driveway. Knowing John wasn't saved, Enoch concluded, "Like King Solomon, the key to learning from your mistakes is by focusing on where you slip, not where you fall. Slipping represents the 'sowing' period. Falling represents the 'reaping' period, or the end result of your deeds and actions.

"Disobeying the Most High God and marrying so many foreign women was where Solomon slipped. I already shared with you some of the undesirable consequences the defiant king reaped for himself and for all of Israel, as a result.

"With that in mind, one question you might want to ask yourself from time to time is, 'What am I sowing right now that I do not want to reap?'"

John was caught off guard by Enoch's question and took a moment to ponder it.

Lydia walked through the front door carrying grocery bags.

"Welcome back, Lydia." Knowing they both read Ecclesiastes last night Enoch said, "I was just giving John a brief history on the life of King Solomon, and what ultimately led him to write the Book of Ecclesiastes. Care to join us?"

Lydia's eyes volleyed back and forth from John to Enoch. "Sure. But let's eat first. I'll make soup and BLT sandwiches."

"Sounds delicious," Enoch said.

"Have you ever read the book of Ecclesiastes?" John asked his wife, as if trying to disqualify her from the conversation.

"Just last night, in fact!" Lydia tried to keep from laughing and went to the kitchen without saying another word.

John turned his head so fast toward Enoch that it nearly snapped off. Just as he was about to inquire, he felt prompted to let it go.

With the week he was having, it sort of figured...

19

LYDIA PREPARED THE TABLE and Enoch blessed the food.

The old man dipped his BLT sandwich in the tomato soup and blew on it. He took a small bite and swallowed. "As I was telling John earlier, with its many dire warnings and constant air of futility, it's easy to see why Ecclesiastes can be such a depressing book to read.

"One of its main focal points is that sustained contentment can never be found in human endeavors or in material things. Even the wisest man that ever lived was forced to conclude that knowledge and wisdom can only take mankind so far. In and of themselves, they leave too many unanswered questions to give anyone a sense of completion.

"But those who read Ecclesiastes closely will see a progression from depressive analysis to hopeful solutions."Enoch could almost see John shrinking in his seat, knowing he leaned more on his intelligence for his day-to-day guidance than anything else in life.

"King Solomon's fall from grace was a culmination of many things going all the way back to his childhood. If you study the first book of Kings in the Old Testament, you will clearly see that his biggest downfall happened at the hands of foreign women. This was a clear violation of what God had instructed for His chosen people.

"The end result was when King Solomon was old, his wives had indeed turned his heart away from God. So much so that he started chasing after other gods. In order to pacify his many wives, the king of Israel built temples and altars to their gods, thus trading the wisdom of God for the wisdom of the world.

"Oftentimes when man has an abundance of money, his need for God decreases. Solomon was no exception. As he continued down that destructive path, he started thinking more highly of himself and less highly of his Maker. So prideful did he become that even the Temple he built for the Lord was eventually called Solomon's temple."

Enoch shook his head, as if out of shame. "The world-weary tone of his writing in Ecclesiastes reflects someone looking back on a life that was long on experience but short on lasting rewards.

"Viewed distinctively through human eyes, Solomon vividly describes his life without God, by using the absurdities of life and pushing them to their logical end-points. He ultimately concluded that life is destined to remain unsatisfying apart from mankind's recognition of God's intervention in all things.

"Solomon repeated the phrase 'under the sun' twenty-nine times, signifying man's view of the world, when God is left out of the picture. He used the word 'vanity' more than thirty times to constantly demonstrate that when man pursues things under the sun, apart from God, life ends up becoming rather pointless, meaningless and even absurd.

"By simply reading it, it becomes crystal clear that Solomon not only saw his departure from his Maker—the very Source of life—we also see him being restored back to God after sincerely repenting, much like his father David had done, after being confronted by the prophet Nathan about his great sin, to include adultery and even murder.

"In that regard, Ecclesiastes could very well have been called, 'Solomon's Book of Confessions.' When someone tries to find meaning in the pursuit of pleasure, the commitment to a job or a career, or through mining intellectual depths, his path is filled with bursts of satisfaction that may shine bright for a time, but they eventually fade upon discovering they are nothing more than dead ends.

"Truth is, anyone can relate to the repentant ruler's hectic journey because it applies to all humans—whether king or common citizen. This is precisely why we occasionally hear stories of celebrities, star athletes and business moguls taking their own lives while still in the prime of life.

"From a worldly standpoint, these people have everything life has to offer. The world is their oyster, as the expression goes. That is, until the moment arrives when they wake one morning feeling incredibly empty inside with no way of explaining it.

"Like everyone else on the planet, they are forced to answer the same question everyone wrestles with at some point in their journey. This question cuts deep to the heart, and transcends all borders, religions and social statuses. That question is, 'What is my purpose for being here?'

"Unable to provide a satisfactory, life-affirming answer, the emptiness they feel intensifies until life eventually dries up and many turn to drugs, alcohol and a myriad of other destructive vices to try filling the deep holes they have inside, but to no avail.

"If fame and fortune could solve all of humanity's problems, the wealthy would truly be blessed. But since it cannot, even if unspoken, the time surely comes when many in the higher tax-brackets struggle to make sense of their lives. With no definitive answer to that simple yet life-affirming question, even their favorite places on earth lose their overall luster, further fueling the emptiness they feel inside.

"To those who believe life would be so much easier and more enjoyable if they only had more money, a bigger house to live in or a nicer car to drive, I say be careful what you wish for. Imagine the paralyzing feeling of having so much money at your disposal, being able to do whatever you want, travel to anyplace on the planet, yet still feeling dreadfully empty inside?

"When individuals reach the highest pinnacles of success, but still cannot satisfy the constant hunger to find true meaning in life, with no place higher to climb, they see it all for what it really is, a chasing after the wind. What's next suddenly turns into what's the point? The hollowness of life starts eating away at their souls. For some, the only escape is to take their own lives.

"Yeshua said, 'What shall it profit a man to gain the whole world yet lose his soul?' Truth is, we all yearn to be part of something that can hardly be put into words. No generation is exempt from this Divine truth. If you find in yourself a desire which no experience in this world can satisfy, the most probable explanation is that you were made for another world."

"That's deep," John said, totally mesmerized by Enoch's words.

"Earthly possessions and pleasures can never satisfy this yearning, John. They were never meant to. At least not permanently. For those who constantly try filling this void with the things of this world, something will always be lacking, something outside themselves that would make sense of life, something man cannot work out on his own.

"Man knows in his heart of hearts there must be a wisdom that makes sense of his foolishness, a moral purity that exposes his wickedness. But man hasn't the resources within himself to figure it out. He needs God.

"So crushed was Solomon in his spirit when he wrote Ecclesiastes that he even compared man to animals, saying man has no advantage over the animal, that the same fate awaits them both.

"As one dies, so dies the other. All have the same breath. All go to the same place; all come from the dust and to the dust all return. When viewed through a human lens, life seems rather pointless for animals who just stand around in a field. Yet it doesn't bother them in the least!

"But for man, the eye never has enough of seeing or the ear its fill of hearing. Whoever loves money never has enough; whoever loves wealth is never satisfied with his income. There are always yearnings for fame, wealth and pleasure; for knowledge and meaning and to know the future. The fact that humans worry about such things and even question their existence is what sets them apart from every other animal.

"Not much has changed since the days of King Solomon. Just like Israel's third king did for so many years before he finally repented, the modern world zealously seeks to discover new ways to live life without Yahweh. They keep themselves busy day and night with numerous projects that become distractions to finding true meaning in life, which is only found in serving God."

Enoch swallowed the last spoonful of tomato soup. "Secular man boasts that his intellect alone is enough to provide the necessary means to eventually create a near-perfect world without the need for God.

"When things go well, such persons are prideful and content. Since this world is all they have, anything that threatens their throne or challenges their intellect is vigorously defended. When things go wrong, the inevitable consequences of a Godless existence loom large and oftentimes leads to loneliness, depression, anxiety, broken relationships, drug and alcohol abuse, and on and on.

"In conclusion, to all who come to understand the Book of Ecclesiastes, Solomon's chief purpose for writing it becomes quite clear: whenever a person lives his life apart from the clear influence of the One who made them, he ends up living a sad and unfulfilled existence. Something will always be lacking. Nothing they say or do can change the fact that God has set eternity in man's heart which can never be pacified by temporal things."

"I have a question."

"Yes, John?"

"You said earlier that the temple Solomon built eventually became a heap of ruins, right?"

"Yes. It was destroyed by the Babylonians in 586 B.C."

"Why would God allow anyone to destroy His earthly dwelling place? Isn't He supposed to be in charge of all things?"

"I can give you two reasons. The first one I already shared with you. Yahweh did it to fulfill His promise, by withdrawing His presence from the Temple when the people became faithless and participated in all sorts of wickedness. Second, though it was a great and marvelous architectural achievement, the temple Solomon built for the Lord was merely a prophetic illustration, a foreshadowing of what was to come.

117

"One temple was destroyed, while the other Temple is still in the process of being built. This Temple will remain forever. Its glory outshines the glory of the old temple. Whereas the stones and wood used for the temple Solomon built were quite expensive, the stones of the new temple were purchased by the blood of Yeshua HaMashiach.

"Yahweh's church, therefore, has become, in effect, His temple on Earth with Christ being the chief Cornerstone. By the grace of God alone, all who belong to Christ have the eternal privilege of being living stones in this house."

"I think you are the wisest man I've ever met in my life," Lydia said. "Everything you say makes perfect sense to me."

"I am only quoting Scripture," Enoch said, leaving it at that.

After just being given so many priceless nuggets of wisdom from their godly house guest, John countered by blurting out one of the stupidest things he could say to his wife at this time, "By the way, I was given the rest of the year off at work and told to get my act together or else."

At first, Lydia allowed her human nature to surface. She felt panicked. But seeing tiny glimpses of the man she married finally surfacing again, after a seven-month drought, she relaxed and decided to go along with it. "I see."

And that was that.

LATER THAT NIGHT, AFTER everyone went to bed, John retreated to his study to read Ecclesiastes a third time.

From there he ventured on to the New Testament...

Lying in a warm bed for the second straight night, Enoch spent much time in prayer and fellowship with his Creator.

He longed to be with Yahweh, so he could once again bask in the Almighty's love in a way he never could on Planet Earth. Even so, he was enjoying this Mission on which he was sent.

After a while, Enoch was still before the Lord waiting for his next instructions. A few minutes later, Yahweh told him what his next step should be.

"As you say, Lord," Enoch said rolling onto his side, quickly falling asleep.

20

3 DAYS BEFORE CHRISTMAS

JOHN JENSEN WOKE AT 10:37 a.m., four hours later than his normal wake up time. After two full days in Enoch's company, followed by reading God's Word until nearly 3 a.m., he didn't need a doctor to diagnose why he felt like he'd been hit by a runaway train.

John changed from pajamas into blue jeans and a brown polo shirt and went downstairs, to find Enoch seated on the couch reading the Bible.

"Good morning, Enoch."

"Good morning, John!" As always, his gravelly voice was full of enthusiasm. He looked very much at home, wearing the old gray slacks and black and white sweater he brought with him. With four walls and a roof encasing him, only one layer of clothing was necessary now.

"I can't believe I slept this late. Where's Lydia?"

"Out Christmas shopping. She told me to tell you she will get the children after school lets out. I believe this is their last day before Christmas break."

John blinked hard a couple of times, realizing he should have known that. "Coffee?"

"I would love a cup."

A few minutes later John rejoined Enoch in the living room.

Blowing into his cup, John took a large gulp of coffee. "I hope my pessimistic viewpoint on life and negative stance on the church hasn't offended you. That wasn't my intention."

Enoch laughed. "I assure you, John, nothing you do or say will ever negatively affect my view on life. Regarding your comments on the church, how could I be offended when, for the most part, I agree with you? But what if I told you the many accusations you have brought against the church aren't even the most crippling."

"And what might that be?"

"The first step downward for any church isn't when members stop tithing," Enoch informed, knowing this was John's biggest gripe, "but when she loses her high opinion of God. So necessary to the church is a

119

lofty view of God that when that view in any way declines, the Church declines along with it.

"The long and turbulent history of Israel demonstrates what sowing a low view of God ultimately reaps. The history of the Church merely confirms it. It hurts my heart seeing so many pastors today having such faulty views of Yahweh God. Because of this their sermons lack reverence and balance. This watered-down gospel they preach only leads to watered-down worship.

"Truth is, an outward form of religion can never provide a substitute to close relationship with Almighty God. When churches merely become places to pacify God with memorized prayers, religious formalism, ritualism and legalism, the Most High finds other people to declare His glory.

"Once Yahweh is elevated to the status He so richly deserves, that church can then come into proper fellowship, and everyone involved will experience unprecedented growth regarding the ways of Yahweh God."

Leaning up in his chair the old man grew more serious. "And, so I ask, John, what kind of view do you have toward God? Is He a big God or is He little?"

"Of course, He's big. After all, He's God, right?"

"How big?"

"Well..." John was stumped. *Time to turn the tables!* "What kind of view do *you* have toward God, Enoch?"

"The God I serve has no origin, no beginning or end. He is limitless yet He never changes. He possesses perfect knowledge and therefore has no need to learn anything. Being the source and author of all things, He didn't create the universe and everything in it to meet some unfulfilled need. His knowledge doesn't arise from things because they are or will be, but because He has ordained them to be.

"Not only does the God I serve know Himself perfectly in all ways, He knows everything that can be known about anything, with a fullness of perfection that includes everything that exists or could have existed anywhere in the universe at any time in the past. His knowledge of the future is just as complete as His knowledge of the past and present."

John raised an eyebrow but remained silent, wondering if this was some memorized speech. It wasn't.

"Yahweh never wonders about anything. Nor does He ever seek information from any other source. He simply has no need. He sustains all but is Himself independent of all. He gives to all but is enriched by no one.

He never discovers anything or requires helpers. He is never surprised, never amazed. Were it possible for anything to occur apart from His permission, then that something would be independent of Him, and Yahweh would at once cease to be Supreme.

"Not only is the Most High mindful of all things, He is mindful of all things simultaneously, including every human being that has ever lived. Every thought, breath, heartbeat, teardrop, every hair on every head are recorded in Heaven's memory." Stroking Freeway's back with his right hand, Enoch said, "Can you tell me how many cats or dogs are on the planet, or how many have roamed the planet before them?"

"Of course not."

"Yahweh can. How about the number of fish swimming beneath the waters? Do you even know how many different underwater species there are?"

"No," came the reply, softly.

"Yahweh knows. Is it possible for you to number the flies and mosquitoes on the planet?"

John shook his head no.

"Yahweh can. After all, it's because of Him that they even have life."

John gasped. "Talk about a supercomputer!"

"Not only that, the Most High is mindful of every leaf on every tree, every blade of grass that has ever grown, every mountain and valley, every raindrop and snowflake, every star and planet, every atom, particle and molecule, not to mention the always-active spirit world which occupies every square inch of the universe. None of it ever escapes His attention for a single second—past, present and future.

"Even more amazing is that El Shaddai knows no one thing better than any other thing, but all things equally well, including you and me. For an infinite mind is as capable of paying the same attention to billions of people at once as if one individual were seeking His attention.

"And this means there is no danger of anyone belonging to Yahweh of ever being ignored or overlooked, despite the multitudes presenting their various petitions before Him, every second of every day."

"That's quite amazing," John remarked.

Enoch eyeballed John carefully. "Yahweh is the God of unsearchable wisdom. Supreme in His Majesty, unique in His excellency, and peerless in His perfections, the Most High has encountered everything imaginable except for one thing."

"What's that?"

"His equal match. It simply doesn't exist anywhere in the universe."

"What about the other so-called gods out there?"

"They are man-made gods only and will not stand the test of time. While this may be a highly-debated topic among humanity, I can assure you it is a total non-issue for the Most High God. In the end, everyone will see for themselves that only Yahweh is the one true God."

Pausing a moment, Enoch said, "How wonderfully sweet is the knowledge that our Heavenly Father knows us so completely and has called all His children in the full knowledge of everything that was against them. Because of this, no enemy can make an accusation stick; no forgotten skeleton or unsuspected weakness in their character can come to light to turn God away from any of His children."

John said nothing. What could he possibly say?

"I can assure you, John, that after just a few brief moments in eternity, those fortunate enough to be there will not be thinking of jobs lost back on Earth or the things they never obtained in life. Instead, when they gaze into His Holiness, they will wish they had prayed more, sacrificed more, given more, loved more and shared the Gospel more."

John lowered his head in shame. "What love indeed..."

"It is right to call our Maker a God of love. But it is equally foolish for anyone to overlook or fail to realize that Jehovah God hates all sin and demands justice for it. Yahweh is the God of mercy and sternness. His love is both gentle and tough. Soon all of creation will observe as the Most High proves it by showing not only how indescribable His love is to those who belong to Him, but also how equally terrible His wrath is, by holding the unconverted in the highest contempt. The misery they will be exposed to on the other side will be merciless and eternal."

John shook his head, "Sounds a little harsh to me."

"Before anyone can truly appreciate the grace of God, they first need to understand they are deserving of His wrath, which amounts to an eternity in hell. Yahweh is justifiably provoked to anger. What He sees transpiring every second of every day is an affront to His holiness. I can assure you He will *never* compromise His holiness by overlooking such evil. This is an impossibility."

"But aren't we supposed to be living in the age of grace? I can't tell you how many times I've heard that preached over the years."

"Like I said earlier, John, Yahweh never changes. He is the very same God in the Old Testament as He is in the New. He has always been a God of mercy and grace. But He also demands justice for sin.

"The Book of Revelation in the New Testament clearly proves that Yahweh may be kind, but certainly not soft. If His love were too soft, it would only encourage sin. If His love were too harsh, it would promote rebellion.

"Nothing represents the conflict of Yahweh's love better than what took place at Calvary. It was the sternness of His love for mankind that moved the Most High to crucify His own Son on the cross, laying on Him the sins of the whole world. We also see it when Messiah cried out on the cross, 'My God, My God, why have you forsaken me?'

"But we also see the tenderness of Yahweh's love as our Savior prayed, 'Father, forgive them for they know not what they do.' Then to the thief Messiah said, 'Today you shall be with me in paradise.' Here we see a condemned sinner hanging on a cross, a breath away from eternal destruction.

"It was only by God's grace and for His name's sake and good pleasure that Yahweh changed the condemned man's heart at that precise moment, opening his eyes to see Yeshua for who He really was, the Savior of the world, despite that He was hanging on the bloody cross next to him. Talk about love!

"Nothing else had the power to save him that day but Yahweh's grace. Those who foolishly think they can somehow live their lives apart from the One who created them, thinking they'll find a way to escape, outsmart or outmaneuver Yahweh's coming judgment, will soon see how foolish they really are, when they end up in hell suffering His merciless vengeance for all eternity.

"Of the greater part of humanity who are already dead, currently awaiting God's judgment, without question, those who are the most shocked by this were churchgoers in life. Imagine the stark terror after exhausting so many years thinking they were serving God and doing His will, having a full expectation of Heaven at the time of their deaths, only to learn everything they did was wasted in vain, a chasing after the wind, if you will..."

Enoch couldn't ignore the deflated expression on the face staring back at him. "Fully expecting to hear Yeshua say, 'Well done thou good and faithful servant,' they will instead hear Him say, 'Depart from Me, for I never knew you!' I am not only talking about common churchgoers, John, but rabbis, pastors, popes, priests and some of those televangelists you referred to the other day. What can be more terrifying than that?"

The hair on the back of John's neck rose like on an animal sensing danger.

Enoch continued, "Imagine suffering Yahweh's merciless judgment for millions and millions of years, then looking ahead and seeing an eternity of torment still before you, as if hardly a second has gone by...

"Terrifying, I know..." There was a faraway expression on Enoch's face, as if he could feel the anguish of those presently inhabiting that awfully dreadful place. "Only Messiah has the power to save anyone from that eternal nightmare..."

John gulped hard, "Why are you telling me this, Enoch?"

"Aside from those who are part of God's covenant of grace, who have been redeemed by the blood of Yeshua, God is under no obligation to keep any man or woman from eternal destruction."

Gazing deep into John's eyes, it was as if the old man was peering into his soul. "This includes you, too, John."

John wanted to reply, but he was too frightened. He looked down at his hands. Every limb quaked in his body just thinking about the possibility of spending an eternity in hell. His stomach twisted in pain.

Without saying another word, John retreated to his study.

21

LATER THAT NIGHT, AFTER the children were tucked in for sleep, Lydia took a hot shower and climbed into bed. She was exhausted after a full day of Christmas shopping.

John and Enoch were in the living room reclining on the sofa.

"Thanks for opening my eyes to just how big God really is. I have a whole new perspective on the meaning of His Sovereignty."

Enoch nodded cautiously, knowing John wasn't finished. His posture and tone of voice dictated that much.

"But to be honest," John offered, carefully, "I've always struggled with the whole Trinity thing. After our talk earlier, I skimmed through the Gospels reading about the life of Jesus. Sorry to say but it's hard for me to imagine Him being anything more than a Prophet.

"If God is so big and nothing escapes His attention, why would He need Jesus to do His bidding in the first place, let alone the Holy Spirit? Doesn't make a whole lot of sense to me."

Crossing one leg over the other Enoch explained, "Everything Yahweh does is for a specific purpose. As we discussed earlier, He is the God of mercy and sternness. He hates sin and demands justice for it. Knowing the law of Moses could save no one, nothing was more important than when the Most High sent His Son to this earth in the likeness of sinful flesh, only He was without sin.

"For two thousand years leading up to the birth of Christ, from Abraham to Messiah, Yahweh chose the Jews to be His people and His representatives on this earth. The Israelites started out knowing the Word of God, but once it ceased being important to them, they lost touch with the Most High as a wayward wife leaves her husband, and continued sinning against Him.

"When Messiah lowered Himself from Heaven, the Jews had drifted so far from their Maker that they didn't recognize Him. Instead of clinging to the only One who could truly save them, they rejected Him and ultimately crucified Him.

"The object of the Jews' rejection became the means to salvation for the whole world. Yahweh removed the Jews from their position of blessing and gave it to the Gentiles, by offering them the opportunity to have a real relationship with Him. From the time of Christ until now, the Gentiles have taken the Gospel to the far ends of the earth. Many have received it with joy and great fervor. Subsequently, most have not."

"I'm still having trouble connecting the dots regarding Jesus."

"Simply believing there is a God, John, and that He is really big isn't enough. Yahweh has explained in the clearest possible language His plan of salvation. Scripture is explicit that all sin will be punished apart from what is covered by the blood covenant of Messiah."

Enoch could tell John still wasn't convinced. "By sending His own Son, Yahweh condemned sin in the flesh in order that the righteous requirement of the law might be fulfilled. Simply put: Yeshua, the sinless One, did what the law, weakened by the flesh, could not do.

"When He was crucified on the cross, God's full wrath and judgment came to rest upon Him. By shedding His own blood, Yeshua paid the ransom to free humanity from sin, death, and hell.

"For this reason, He is the Mediator of the new covenant, setting all who have been called by God free from the penalty of the sins they committed under the first covenant. Without this new covenant, God's Law would still need to be satisfied, and no one could come into proper relationship with the Most High."

Enoch paused to give John the opportunity to ask questions. When he remained silent, Enoch went on, "Scripture states that to those who are perishing, the cross is utter foolishness, but to those who are being saved it is the power of God.

"To those who are being saved, faith in Christ isn't merely an intellectual assent, but a total transformation, a total surrender of the heart and mind, based on the overwhelming evidence of Yeshua's life, death and resurrection. All are well documented in the pages of the Book you are reading in your study."

Finally, John said, "But what about the majority in the world who believe all roads lead to God, with or without Jesus?"

"They are right."

"What? Really? You agree with them?"

"Absolutely. Despite what one chooses to believe in this lifetime, it *will* ultimately lead them to Yahweh God."

"Even those who proclaim to be Satan worshippers?"

"Yes. All roads, including those marked science, medicine, atheism, agnosticism and humanism."

"I can't believe I'm hearing this from you."

"You should believe it, John, because it's true. All roads do lead to God. But then comes the judgment. All who reject Christ this side of the grave will be one-hundred percent convinced of His true identity on the other side. But by then it will be too late.

"On bended knee, before being banished from God's presence for all eternity, anyone whose names aren't found written in the Lamb's Book of Life will have to give an account for every sin they committed in life, before openly confessing Yeshua as KING of kings and LORD of Lords."

John said, "Okay, for argument's sake let's assume what you're saying is true, that Jesus is humanity's only Bridge to God. Bearing that in mind, how does someone know if they are among God's chosen?"

"Simple. They respond to the Call. On many occasions, Messiah said, 'He who has ears to hear, let him hear.' Sadly, many people hear the call of God, but only few respond. They are the ones who are truly hearing.

"But only because God first opened their ears to the saving knowledge of the Gospel. Otherwise it would be impossible for them to be saved. Once God creates new life, He grants repentance and gives faith. There is no other way."

John scratched his chin, "Of those who have ears to hear, as you say, where's the proof of their salvation? I think it's a fair question, given the current climate of the church today."

Nodding agreement Enoch explained, "Once Yahweh breathes regenerating life into a person, what once was dry and boring in God's Holy Word jumps off the pages and becomes alive and riveting. Words explode in their hearts and minds like no other sensation.

"The more Yahweh reveals Himself, the less the things of this world matter to them. Even when driving their cars or doing chores at home, nothing can stop their thoughts from drifting toward God. That's the work of the Holy Spirit drawing them closer to their Maker."

"Can these people ever lose their salvation?"

"No," Enoch vowed, without flinching. "Messiah Himself said that all that the Father gives Him will come to Him, and whoever comes to Him will never be driven away. There is therefore now no condemnation for those who are in Christ Jesus. Yahweh disciplines His children whenever it is necessary, but they are never in danger of eternal condemnation. Remember the new Temple we discussed the other day?"

"Yes."

127

"Those who belong to this eternal dwelling place are no longer foreigners and strangers, but fellow citizens with God's people. They are members of Yahweh's household which is built on the foundation of the apostles and the prophets, with Christ Jesus himself as the chief Cornerstone. In Him the whole building is joined together and rises to become a holy temple in the Lord. This Temple will never be destroyed, John, nor will anyone belonging to it.

"But much like the rock quarried by Solomon's workers needed to be cut and shaped before being added to the temple he built, likewise, it takes the work of a skilled Craftsman, through sanctification, for anyone to become living stones in God's spiritual house.

"But everyone God calls can be confident that He who began a good work in them will carry it on to completion until the day Christ appears a second time; not to bear sin, but to bring salvation to those who trust in Him.

"In the final analysis, only two things will last for all of eternity—the soul of man and the Word of God. Like King Solomon said, everything else is just chasing after the wind. The soul Yahweh placed inside you at conception will live forever someplace. Bearing that in mind, I can assure you the greatest blessing and most secure feeling this side of eternity is knowing you are counted a child of the Most High God."

When John remained silent Enoch continued, "Those who are not children of the covenant, on the other hand, who disbelieve all the promises and disregard the Mediator of the covenant will have no share in the promises of the covenant.

"In the end, John, any rule or law or people that are against the Word of God are diametrically opposed to the Sovereign Creator of the universe. The fate that awaits them will be the full fierceness of Yahweh's judgment."

A smile crossed Enoch's face. "But Messiah will never turn away anyone who comes to Him wanting the salvation He freely offers. The love His followers will experience in Heaven can never be measured in human terms."

John brushed off a shiver. "Interesting points you make. I'll keep everything you said in mind."

At that, John went to his study, hoping to validate the many things Enoch said about Jesus being the only Bridge to God.

But instead of words jumping off the pages of the Gospels and exploding in his heart and mind, John kept stumbling on Jesus' many statements of Truth. He was completely unaware that the enemy of his soul was doing all he could to cloud his mind and keep his spiritual ears and eyes from being opened.

But Enoch knew what was happening. Lying in a warm comfortable bed for the third straight night, the old man was prostrate before his Maker, praising Yahweh with all that was in him, rebuking Satan, and praying that John would finally see Yeshua for who He really was: The Way, the Truth and the Life, and that no one comes to the Father except through Him.

A few moments later, Yahweh prompted Enoch in his spirit. The message was crystal clear: John had already heard and read enough this week. His mind was on overload.

What he needed now was to see the proof of the Holy Spirit manifested in the lives of others. Only then would his eyes and ears be opened to Jesus.

"As you say, Lord," Enoch said rolling onto his side, quickly falling asleep.

129

22

2 DAYS BEFORE CHRISTMAS

"MOM? DAD?" THE MOMENT John came out of his study, empty coffee cup in hand, Matthew jumped up off the living room couch and dashed to the kitchen.

Lifting herself up off the living room floor, Grace followed her older brother. Lydia was already in the kitchen mixing ingredients for another batch of holiday cookies, her third of the day.

"Yes, son?" John refilled his coffee cup. His mind was still focused on what he'd just read in the Gospel of John.

The children stood side by side, thrilled to be addressing their parents together again. To a ten and seven-year-old, seven months was like an eternity.

Speaking on behalf of them both, Matthew said, "Would it be okay if we wrapped gifts for everyone down at the park for Christmas?"

John looked down at his feet.

"What kind of gifts do you have in mind?" Lydia asked, knowing they couldn't afford it this year.

"Things they need like socks, hats, gloves and underwear."

"How many people are you looking to shop for?"

"Everyone," Grace answered, thrilled by the possibility.

"As in fifty people?"

"Mm-hmm," Matthew and Grace said at the same time.

Lydia glanced at John. "That could be expensive, kids."

"Even if it means getting less this year," Matthew added, "or using some of the money grandma and grandpa put in our savings accounts, we want to do it."

"We're both willing!" Grace was unable to conceal her excitement. They looked like two soldiers awaiting marching orders, only they were the ones giving the orders. Sort of, anyway.

"Enoch was right; it feels good to be a blessing to others."

"Yeah, we want to keep the blessings flowing this Christmas," Grace said in reply to her brother's comment.

John and Lydia were both rendered silent. It's not every day that parents are taught valuable life lessons like this from their own children.

John finally said, "Are you sure it's what you want?" Though seized with fear wondering how he would pay next month's bills, the pride he felt for his two children—children he'd neglected all this time—out-muscled his fears for the time being. He refused to let his shrinking finances ruin this precious family moment.

"Yes, Daddy, we're sure," said Grace, looking up at her brother glowingly. "More than sure."

"How much were you planning to spend on everyone?"

Matthew said, "After doing some calculations, we were thinking fifteen dollars each."

"For fifty people? That comes to seven-hundred and fifty dollars!" John gulped. *The exact amount of my Christmas bonus. How strange...*

Lydia shot a quick glance at Enoch. It was evident that the jolly old man was thoroughly enjoying what was transpiring between them. *The children are really getting it,* he thought.

John looked at Lydia and shrugged his shoulders, then nodded his head.

Lydia said to her children, "After dinner, we'll go to Walmart."

"Yippie!" Grace exclaimed.

Matthew just smiled.

"You might want to try the Salvation Army thrift store first," John suggested. "Definitely will be cheaper there. This way, you'll be able to get more bang for your buck."

"Good thinking." Lydia was warmed by her husband's sudden involvement. *Small but steady steps, just like Enoch said!*

"Wanna come with us, Enoch?" Grace said.

"The stores will be crowded, honey. Why don't we let Enoch rest?" Lydia knew she was being selfish, but in a good way. If the key to seeing even more positive change in her husband came down to how much alone time he spent with Enoch, God had just given her another opportunity to make it happen.

"Okay," came Grace's reply without protest.

John and Enoch were on the couch discussing the Word of God when Lydia and the children came home three hours later. All three were carrying bags.

131

Just as John had suggested, they found everything they needed at the thrift store, for a fraction of what they would have spent elsewhere. From there they went to the local Dollar Store and purchased 50 stockings, five boxes of candy canes and lots of wrapping paper.

"Anymore bags in the car?" John asked.

"Yes. Two big bags," said Lydia.

John went out to fetch them, then retreated to his study without saying another word to anyone.

Tears rushed to Lydia's eyes. She thought for sure John would want to watch his children wrapping gifts for the homeless, especially knowing they'd concocted the idea out of the goodness of their hearts.

It seemed like he only wanted to spend time with Enoch. But what Lydia didn't know was that John was doing it for their benefit. He didn't want to dampen the mood for everyone else.

After changing into pajamas, the kids raced back down the stairs and dumped the contents inside the bags onto the floor, so they could mix and match everything before wrapping it all.

"Look what I got for Suzie, Enoch!" Grace held up a pair of pink gloves, with the childlike excitement of someone who would soon be receiving a gift, not giving one.

"I am certain she will like them," Enoch insisted. "Pink just happens to be her favorite color."

"Perfect!" Grace smiled brightly.

Matthew held up a *Daddy and Me* picture frame. "I got this for Pedro for the only picture he still has of him and his daughter, Erica. Hope he likes it."

Enoch was aglow, "I can assure you he will like it above all other things."

"We got you something, too," Grace said.

Enoch raised an eyebrow, "Really?"

"Uh-huh, but first we need to wrap it, so you can open it."

"As you say, dear Grace."

Lydia turned on Christmas music and joined her children on the living room floor.

"Mommy, can we write everyone's names on the stockings?"

"How, sweetheart, when we don't even know many of their names?"

Grace looked dejected.

"Will you use a marker?" Enoch probed, undeterred by Lydia's protest.

"Actually, I was thinking we can glue their names on the stockings then cover it with shiny glitter. I have lots of it up in my room."

"What a splendid idea, Grace." Enoch leaned forward in his chair, "Tell you what; start with the names of the people you know. When you're ready for more names, just let me know."

Without the slightest protest or hesitation, Grace raced up the stairs. A moment later she was back with the glitter and Elmer's glue.

Lydia wondered how in the world this would be possible, but she remained silent and watched as her daughter spread an old sheet on the carpeted floor, then placed four stockings on it.

Using Elmer's glue, in cursive, Grace wrote the names Leroy, Pedro, Tiwanna and Suzie at the top of each of them. She covered Tiwanna's and Suzie's names with red, green and silver glitter. Matthew did the same to the stockings marked for Leroy and Pedro.

Finished, Matthew said, "Next?"

From memory, the old man said, "Okay. Let's do Tiwanna's best friend, Wanda, and the three young musicians who are always strumming their guitars late into the night. Their names are Troy, Dillon and Rocky."

The three Jensen family members went back to work.

Finished with the next four, Matthew and Grace both said, "Next?"

Without flinching, Enoch provided them with four more names. Then four more. Then four more.

Halfway through, Lydia couldn't help but marvel. "Your mind's as sharp as a steel trap. But how can you know who will be at the park and who won't be?"

"Oh, ye of little faith," Enoch said, sort of jokingly.

Lydia got the point and went back to work. The only time she took a break was to take video and more pictures of her children and Enoch.

She couldn't remember a time when her children looked any happier or more full of joy than right now. What she saw on their faces was simply incredible.

Thirty minutes later, each of the 50 stockings had someone's name written on it. As the glue dried, Lydia, Matthew and Grace wrapped socks, hats, gloves and underwear—all individually—then placed them inside the stockings.

Foot perched on a padded footstool, Enoch was nearly moved to tears witnessing this labor of love for his friends at the city park. He knew Yahweh was watching and smiling.

Just before 10 p.m. the 50 stockings were filled to the brim with gifts and topped off with candy canes. Matthew and Grace carefully placed each stocking upright inside two wooden fruit crates.

After that, the children scurried off to the kitchen to wrap Enoch's gifts, then watched with great anticipation as their house guest carefully unwrapped each of the four boxes. Inside one of them was a pair of tan slacks. Another box had a thick red sweater inside. Another had underwear and new socks. The fourth box had shoes inside.

"For Christmas Eve church service," Matthew said.

Enoch placed the boxes on the floor beside him and gathered Matthew and Grace into his arms. "Thank you, children. I will wear these things proudly."

John should be witnessing this, Lydia thought, turning off the video camera on her phone. She ached for her husband. "Time for bed, kids," she declared.

"Do we have to?" Matthew protested.

"Yes. We have a busy day tomorrow."

"Okay," Matthew said in defeat.

"Enoch?"

"Yes, Grace?" the old man said.

"Can you be my best friend?"

Enoch shot a quick glance at Lydia, before steadying his gaze onto Grace. "No, but I would be honored to be your second-best friend. Yeshua must always be your best Friend and first love."

"Okay. Thanks, second best friend!" Grace embraced Enoch again.

The children ascended the stairs, both eager for the sun to rise so they could hand out gifts to many at the city park. What made this already gratifying moment even more special for Lydia, was that Matthew and Grace had no expectation of receiving a single gift. Only giving them.

Enoch silently praised his Maker for providing the provisions to make this special moment possible.

23

JOHN JENSEN REMAINED IN his study the entire time. His Bible was open. But try as he might, he couldn't concentrate on what he was reading. His mind was too cluttered.

Not only that, tears kept stinging his eyes, making reading impossible. He removed his reading glasses and placed them on his desk. How could he not be emotional knowing what was taking place in the other room?

He couldn't be any prouder of Matthew and Grace. Lydia too. Seeing how on-track their lives were made it difficult to be in their presence, because it further magnified just how off-track his life was.

John rose from his chair and paced the small floor of his study, trying to decide if he should do it or not.

Staring at his college degree hanging on the wall, something Enoch said the other day kept attacking his mind. "It's not old age that slows most Christians down," he had said, "it's comfort."

Enoch also said something about believers in the western world willingly giving money for good causes, but only a few were willing to step outside their comfort zones and go into the trenches with those who truly have nothing.

With the decision made, he made a phone call. As Lydia tucked the kids in bed for the night, John tiptoed out the back door without saying a word to anyone.

He went to the garage and changed into clothing he put in there when Lydia and the kids went Christmas shopping earlier—long john underwear, blue jeans that were ripped at the knees, a thick gray hoodie, two pairs of socks, old construction boots, gloves and a thick parka coat—then drove off into the night.

From Grace's bedroom window, Lydia saw her husband pulling out of the driveway. A million thoughts assaulted her mind. Where could he possibly be going at this late hour?

Lydia did a good job all week by honoring Enoch's wishes to give John space. But with Christmas Eve just two hours away, it was never more difficult to go along with the plan, especially seeing how John was missing out on so much.

Little did she know her husband was acting under God's influence. Even John didn't know it, not entirely, anyway...

His first stop was at his favorite pizzeria. The song *White Christmas* by the late Bing Crosby was playing on the radio. The Christmas spirit was alive and well at this popular eatery; at least the worldly version of it.

"Merry Christmas, John," said Anthony, the pizza shop owner.

"Same to you, Anthony. Is my order ready?"

Anthony nodded yes. "That's a big order. Christmas party?"

John took a second to ponder Anthony's words, "Something like that."

"Hope everyone enjoys the pizza."

"I'm sure they will."

"That's what I like to hear. Total comes to one-hundred and forty-three dollars and seventy-nine cents," the pizza shop owner said. "Will that be cash or credit?"

Cash? What cash? "Credit." John handed Anthony his credit card. *If I keep this up, we'll soon be living at the very place I'm going!*

Uncertain future or not, John decided not to worry about his mounting financial problems for now, so he could focus his attention on the people he was going to spend time with. Compared to the constant problems they wrestled with each day he had no right to complain about anything.

Driving to the city park, the smell of pizza permeated every inch of his vehicle. John used this time to reflect on how drastically his attitude had changed since his first visit to the park, when he went to see what all the hoopla was about.

His motivation for going the second time was more out of guilt than anything else, knowing he'd greatly disappointed his family, especially his little girl. This time he was going because he truly wanted to, with no pretensions or ulterior motives.

Anticipation and excitement pumped through his heart. Was this vertical giving? John was unsure. But it sure felt like it. He liked the feeling.

Whereas the shopping malls were undoubtedly filled to the brim with anxious shoppers looking for last-minute gifts for friends, co-workers and loved ones, parking spaces were plentiful at this place. In fact, his was the only vehicle parked on this dimly-lit side of the street.

John got out of his car and left for the darkened city park, totally void of holiday lights and Christmas music. It was a frigid starry night.

Bundled up from head to toe, no one recognized him at first. "Greetings everyone!" he shouted, not wanting anyone to think he came to cause trouble for coming at this late hour, totally unannounced. "I come in peace, wishing you all a Merry Christmas!"

Tiwanna recognized the voice, but it sounded so much more cheerful now. And upbeat. "Is that you, John?"

John inched in closer, "It is I! I come bearing gifts. Instead of twelve drummers drumming, I brought twelve pizzas instead."

His comment elicited laughter from some.

Squinting in the darkness, John mentally tallied the number of people he saw. *Roughly fifty. Perfect, two slices each!* "Can I get some volunteers to help carry the food from my car?"

"Yes sir," Leroy said. Nodding at Troy, Dillon and Rocky, they rose to their feet and followed John to his car.

A moment later, each man came back carrying four pizzas each. John grabbed the stack of paper plates Anthony had given him at the pizzeria, then opened the trunk and grabbed the sleeping bag and three battery-operated lanterns he placed there before leaving the house.

Once everyone was seated, Tiwanna said, "Quiet down y'all, Leroy's about to pray."

Since Enoch had served as spiritual leader for so many months and prayed before each meal, this change of protocol still needed some adjusting to. Pedro would have been considered for the position as well, but soon-to-be no longer homeless, there was no need to cast votes.

Leroy finished praying and everyone interested said, "Amen!"

John turned on the lanterns to illuminate the pizza boxes. "All boxes marked with a 'C' are cheese only. Boxes marked with 'P' are pepperoni. 'S' is sausage. 'M' is mushroom. Dig in before it gets cold."

After a few had taken their share, John grabbed two slices of pepperoni and placed them on Suzie's lap. The old handicapped woman was bundled up so much that her wheelchair was barely visible.

Kissing her icy cold chapped right cheek, John said, "Merry Christmas, Suzie. It's nice to formally meet you. Lydia and the kids just adore you."

"They do?" Her voice shivered in the cold. "So nice to hear that."

John nodded yes and smiled warmly. The radiant glow on his face warmed Suzie greatly inside.

"Thanks for the pizza," Suzie said, her breath visible in the winter air.

"Believe me when I say, it's my pleasure." It finally felt like Christmas. *Yes!*

137

After everyone had served themselves, John grabbed a slice for himself.

If the stiff cold breeze did any good, it carried away much of the combined stench of body odor, unwashed clothing, stale cigarettes, alcohol and marijuana joints, that filled John's nostrils last time. The only thing he smelled now was pizza wafting in the air.

Conversation was lively as they ate their food. John listened and observed in silence. Many of them had lively personalities and were hilariously funny. Some were a bit too brash for his taste, but all seemed eager to share their stories with anyone who cared to listen.

They were anything but boring.

Taking the last bite of his pizza, John sent a text message to Lydia: *Won't be home tonight. But don't worry, I'm fine. See you tomorrow.*

Wanting to experience life apart from the "real world", he turned off his cell phone without waiting for his wife to reply, then spread his sleeping bag out on the frozen ground.

John lay flat on his back gazing skyward. Aside from the tops of the massive, leafless oak trees bending obediently to the constant wind, and his visible breath rising up into the atmosphere, nothing else obstructed the sprawling view above him. And what a view it was!

"Sure is cold," he said to no one in particular, rubbing his gloved hands together for added warmth.

"This ain't nothing," Leroy said, mildly surprised John was still among them after all the food was gone. It was quite uncommon. "Wait 'til January and February. Then again, you'll be safe and warm back in your home."

"Perhaps you won't be here either, right?"

"Whether God blesses me with a roof over my head in the future, or if He wants me to stay here to be His witness, it's His call."

"I don't get it, Leroy. Why would God want you to remain homeless?"

"Until you're put in a position of total dependency on Christ and not your own abilities, you'll never truly know what it means to be fully alive as one of His followers. If I'm here, I'm here for a reason."

"That's deep," John said. *Wish I had that kind of faith...*

"Don't get me wrong: I'm not saying I like being homeless. I don't. But I do like being stripped away of the world. By having nothing, I'm not weighed down by the things that ensnare most others. How funny though that you're sleeping here while Enoch is safe and warm in your house!"

Leroy said it so loud that many laughed.

John laughed too, then grew serious again and focused on the magnificent sky above him.

"Impressive handiwork, wouldn't you agree?" Pedro said to John, also looking skyward.

"It really is spectacular. So peaceful."

"We may not have ESPN or HBO like you," Leroy said, interjecting, "but look at what we get to see every night for free, when it isn't cloudy, that is."

"This very well may be the first time I've ever really looked into the endless tapestry above me. I feel so small." John's mind drifted back to his conversation with Enoch. It was too mind-blowing to try wrapping his mind around. "He really is a big God!"

"Is He ever!" Pedro said in reply. "And this is only a tiny fraction of the vast expanse of universe He created. When it's all said and done, perhaps man will discover one-one-millionth of one percent of it. Which begs the question, if man will never discover most of it, why is it even there?"

"Never thought about that before," John confessed.

"Personally, I think the two main reasons are to glorify the One who created it all, and also bring forth His plan of redemption. After all, this is the planet and universe God created to redeem His people."

Pedro shook his head, "I've often wondered how any scientist or physicist could ever deny there was a God, with all this constantly staring back at them." His right arm arced the sky like a rainbow. "The deeper they explore the heavens should only further deepen their belief in a Creator all the more. Apparently, that's not the case for most."

"Never thought about that before either," John admitted. Always one to enjoy discussing worthwhile matters, it suddenly dawned on him that many of his past so-called "intelligent discussions" weren't so worthwhile after all.

"Sure gonna miss this view."

"Are you leaving, Pedro?"

"I move into my own place January first."

"That's terrific," John declared. "Good luck in your new home."

"It's only a supervised room for now, which means no one else can stay there but me. But we all have to start somewhere, right?"

"Right."

"But I'll surely miss having this view as my ceiling each night."

"I guess this must be the worst time to be homeless," John said, cautiously.

"Yes and no," Leroy said. "While there's never a good time to be homeless, at least the bugs are gone. Nothing worse than trying to sleep in the stifling heat and humidity of summer, with hundreds of insects on the ground and in the air constantly feasting on you. Least they're not around this time of year."

"Don't forget stray dogs and rodents," Tiwanna interjected.

"Yeah, them too. Another advantage is when it gets too cold in winter, we're taken to shelters for the night. But without a doubt, the best time to be homeless is fall and spring, when the weather's near-perfect."

"Unless it rains," Pedro added, rolling onto his side. He was buried beneath every article of clothing he owned.

"I heard that," Tiwanna said matter-of-factly. "Especially when a storm sneaks up on us in the middle of the night, when we're already settled in. Even if it only rains for ten minutes, everything gets soaked and we're forced to collect our belongings and seek dry shelter."

"The things most people take for granted..." John said, knowing he was one of them.

"Yeah. And it's a million times worse when I'm sick or have my monthly cycle. Sometimes it doesn't take gunshots or loud thunder to frighten me. Sometimes I get scared for no reason at all, and just want someone to hold me."

The way Tiwanna said it made John want to hug her.

Sighing, Leroy continued, "But at the end of the day, I'd have to say Christmas *is* the worst time for anyone to be homeless. As the world celebrates with family and friends, we're reminded once again that we lost everything and have no one to lean on except those here at the park."

"True that, brother Leroy," Tiwanna said. "No doubt this is the time of year when our many failures and shortcomings turn inward to feast on our insides. Last Christmas I felt so unworthy of taking up space on this cruel planet. Came close to ending my life for real."

"Really?" John said.

Tiwanna nodded then blinked tears from her eyes.

"To be scorned and hated by so many strangers all year long, just for being homeless, is already difficult enough to cope with," Pedro said, shaking his head, "but when it happens at Christmas, it stings even more. It's enough to fill many homeless folks with dark and sinister thoughts."

140

Knowing this would be when Enoch would apply God's Word to the discussion, Leroy decided it was time to redirect the conversation. "But now that the three of us are true children of the living God, our present sufferings aren't even worth comparing to what awaits us on the other side."

"Praise Jesus!" Tiwanna said.

"You see, John, despite the harsh perils we battle every day, once we leave this planet, we'll never be homeless again. Jesus' promise of eternal dwelling places applies to us too."

"Amen to that," Wanda declared, with a voice that was glad. Not one to speak much, she made up for it by being a very good listener. The many messages she'd heard preached by Enoch at this place were slowly transforming her from the inside out.

"I can't wait to no longer need this wheelchair," Suzie declared.

"Hallelujah!" Pedro shouted, greatly impressed by his accountability partner's growing faith in her Maker.

Many others repeated the joyful proclamation.

John was rendered speechless. Despite the great misfortune of being both crippled and homeless, her faith in God was rock-solid. *How remarkable!*

Leroy said, "As children of God, we cling to the promise each day that we win in the end, no matter what people may say or think about us in this lifetime."

"Yeah. Society may see us as ruined people," Tiwanna added, "but Jesus sees us as people worth dying for. Talk about blessed!" the homeless woman exclaimed, teary-eyed. "Why can't His followers be more like Him?"

John's mind was completely blown. Here he was laying on the frozen grass in the dead of night, in the cold of winter, with a bunch of street people who had nothing in life but the clothes on their backs, and a few backpacks full of things mainstream society would consider worthless.

The way they could turn their negative situation around so quickly by praising God was both impressive and inspiring. "I can't help but be amazed by your overall outlook on life."

"We're just resting in God's future promises, John, not stressing in them," Pedro confided.

Resting in the promises, John thought. *Those comforting words again.*

141

Tiwanna saw Suzie yawning and nudged Leroy. "Gather round, y'all, so we can pray. Some of us need to sleep."

Those who were interested formed a circle and held hands. "Father God, thanks for blessing us with another precious 24 hours of life. My hope is that our thoughts, actions and deeds were pleasing in Your sight. I ask a special blessing on everyone You sent to feed and encourage us today, including John.

"Please protect their families and meet their needs this Christmas season. For those who don't belong to You, may they come to learn the true meaning of Christmas this year. Bless your homeless servants with a peaceful night's sleep, in Jesus' name we pray, Amen!"

"Amen!"

Laying on his belly, hands under his chin resting on elbows, John observed in stunned silence as two men lifted Suzie out of her wheelchair, gently placing her onto a sleeping bag already laid out for her.

Before zipping it up, like two nurses caring for a patient, they made sure the handicapped woman was completely bundled up from head to toe.

"Hope your neck feels better in the morning," one of them said to her.

"Thank you, William." Then to John, she said, "Thanks again for the pizza. It was a tasty Christmas treat."

"You're welcome, Suzie," John replied.

"Thanks for the pizza, John," Wanda said, rolling onto her side.

"Yeah, thanks for the pizza," someone else yelled.

Then another.

Then another.

After a few moments of complete silence, John finally whispered in the darkness, "What time do you think it is?"

"Probably close to midnight," Pedro replied, in a whisper.

John reached into his pants pocket for his cell phone and turned it on. It took a moment for his eyes to adjust to the bright luminescent light. "12:03 a.m. to be exact. Let me be the first to say Merry Christmas Eve, guys."

"Same to you, John."

Tiwanna started singing *Silent Night*. Leroy and Pedro quickly joined in. The thunderous bass in Leroy's voice rocked the frigid night air.

John listened and star-gazed. His heart was bursting inside his chest like never before. How ironic that it took seeing his two kids selfless generosity, followed by spending time at a humble homeless community, of all places, to finally see true Christian love at work.

First to hear Leroy praying for those who had warm homes to live in, when he had no place to lay his head; that was touching enough. Then the way the two men helped Suzie out of her wheelchair into her sleeping bag.

These things convicted John deep inside and caused him to pause and examine his own life. *Is this the work of the Holy Spirit?*

Whether it was or not, one thing was undeniable: John Jensen never felt more honored to be at any other place, than right here right now.

If it's true that those who have nothing usually end up giving the most, John now understood that comment completely. All he did was bring the pizza. They provided everything else. The $143.79 he spent was well worth the privilege of being in such distinguished company. *Go figure!*

The second time through the song, John joined in the singing as many slowly dozed off.

24

AFTER MANY HAD SETTLED in for the night, in a near whisper Leroy said, "Shouldn't you be heading home? After all, it's Christmas Eve."

"If it's okay with you, I'd like to spend the night here." John's head was resting on his hands like two gloved bony pillows.

"Seriously?" Tiwanna was astonished by what she'd just heard. She turned to face John. The two were sandwiched in between Pedro and Leroy. Pedro was on Tiwanna's left. Leroy was on John's right.

"I confess my reason for coming at this late hour was purely selfish."

"In what way, John?" Tiwanna asked quizzically.

"I wanted to have you all to myself."

Tiwanna's thick lips curled into an easy smile, and the few teeth she still had in her mouth were illuminated by the three lanterns. "That's the nicest thing an outsider has said at this place in a very long time. Your words tasted better in my mouth than even the pizza."

Leroy and Pedro remained silent, but the softened expressions on their faces spoke volumes. Both men were greatly warmed by what they'd just heard.

"It's the truth. Besides, this is the most peace I've felt in too long to remember," John said softly, not wanting to wake anyone, especially Suzie.

"Don't get too used to it. This isn't the norm," said Pedro, considering just how ridiculous, yet beautiful, it was that a man with a warm bed and home chose to sleep at the frigid cold park with them this night. "Now that Enoch's gone, I'm reminded again that life on the streets is always difficult and seldom peaceful. What you feel now could evaporate at any moment. It wouldn't take much for this place to be filled with chaos again."

"Yeah," Leroy said, "Life on the street is always dangerous. It's unedited, uncensored and quite raw. And there's never a shortage of thieves and hustlers. We always need to be on the constant lookout."

"True that," Tiwanna replied.

John's eyes widened in panic; his face crumbled in anguish.

Leroy went on, "You should have seen this place before Enoch arrived. It was like a war zone. Drug dealers and hustlers as far as the eye could see; bullets whizzing by our heads at any given time."

"I remember hearing about it on the news."

"Believe me, John, TV reporters and cameras do no justice. To see people tearing wildly at each other, blood being spilled in front of your eyes is terrifying to witness. Unlike the fistfights you see in the movies where everyone cheers, when fights break out here, people tremble with fear. Especially women. As a one-time participant myself, I can tell you it's nothing you ever want to encounter."

"Sounds scary," John said. He was never more thankful for the current peace at the park.

"And impossible to get used to. But when you're homeless, where can you go to escape it?" Tiwanna said. "You may be homeless for one night, John, but you're not really homeless. You can get in your car and drive back to your warm house any time you want to. Most of us living on the streets don't have that luxury."

"Hmm, just when I was starting to feel like a rugged wilderness man! Gee thanks, Tiwanna!"

Tiwanna giggled. "Truth is, we're not even supposed to sleep in the park. Soon after Enoch came, the cops stopped giving us a hard time. They even designated this small area just for us. As long as we maintain the peace and quiet and clean up after ourselves and don't panhandle on park grounds, they usually leave us alone."

She frowned. "Now that he's gone, I pray each night the police won't change their minds and make us leave in the middle of the night."

"Where would you sleep if that happens?"

"You name it, in the woods, under bridges, in vacant garages and trailers. If we're lucky, we get to squat in old warehouses, dilapidated homes, or motels for a night or two before moving on.

"Wanda and I once slept in a closed-down car wash for nearly a month, before we got trespassed. Wasn't so bad except for the rats and the constant noise from the breeze pressing through the cracks."

"A car wash, huh?" John said more to himself than to Tiwanna.

"Yeah, and every time we're forced to relocate, there's always the chance of being mugged by someone or even worse. That's why most homeless people tend to cling to the places where they settle."

"Sometimes I'm happy having nothing. Difficult sleeping knowing someone could steal my stuff at any time. Like brother Leroy said, there will never be a shortage of thieves and hustlers living on the streets."

"Wasn't there a murder here last year?" John asked.

145

"Yeah. Friend of mine," Leroy said, with a deep sigh. "Shot and killed by a rival drug dealer. We were partners in crime." Noticing John's "You used to be a drug dealer?" expression, Leroy said, "One advantage to living on the streets is that we always keep it real. Unlike the rest of society, we have nothing to hide. No secrets. There's something freeing about always being honest. That's how we sleep at night."

"Sorry. Just hard for me to imagine you being a drug dealer."

"Used to be, John, used to be. Anyway, DeSean's death really shook me up. Even when I was far away from God, I always believed the Bible's version of Heaven and hell. Seeing his lifeless body on the grass, those two eternal places loomed large in my mind.

"If DeSean left this planet without first trusting in Jesus, which, as a self-professed atheist, appears to be the case," Leroy said, shaking his head sadly, "he's suffering so much more torment now than he ever did on the streets.

"Shoot, this life's a breeze compared to that horrific dwelling place. Despite how hopeless his life may have seemed here at the park, he would do anything to trade places with us, just to have an opportunity to obtain salvation. But it's too late for him. Like everyone else in hell, he's doomed for all eternity."

John bit his lower lip. Try as he might, he couldn't stop his heart from beating wildly in his chest.

"When I finally sobered up the next morning, it dawned on me that had I been killed that night, I'd be in hell too. Scared me straight, man. I prayed that God would send someone to straighten me out before it was too late. That's when Enoch appeared."

"Does anyone know where he came from?" John asked.

"No."

"Has anyone asked him?"

"Of course, we have," Tiwanna said, "but he seems content to leave it a mystery."

"We may not know where he came from," said Pedro, "but believe me when I say, he was answered prayer for so many here. God used him to completely turn so many lives around, including the three of us."

"Yeah, before the old man came," Leroy confessed, "I was always looking for a reason to argue with anyone. All someone had to do was look at me the wrong way, and I was ready for a fistfight. I may be old, but I can still handle myself. Right, Pedro?"

Pedro nodded yes.

"Ha! You're nothing but a big Teddy bear, Leroy!" Tiwanna's comment made Leroy and Pedro laugh.

Leroy grew serious again. "I must say, the ones who bothered me most back then were those proclaiming to be something they were not."

"Yeah, like who?"

"Fake Christians, mostly. Because we keep it real here with nothing to hide, it's easy for us to spot fake or pretentious people a mile away. Including churchgoers. I believe many who come here are the real deal, but not all. Some spew a bunch of packaged Christian catchphrases as if their lives were so on-track. In truth, they're just as lost as the unconverted. It's not the words they speak but the lives they lead that reveals their true inner selves."

"Always had a problem with hypocritical Christians myself," John remarked, realizing how foolishly hypocritical it was for him to say such a thing when he was the biggest hypocrite of all.

Leroy went on, "In truth, we're all hypocrites and terrible followers of Jesus at times. But praise God for Enoch. I can't begin to tell you how much God used the old man to help transform this once angry black man, from the inside out.

"His willingness to never let the negative opinions of others affect him taught me firsthand that the only person I can control is myself. At the end of the day, all that matters is how God sees me."

Pedro interjected, "Whenever I see people walk by wearing thousand-dollar suits and dresses, I can't help but wonder if they have eternal security or not. They can have all the money in the world. Problem is they won't live on this planet forever. And they can't take it with them when they're gone. The security most cling to is false and temporary. I don't envy them. Instead I pray for them."

"In truth, they used to make me so envious," Tiwanna confessed. "For many years, I felt society had gypped me of something and had yet to pay the bill. In my mind, life on the streets was always 'us versus them'.

"Since I had nothing, and they had everything, I was always trying to get over on anyone I could, including those who came here out of the goodness of their hearts to feed us. It was all about me. Enoch changed everything…"

Nodding agreement, Leroy said, "What I'm about to tell you I'd never admit a few months ago. Accept it as insider secrets. Some folks living

147

here have mastered the art of looking and sounding so pitiful that good-intentioned citizens who feed us practically throw money at them.

"With fake tears in their eyes, they make up all kinds of excuses, saying they need money for food, or for bus passes, so they can apply for jobs in the morning, and on and on. But more times than not it's all lies. The money's used for drugs or alcohol."

Leroy eyeballed John, "I know what I'm talking about because it used to be me."

"Me too," Tiwanna said.

"Also guilty," Pedro said. "Can't say I blame ordinary people for not wanting to come here anymore. We've turned the city park into one big racket."

Leroy continued, "Truth is, only a few panhandlers on street corners holding cardboard signs use what they collect for food and housing. Most use it to fuel their bad habits. And what the public doesn't know is that some make as much as fifty to two-hundred bucks an hour standing on corners with cardboard signs."

"Are you serious?"

"Yup. Some collect more in a few hours than most folks earn working full time jobs." Leroy grimaced. "With that kind of money, they could live better than most. But the constant pull of drugs and alcohol is very strong on an addict. They'd rather have those things than a roof over their heads. And they'll do anything to get them."

"It's common seeing women and even men selling themselves dirt cheap, if you know what I mean, just to support their addictions. Many even sell the food stamp credits they get each month for pennies on the dollar for the same reason. Even the gift cards we get on occasion from good Samaritans for fast food end up being sold for money. If something's redeemable, they'll find a way to turn it into quick cash."

John shook his head in disbelief.

"But you never have to worry about Lydia and the kids," Leroy said. "We got their backs. But you may wanna tell your wife to leave her handbag at home when she comes to feed us. The moment she starts handing out money, many will expect it at each feeding."

What money? We're as broke as you are! "Thanks for the tip. Leroy."

Pedro said, "Don't worry, John, every cent of the fifty bucks you gave us last time all went for good. Had you given it to us a few months ago, it would have been drunk, snorted or smoked ten minutes after you were gone."

"True that," Tiwanna exclaimed.

John turned to face Leroy, "I must ask, Leroy, why are you so insistent on not giving money to anyone?"

Leroy shifted his body on the blanket. "If someone you loved had a serious drug or alcohol addiction, would you give them money knowing it would be spent on those things?"

"Of course, not."

"Well, street people are made in God's image too. Jesus delivered me from the bondage of drugs and alcohol and so many other vices. If He can straighten me out, He can straighten anyone out. Jesus is all they need.

"The more sober they are, the better chance we have to share God's Word in a way they can best understand it. So, by not giving them money, which will only be used for bad things anyway, you're actually helping our cause here."

"That's very noble of you, Leroy." *Just when I thought I heard it all. Homeless people telling me not to give money to their own kind...*

"That's why if God wants me to stay here for His purpose and glory, I'm willing to stay. Besides, how can I leave with so much work to do? I know Satan's gonna do all he can to try and reclaim this territory. Someone has to step up in the old man's absence and lead the battle. I figured why not me?"

"Amen to that, brother," said Pedro.

"After so many years working the streets for my own personal gain, it feels good to be working for Jesus now. After all, He died for me, a former drug dealer. Imagine that..." Leroy's voice trailed off.

The way he said it so tenderly nearly brought John to tears.

"Are you saying you'll remain homeless?"

"If that's what God wants, yes! Once God saves us, John, He gives us different callings. Anyone who thinks following Jesus will suddenly relieve them of all their earthly problems better think again.

"It took a long time for me to finally realize the Apostle Paul never glamorized the Gospel, by preaching a message on personal success or comfort like many preach from the pulpits today. He preached on self-sacrifice, faith and obedience to God above all other things.

"If you compare Paul's message to the 'lap of luxury' message many in the world preach today, you'll see there's no comparison. You can't be Christ's servant if you're not willing to follow Him, cross and all. Only then can anyone live a life worthy of the Gospel.

Leroy exhaled deeply, "Besides, after so many years out here in the trenches, I can relate first-hand to what they're going through. And there's something to be said about making a difference at the very edge of darkness.

"Shoot, my struggles are nothing," he said, the atmosphere struggling to soak up his deep, booming voice, "when compared to the hundreds of thousands in the world who are in prison because of their faith in Jesus."

"Preach on, brother Leroy!" Wanda inched in closer to hear more of the conversation.

"A few months ago, I never understood how anyone could go through all that for their faith. Prison? Are you kidding me? Now that I've been transformed by the power of the Holy Spirit, I finally get it. And believe me when I say, I'll never deny Jesus, no matter what the world tries doing to me. Even if I have to go to prison someday for my faith, so be it."

"I must say, Leroy, your faith in Jesus is remarkable."

"It all comes down to who is seated on the throne of your life, John," Pedro said. "Jesus already is Lord over all of creation. Nothing can change that. Those who don't believe it now will be fully convinced when God separates the wheat from the chaff; some to everlasting life, the rest to shame and everlasting contempt."

"No one has the power to stop this Divine appointment from happening," Leroy said with authority, his words exploding into clouds in the frigid night air. "Not Bill Gates. Not Donald Trump. And certainly not you. And so I ask, John, who is seated on the throne of your life?"

John gulped hard without knowing why. Or did he?

25

"BEFORE YOU ANSWER THAT I want you to do something for me." Feeling prompted in his spirit, Leroy sat straight up so he could face his kind visitor. It was time to get even more serious with him.

"What is it?" John Jensen's heart pumped wildly in his chest again, sort of knowing where the conversation was going.

"Try fast-forwarding to the end of your life. Nothing you can do to escape it anyway."

"Okay, I'll try."

Leroy paused a few moments. "When that inescapable moment invades your life and you're standing before God completely naked, stripped away of all other things, will the One who created you welcome you home as His son, or will He treat you as an object of His eternal wrath?"

"Hmm..." John stiffened up. "I've always professed faith in Jesus."

"Yeah, me too, after saying an emotional prayer in church many years ago. But in truth I wasn't saved. From day one, I was shown the worst examples of what the Christian life was supposed to be like from members of my own church. They openly proclaimed they were saved, but you'd never know it by how they lived their lives. They were no different than the rest of the world."

John sighed, "I know what you mean." *Do I ever!*

"To be honest, most at my church were true followers, but the few bad apples ruined the whole bunch, for letting me think God's grace gave me a license to keep on sinning without any repercussions.

"Don't get me wrong, John, I was thrilled at first thinking I could keep selling drugs and engaging in all sorts of wickedness, just like them, knowing I was saved no matter what. It was like having the best of both worlds."

Leroy grunted. "Who was I kidding? I knew God was greatly disappointed with me. I felt it deep inside. But it never stopped me from sinning. That all changed on Enoch's third day at the park, when I was finally sober enough to have a decent conversation with the old man.

"For hours on end he listened as I mourned DeSean's death, and angrily blamed everyone and everything for what had become my life.

"When I finally ran out of words to say, Enoch looked me square in the eye and said, 'You're very good at pointing out the sin in others, Leroy, but what about your own sins?' I got all puffed up inside and wanted to shout, 'Oh no, you didn't just say that to me!', but the old man was right. His next words impacted me greatly.

As lovingly and gently as he could, he said, 'In order to hate the sin in the world, you first have to hate the sin in yourself.' BAM! The old man hit the nail right on the head," Leroy yelled, a little too loudly, momentarily rustling some from their sleep.

Leroy toned it down a couple notches. "Enoch was right. I hated everyone's sin but my own. What a hypocrite I was!" He snorted. "Because my relationship with God wasn't authentic, it never bothered me that my sinful lifestyle wasn't pleasing to Him. So I just kept on sinning."

John winced in the darkness and kept listening.

"I spent that whole day reading God's Word and taking a good, hard look at my life. For the first time I saw just how offensive *my* sins really were to a Holy and just God. I finally understood that His eyes were too holy and pure to look at me, let alone tolerate my sin.

"Needless to say, I didn't sleep much that night. I tossed and turned unable to stop thinking about DeSean's whereabouts, knowing that would have been my final destination had I been killed that night. The next day I told Enoch I wanted to rededicate my life to Jesus."

Leroy chuckled shamefully. "I'll never forget the look he gave me. It screamed, 'Rededicate?' Once again, the old man saw right through me. I didn't need to rededicate anything. Like many in the world who proclaimed to be Christians, I was spiritually dead and needed God's regeneration, so I could finally be saved for real. I mean think about it, what can anyone do for themselves if they're dead?"

"Nothing, I suppose," John said.

"Correct! When Enoch entered into my life, I was physically alive, but spiritually I was as dead as roadkill. Just like you, God breathed life into my human body at birth. But due to the sin nature I inherited from my parents, which dates all the way back to Adam and Eve, I entered this world physically alive but spiritually dead.

"John three-eighteen states, 'Whoever believes in him is not condemned, but whoever does not believe is condemned already, because he has not believed in the name of the only Son of God.' Did you hear me,

John?" Leroy exclaimed, "Condemned *already* in the eyes of a Holy and just God!"

John gulped hard then shivered.

Leroy sighed, "Scary stuff, I know. The more I realized how deserving I was of hell, yet Jesus was still willing to take my countless sins and shame as if they were His own, the more I finally understood just how amazing God's grace really was. The Most High changed my heart that day and breathed new life into my dead, sin-stained body."

Leroy became teary-eyed, "That's the day I fell in love with Jesus for real and decided to live my life for Him. It's impossible to be saved any other way, John. Enoch taught me that the God we serve can only be known as He's revealed to the heart by the Holy Spirit through the Word. Thanks to him, I finally know how it feels to have eternal security.

Leroy took another deep breath and exhaled, "I may be homeless, but now that I see God's miraculous City on a hill, knowing it's my final destination makes all my struggles in this fallen world seem like nothing."

"Amen, brother," Pedro said.

"Been reading the Bible every day since. Still don't understand it all. And to be honest, some parts still offend my human nature."

"Yeah, like what?" John couldn't help but be drawn even further into the discussion.

"Where shall I start? For one thing, the many wars where orders were given to leave no survivors, not even women, children or livestock. That doesn't sound like love to me, but sheer madness."

Tiwanna grimaced, "I keep telling you both, if more women were in charge down here, there'd be less wars being waged in the world."

"Here we go again," Pedro replied, jokingly.

"Just saying..." Tiwanna nudged Pedro's arm. "In all seriousness, I also struggle with God's Word at times; especially the parts on forgiveness. It used to enrage me hearing stories of convicted rapists claiming they were forgiven by God, after confessing their sins in prison and becoming Christians."

Tiwanna sighed. "As a rape victim myself, it's impossible to forget the evil I saw in the eyes of the men who violated me. To this day, it's difficult for my human side to accept what they did. I had so much hatred in my heart for the longest time.

Tiwanna did all she could to pull herself together, so she wouldn't burst out in tears, "But now that I've been given a deeper glimpse into

God's amazing grace, I've come to realize my sins are just as offensive to God and I need His grace and mercy just as much as any murderer or rapist on the planet."

"Amen to that, Tiwanna," Leroy said. He wanted to shout, "Woo hoo!"

"Here's how far I've come in my walk with Jesus," the forever-changed woman said, "Though I still don't understand all of God's Word, nor will I ever, at least not in this temporary shell of a body, I accept it as the highest authority over my life, whether it sometimes offends my sensibilities or not."

The way Tiwanna said it gripped John in his spirit like never before. What always sounded weak-minded to him wasn't so weak-minded after all. It was starting to make perfect sense.

"Let me put it this way, John," Leroy said, "if God's Word declared that all males age 53 like myself had to dress a certain way or weren't allowed to speak in church, though it might ruffle my feathers and offend my human side, this former angry drug dealer would do his best to honor God's command, knowing He knows what's best for me at all times. If it's in His Word, it's there for a definite reason, whether I understand it or not."

"Preach on, brother Leroy," said Tiwanna.

"At the end of the day," Pedro opined softly, "God's Word wasn't written for us to question or examine it. It was written to question and examine us. He is the Potter. We are the clay."

"And so I ask, John," Leroy said, almost sternly, "if your life came to an end today, would Jesus be your greatest hope or worst nightmare?"

John flinched. *Hmm...* "Well, in fairness..."

Leroy cut him off. "Fairness? In the eyes of a holy God, you're in no position for fairness. None of us are. If God were to be fair to you, He would rightly send you straight to hell! The Bible tells us in Luke chapter twelve, verses four and five not to fear those who kill the body, but He who has authority to cast into hell."

Sensing John's chief motivation for feeding them was to somehow earn extra credit with God, Pedro said, "You did a very good thing tonight, John. Generous as it was, if you haven't been truly converted, your kind deeds did nothing to bring you any closer to God. If anything, because tomorrow is promised to no one, if you remain unconverted, guess you can say your kind deeds actually brought you closer to hell than to Heaven."

"Ouch," John bellowed, chuckling without humor.

"Sounds mean, I know," Pedro replied, seeing John squirming uncomfortably in the darkness, "but because God has bound all men to sin, if you're not counted among the converted, your righteousness or good works are seen by God as nothing more than filthy rags.

"Ephesians two, verses eight and nine says we are saved by grace, through faith, and not by works, so that no one can boast. Verse ten declares that we are God's handiwork, created in Christ Jesus to do good works, which God prepared in advance for us to do."

Exhaling deeply, Pedro went on, "If there's one thing you take from this discussion, never forget that God's salvation has nothing to do with works, fairness, or what we think we deserve, and everything to do with His unmerited mercy, grace and forgiveness.

"Without those things, you'll never come into proper fellowship with the One who created you, no matter how many nice things you do for others, or how many times you're seen in church going through the motions. Noble as those things may seem, they can never atone for your sins in life. Only Jesus can."

Pedro paused a moment, so his words would resonate. "What you saw here tonight, my friend, was nothing more than God's Word in motion carried out by souls that have surrendered to the pull of the Holy Spirit. In and of ourselves, we're completely incapable of extending such kindness to others. Only those who live their lives according to the Scriptures can demonstrate this kind of sacrificial love."

Leroy chimed in, "Jeremiah seventeen-nine states, 'The heart is deceitful above all things, and desperately sick; who can understand it?' This Scripture applies to all humans, John, saved or not. Shoot, how else could this one-time self-centered drug dealer be capable of showing genuine kindness toward anyone? It's only by God's power, nothing else."

"Do you feel safe here with us?" Tiwanna asked in the darkness.

"Completely," John said, without hesitation.

Pedro said, "Think about what you just said. Even after we told you the many bad things we did, just a few months ago, you still feel perfectly safe with us. Doesn't that blow your mind?"

"Now that you put it that way, yes!"

"That's the evidence of the Holy Spirit living in us. Believe me when I say, you wouldn't have felt safe with us just a few short months ago."

John Jensen shook his head in awe. Was God using these three servants of His to validate the presence of the Holy Spirit to him? It sure felt that way.

"If there's one thing Enoch's example confirmed to me," Tiwanna said, "it's that the world needs more Christians to be who they say they are."

"Could you imagine the revival on this planet if there were a million more believers like the old man?" Pedro asked. "That's my new goal in life: to be who I say I am in Christ Jesus. It all starts with me. If I do my best to let others see Jesus in me, hopefully it'll help offset the bad actions of the many fake Christians in the world."

Leroy shook his head. "We live in a crazy world. Even a hardcore atheist won't deny society's coming apart at the seams. Everyone can hear the time bomb ticking. The only question is, when will it finally go off? Yet, despite all that, many live as if they have all the time in the world to get right with God.

"I was with DeSean when he died. We spent that whole day together. I can assure you he had no expectation of dying that day. God's mercy may be new every morning. But like Pedro said, with tomorrow promised to no one, who really knows how many mornings we have left on Earth to receive it? Do you, John?"

"No," came the reply softly.

"The only reason the unconverted in the world are not in hell this very moment, is that God's hand is keeping them from falling into the eternal fire. The day of mercy has already passed for my late friend, DeSean.

"The many material things he loved so much and placed before God in this lifetime, to the point of near-worship, are the things he now detests with a hatred that will only intensify as the ages slowly pass. From here on out, even his most desperate cries for mercy will be in vain."

"Scary stuff," Tiwanna said.

"If you don't belong to Jesus, and you're relying on your own righteousness or good works to get you into Heaven, let me just say that if God withdrew His hand from you this day, the moment He let go of you, your so-called righteousness would no better support you and keep you out of hell than a sheet of paper trying to stop a speeding bullet. In the end, you'll either be forgiven or forsaken. The choice is yours."

At that, Leroy laid down and the conversation came to an end. He could tell just by looking at John that his words had landed hard.

John remained silent and considered all that he had heard.

156

ENOCH SPENT AN HOUR in prayer at the Jensen residence, rejoicing in the presence of his Maker. Only someone who had actually been in Yahweh's presence could worship Him so intimately and affectionately.

Lying in complete darkness awaiting his next instructions from above, Enoch had an overwhelming sensation that something incredible had taken place at the city park.

Yahweh confirmed it by revealing that the Holy Spirit was put on full display for John to witness, in the actions of Enoch's beloved disciples at the park. All John needed now was to be convinced that Jesus really was the Son of Yahweh, and the only Bridge to salvation.

"As you say, Lord," Enoch whispered rolling onto his side, sensing his time on earth was drawing near...

26

CHRISTMAS EVE MORNING

JOHN'S EYES POPPED OPEN early the next day when a strong gust of cold wind roused him from his sleep. He blinked a few times totally amazed he slept at all. Ironically, the frigid cold air had little to do with it.

It all came down to the many frightening thoughts invading his mind, stemming from last night's deep discussion with his three homeless friends. How could anyone sleep after that?

Rising on shaky legs, John groaned and stretched his body, watching the partly cloudy sky slowly brighten above him, filling the atmosphere with radiant light. *So beautiful!*

For the first time in a long time, even chilled to the bone, whereas the battery-operated lanterns he brought with him had gone out long ago, John felt fully alive. His senses were on full alert.

"I did it! I survived a night out on the streets!" John looked skyward, "Thank You, God, for this beautiful day."

Knowing his family would be coming to the park in a few hours, John needed to move his car so they wouldn't see it. He started the vehicle and was tempted to turn on the heat—very tempted, in fact—but he refrained.

Finding a parking space, he locked his car and walked the streets of his city trying to warm himself.

Dressed in the shabbiest clothing he owned, hoodie covering his head, blanket draped over him for added warmth, and a few days' worth of stubble on his face from not shaving, John looked...well, homeless. It wasn't easy walking when weighted down by so much clothing.

Okay, so I'm homeless for the time being. Now what? Where to go and what to do?

Each time a car passed by John ducked his head hoping he wouldn't be seen by anyone he knew. Then again, did anyone see him? Really see him? Though it was only one night, the slow spiral into near-invisibility had already begun.

With most businesses closed for the holiday, the streets weren't nearly as crowded as usual. Still, those who were out shopping did their best to avoid making eye contact with him. Just one glance would force them to admit he really existed, thus obligating them to help him in some way.

It was so much easier to blink him away and keep walking.

John knew exactly how they felt. After all, that was him just 24 hours ago. He went in search of a restroom. He entered inside a convenience store. The heat felt good on his face.

An overweight middle-age female clerk glared at him, totally stone-faced. Her arms were crossed over her chest.

Here goes nothing! Clearing his throat, John suddenly felt nervous. "Merry Christmas! May I please use your restroom?"

"It's out of order," she snapped. Just then, a well-dressed man with a clean-cut appearance came out of the men's room.

John pleaded with her, "Please, I really need to go."

"Restrooms are for customers only," she hissed, with a hatred in her voice John had never heard spewed at him before. "Find someplace else to go!"

John felt like protesting more. He was tempted to tell her he wasn't really homeless. Instead, he left the store looking for someplace else to go.

After three more rejections, he was forced to relieve himself behind a dumpster behind a row of stores on Main Street. Being bundled up made it even more difficult. And with no way of washing his hands, he felt dirty, incredibly dirty; and worthless all the way down to his soul.

John was starting to feel the unmistakable indignity of being homeless, and it hadn't even been one day yet. He walked past a candy store that was crowded with many customers.

A young woman, perhaps a college student home for the holidays cheerfully said, "Merry Christmas!"

"Wow! I thought I was invisible!" John said sadly, his metaphor feeling all too real to him.

"Of course, I see you," said the young woman, holding bags full of wrapped gifts in her hands. What separated her from the rest of the last-minute holiday shoppers was that she actually looked joyous.

Everyone else looked rushed, panicked even, trying to beat the clock and finish their shopping before the stores closed for the season.

"Most people ignore me as if I don't even exist," John Jensen said, feeling as if he'd been homeless forever. *And to think that millions of street people deal with this harshness every day! How do they do it?*

"How long have you been homeless?"

159

"Just recently."

"Can I buy you a cup of coffee or food or something?"

When John hesitated, the woman's brow furrowed; her facial expression turned skeptical. "Look, it'll be my pleasure to buy you food. But as a Christian, I can't in good conscience give you money knowing it might be used for drugs or alcohol. Do you understand?"

Everything John liked about her dissipated the moment she pre-judged him, without even knowing who he was. It's not what she said—he wouldn't want to fund someone's addiction either—but how she said it, not to mention the condescending look on her face. It turned him off.

He wanted to say, "I never did drugs in my life! And besides, I didn't ask for money. You offered!" Instead he said, "Hope you have a Merry Christmas."

"You too. Hope you land back on your feet again soon," she said, walking away.

Yeah, sure you do...

"SMELLS GOOD IN HERE," Enoch said to Lydia, entering the kitchen for his morning cup of coffee.

"Thanks. Have you seen John?"

"No, I haven't," came the reply.

"He sent a text message last night saying he wouldn't be coming home. Hope he's okay."

"Let's just trust that John has Yahweh's full hedge of protection, and wherever he is, he's okay."

The way Enoch said it put Lydia's mind at ease. She removed kielbasa from the oven and cut it into sandwich-sized pieces, then dumped it into a large pot full of sauerkraut. In another large pot, she stirred the meatballs simmering in her homemade gravy. "Food's just about ready."

Enoch smiled. He was eager to see his friends again.

They arrived at the park just before noon with a minivan full of hot food and gifts.

Everyone at the park rejoiced upon seeing Enoch again, after a four-day hiatus. It felt more like four weeks. Just seeing him was a blessing.

Matthew and Grace were wildly energized, eager to get started.

"Merry Christmas, Suzie!" Lydia kissed her rosy, frozen cheeks.

"Same to you, Lydia! Thanks for the pizza last night."

"Pizza? What pizza?"

"Didn't John tell you? Oh my..."

"Tell me what?"

"I thought you knew. Last night your husband suddenly showed up with boxes of pizza for everyone. He even slept here."

"What?! Are you serious?" Lydia's eyes darted left to right to see if John was still around. She didn't see him.

"Perhaps I said too much."

Tears rushed to Lydia's eyes. "Don't feel bad. You just made my whole day. It's like you gave me an early Christmas present."

"My pleasure," Suzie said, just grateful to be giving something good to somebody again.

"Gather around everyone, Enoch's about to pray," Leroy said, temporarily relieved of prayer duty.

Since Troy, Dillon and Rocky were fairly sober-minded, and would remain so until the first of the month, Tiwanna said, "Why don't the three of you play Christmas songs to help usher in some holiday cheer?"

"No problem." In between bites of food, the three scrawny musicians strummed their instruments as everyone ate their meals. Many sang the lyrics to the songs.

After performing a few mainstream Christmas carols, Grace asked, "Do you know 'Happy Birthday Jesus?'"

Dillon started playing the mainstream "Happy Birthday" theme song.

Grace giggled. "Not that song!"

"How's it go then?"

You could hear a pin drop when Grace started singing. Her soft, gentle voice warmed the hearts of everyone within earshot. She sounded like an angel.

Happy birthday, Jesus,
I'm so glad it's Christmas,
All the tinsel and lights and the presents are nice
but the real Gift is You,
Happy birthday, Jesus,
I'm so glad it's Christmas,
all the carols and bells make the holiday swell
and it's all about You
Happy Birthday, Jesus,
Jesus, I love You.

161

Troy was the first to catch on. He started strumming away, nodding for Dillon and Rocky to join him. Both quickly caught on, their instruments harmonizing in near-perfection.

The second time through, save for those who were trying to sleep, most were happy to lend their voices to the *City Park Homeless Community Choir.* Those who didn't know the lyrics hummed along.

Using her mobile device, Lydia recorded it all, anxious to upload the newly-shot video onto her Facebook account. She already anticipated many heartfelt comments when she got home. *More Christmas presents!*

Once everyone was finished eating, Matthew and Grace uncovered the two crates, revealing the 50 holiday stockings for all to see. One by one the children handed out gifts, calling each person by name.

Many posed for pictures with the two youngsters holding their stockings. Those still hungover from last night mumbled a simple "thank you" before rolling onto their sides, hoping to sleep again.

Matthew and Grace didn't take it personally. Just to have the distinct privilege of giving for the sake of giving, with no strings attached, was all the gift they needed in return.

Knowing this was her kids' shining moment, Lydia kept recording. *I wish John was here to see it*, she thought sadly.

27

CAMPED OUT AT THE opposite end of the park, John Jensen watched from behind a thick oak tree, doing his best to remain incognito. His head popped out for a few moments or so before retreating again.

He didn't want his children to spot him and say, "Look! Let's give that homeless man a stocking too!"

He cracked up at the thought. It felt good to laugh at silly things again.

John rubbed his hands together to get some feeling back to his frozen fingers. There was no way he was leaving for the warmth of home now.

After successfully playing the star role in *The Grinch Who Stole Seven Months*, the ice surrounding his frozen heart was slowly melting, just in time for Christmas. It felt good.

Even from a hundred yards away, he couldn't help but be deeply moved watching his children passing out gifts to many who were complete strangers. The fact that they were willing to forfeit their own gifts this year, to make this beautiful moment possible, was beyond words.

What children did such things? Only those who truly understood it's better to give than to receive, John concluded.

And they were right. John couldn't deny the times he felt best about himself this week, were when he was giving to others.

The 30 tacos his first visit to this place. The $50 he donated the following day for food and hot coffee. The twelve pizzas last night.

But nothing topped what was transpiring before his eyes right now. It was another example of true Christianity at work.

Even pedestrians who normally ignored the many unfortunates living at this place couldn't help but take notice. Perhaps they thought it was a one-way gift-giving occasion but, after last night's awesome experience, John knew nothing could be further from the truth.

True, material gifts were only being given from one side, but the feeling the givers—his own children—received from doing this to the least of these, could never be measured in worldly terms.

John felt like he was receiving a precious gift by simply observing.

He watched Matthew and Pedro embracing for the longest time, after Pedro opened the gift Matthew got just for him.

The soon-to-be no longer homeless man wiped his eyes, then removed a picture from his wallet of himself and his daughter, Erica, very carefully placing it inside the picture frame.

Kissing his daughter's image, Pedro said, "This will go on the table next to my bed when I move in next week."

"Glad you like it, Pedro." They fist-bumped.

John couldn't hear the exchange of words between them, but that didn't prevent tears from streaming down his icy-cold cheeks.

The look on Pedro's face said it all: though it only cost Matthew a dollar, to Pedro it was priceless.

"What you are witnessing, John, is Christmas being celebrated in a way that brings glory to the Most High."

Startled, John craned his neck back and was shocked to see Enoch standing behind him. "Whoa! How'd you do that?"

"Do what?"

"Sneak up on me like that? I'm certain I saw you standing over there a few seconds ago," John said, pointing to the homeless setting. "I know you're young at heart and all, but not even someone with the stamina of a twenty-year-old track star could have made it here so quickly. I'm tired but not that tired."

Enoch belly laughed and left it at that.

Wiping tears from the two drenched globes filling his eye sockets, John said, "This is one of the most beautiful sights I've ever seen in my life!"

When Enoch didn't reply, John craned his neck back to find no one there. Only air. "What's going on!" He looked back to where his family was gathered. Sure enough, the old man was seated on a blanket apparently in mid-conversation with his former parkies.

What in the world? Is my frozen mind playing tricks on me? Was it a hallucination? No, there was no doubt in his mind that Enoch *was* standing behind him a few short moments ago. It was as real to him as last night's phenomenal experience with Leroy, Pedro and Tiwanna.

John Jensen shook his head and watched with a new sense of wonderment...

WHEN THE LAST STOCKING was handed out, Lydia covered her mouth with her left hand and gasped. Not only were there 50 street people among them—and only 50—each one whose name was written on the gift-filled stockings was present to receive them.

How could Enoch have possibly known that, when people came and went from this place all the time?

"How did you do that?"

"Do what, Lydia?"

Seeing the twinkle in Enoch's eye, Lydia smiled. "Oh, nothing.

JOHN LEFT THE CITY park desperate for the warmth of a hot shower. He raced home not wanting his family to see him looking like this. But Freeway didn't seem to mind. The moment John arrived home, she was ready and waiting to shower her master with lots of love.

After showering and shaving John got dressed for church and went downstairs. He struck a match to the newspaper inside the fireplace, then paused to watch the paper curl and blacken, before spreading to the small twigs and branches. As the fire slowly roared to life, John counted it a blessing to appreciate the little things in life again.

John turned on the Christmas tree lights and sat on the couch. Staring at the hundreds of bright colorful lights, with so many gifts already received, it felt like Christmas had already come and gone.

Whatever was underneath the tree in the morning could never compare to what had already been given and received.

For some people, it takes many years, or even a lifetime of searching to finally be awakened from within. Others go to their graves without it ever happening to them. But sometimes only a small glimpse is needed...

John Jensen felt fortunate to fall into the "small glimpse" category. All it took for him was a few days with a homeless man living under his roof, then having a life-transforming experience in a humble, homeless community.

Having the unspeakable privilege of spending a night with a bunch of poor, forgotten souls—on their own turf—taught him more about what it means to have genuine faith in God, than any other place on earth.

Sometimes you really must lose everything to finally understand...

Aside from Enoch, a man no one could deny was special, Leroy, Pedro and Tiwanna were quite special themselves. They were three of the most authentic people John Jensen had ever met. Even if they didn't know it, they reinstated his will to want to be a better man. They also challenged him to start making a positive difference in the lives of others again.

Without a doubt, this week turned out to be a seminal moment for him. Yet something was clearly amiss. It was nowhere near complete.

A few minutes later, John heard the car pull into the driveway. Freeway's ears perked up. She raced to the front door, her tail wagging uncontrollably.

Freeway looked like John felt. If he had a tail it would be wagging too.

The children burst through the door eager to share the experience they had with their father. Though John was there to witness it all, he listened as if hearing it for the very first time. The glow on his kids' faces, as they explained every last detail, was too incredible to ignore or overlook.

Lydia observed her husband listening attentively to everything the children told him, looking handsome as ever in his red sweater, and could only smile.

No words were exchanged between the married couple, but even without asking it was apparent that John's compass had been severely redirected over the past 24 hours.

He was finally headed in the right direction again. *Hallelujah!*

"Upstairs you two," Lydia said to Matthew and Grace, once they finished telling their father everything. "Can't be late for church."

When Lydia followed the kids upstairs, John turned to face Enoch. His arms were folded across his chest. He bit his lower lip and said, "Can I ask you something?"

"Yes, John?" Enoch was stroking Freeway's fur.

John pointed his left finger at his house guest and opened his mouth, but no words came out. "Hmm, forget it. Perhaps it was just my imagination." *It wasn't my imagination. It really happened!*

"As you say, John."

When Lydia and the children came downstairs, John poked and stirred the ashes to extinguish the fire, leaving only a few small pieces of wood to smolder. Certainly nothing to cause concern.

At that, everyone piled into the minivan and left for church. No one was more eager to get there than John. He had a premonition that he might be seeing the reenactment of the birth of Christ, really seeing it, for the very first time.

John felt childlike again. It felt good...

166

28

CHRISTMAS EVE NIGHT

THE JENSENS AND ENOCH returned home from church just before 8 p.m. Lydia cherished that they all got to enjoy the Christmas concert together, without the children rushing off to Sunday school classes.

Having Enoch with them was an added blessing. But Lydia would have loved it even more had all her friends from the park been able to join them. But there wasn't an extra ticket to be found; the concert was completely sold out.

What came as little surprise was that Enoch was treated with a level of dignity and respect that he should have received all along.

The Jensens knew why: their house guest was properly dressed and groomed for the occasion. Most were unaware their guest was the same homeless person who was mocked and ridiculed the past few weeks, at this place of worship.

Suddenly on their good side, had he requested a front row seat, they would have moved mountains to make it happen for the elderly gentleman.

Betty Rainer was one of the few to recognize him. She flashed one of her, "That's more like it" looks, without missing a stride on her way to the front row.

Because it was Christmas, Lydia let it go. She would keep praying that God would change her former spiritual mentor's heart.

Upon arriving home, Freeway was at the front door chomping at the bit to greet everyone. Alex, on the other hand, couldn't be bothered.

Lying on the windowsill in his own little world, the six-year-old feline was more interested in the many Christmas lights squaring the front window, illuminating his white fur, to pay much mind to anything else, including those who faithfully housed and fed him.

Keeping in tradition with something Lydia did each Christmas Eve, seven gifts were already beneath the tree waiting for them when they walked through the front door. Lydia placed them there before church as everyone waited in the car.

167

Normally there were six gifts: one for each family member, including Alex and Freeway. The seventh gift was for Enoch, the newest "honorary" family member.

Although the kids knew what was inside the wrapped packages—matching pajamas for the humans and pet toys for Freeway and Alex—it was something they looked forward to each year.

It was the Jensens' "official" way of ringing in the Christmas season.

Enoch also got fuzzy slippers to go along with his pajamas. So, in that sense he received two gifts. Everyone changed into their new pajamas and reassembled at the dining room table for a bite to eat.

John and Lydia both drank eggnog. Enoch and the children opted for hot chocolate instead, loaded with lots of marshmallows.

"Enoch?"

"Yes, Grace?" the old man said, taking a sip of his beverage.

"After we eat, can you read 'Twas The Night Before Christmas' to us?"

Enoch shot a quick glance at John and Lydia.

"It's our Christmas Eve tradition," John said.

"It would be my pleasure, Grace."

"Oh, goodie. Thanks, second best friend."

After Lydia finished cleaning the kitchen, she joined everyone in the living room and sat next to her husband.

For the first time in forever, at least it seemed like forever, John was eager to spend time with his family again. Not because he had to. He wanted to. He looked at his watch. *This time last night I was at the pizzeria...*He smiled warmly at the thought.

"I must say, these slippers are the most comfortable apparel my feet have ever touched," Enoch declared, with great satisfaction.

Laughter filled the living room.

Alex finally grew tired of the windowsill and snuggled next to Lydia on the couch. *You treat Enoch like many at church do!* She chuckled to herself.

Freeway, on the other hand, couldn't get enough of the old man. She lay on the floor beside him, as if also waiting for the story to begin.

Lydia drank it all in. The lit Christmas tree. The evergreen garlands hung throughout the house. The lights and electric candles shining brightly in the windows for all outsiders to see. The pleasant aroma wafting in the air from the cinnamon-scented candle burning on the coffee table. But mostly, it was her husband's slow but steady progression.

This was turning out to be the best Christmas ever. It was about to get even better...

Enoch reached for the leather-bound book that had been handed down three generations in Lydia's family. "Ready children?"

"Can I sit on your lap?"

"Sure, you can, Grace." If Enoch was uneasy with her request, he didn't show it. Once Grace was settled on his lap, he opened the book to page one and began reading, "Twas the night before Christmas and all through the house. Not a creature was stirring, not even a mouse..."

On and on Enoch read the timeless work of fiction in his deep, gravelly voice. Lydia recorded it on her phone, savoring every second of this precious family moment. She was desperate to ask John a million questions about last night's experience, but now wasn't the time.

With peace hovering thick in the air for a change, she would remain patient until her husband was ready to open up to her.

Seeing her youngest child sitting on the lap of this bearded, jolly old house guest, if she tried explaining the scene to an outsider, they'd probably conclude that Grace was sitting on Santa's lap.

Only he wasn't Santa Claus. The question was, who was he and where did he come from? Even after having him as a guest in her house the past few nights, Enoch was still a deep mystery to her.

At any rate, if Betty Rainer could only be here to witness it for herself, perhaps then she would finally be ashamed of her actions and repent of her judgmental ways.

"...and to all a good night," Enoch said, closing the book.

As was the custom, the Jensens started clapping their hands.

"Can you read it again?" Grace pleaded. This was, by far, the best rendition of the timeless Christmas classic she had ever heard.

"Once is enough, sweetheart," said John.

"It's a nice story, children," Enoch said, "but I prefer to tell the real Christmas story, rather than some mythical figure flying on reindeer who is never even mentioned in the Scriptures."

"It's okay. We no longer believe in Santa Claus," Matthew said, speaking on behalf of himself and his kid sister.

Enoch smiled. "You've come so far this week, children. While the reenactment at church was quite accurate, why don't we take it a little further?"

"Yippie!" said Grace, always up for hearing another story.

169

"Even though we're not called to celebrate Yeshua's birth, only His death and resurrection, I'd like to give you a more accurate account of what really took place way back when. This way you will be able to better explain it to others in the future. But in order to tell it, you will need your Bibles."

"Okay," Matthew said.

Grace jumped down off of Enoch's lap and raced upstairs with Matthew to retrieve their Bibles from their bedrooms. A moment later, they were back. Grace once again sat on Enoch's lap.

John excused himself to fetch his Bible from his study to share with Lydia.

A moment of anticipated silence ensued. Fuzzy slippers perched on a padded footstool, Enoch let his eyes wander from one family member to the next. "Children, turn if you will to the Gospel of Luke, chapter one."

John and Lydia did the same.

Closing his eyes, Enoch recited the entire first chapter of Luke from memory.

What the Jensens didn't realize was that each heard Enoch's words in the exact translation in which their Bibles were printed. John and Lydia heard him reciting from the King James version. Matthew heard it in the English Standard Version. Grace heard it recited in her NIV teenage adventure Bible, even though she was only seven. Only Enoch was aware of it.

Glancing at John and Lydia, Enoch said, "Did you know Luke chapter one is the longest chapter in the entire New Testament?"

Both shook their heads no.

"And for good reason. So important was this Divine moment in history leading up to the birth of Yeshua that Luke was careful to write an orderly account of the two humble servants Yahweh used to start the process that would forever change the world."

"Six months before Joseph and Mary came into the story, Zechariah was visited by an angel of the Lord. Much like Joseph and Mary, Zechariah and Elizabeth weren't born into wealth or royalty. Their only qualifications were that both were righteous before God, walking blamelessly in His commandments and statutes.

"According to the custom of the priesthood, Zechariah was chosen by lot to enter the temple of the Lord and burn incense. While he was in there, everyone outside prayed. And that's when the angel Gabriel appeared, standing on the right side of the altar of incense.

"As you can imagine, Grace," Enoch added, growing more animated, "Zechariah was deeply troubled when he saw him. Fear fell upon him."

"I'd be scared, too," she said.

Enoch gave her a comforting squeeze. "But Gabriel told him not to be afraid, for his prayer had been heard, and his wife Elizabeth would bear him a son, who would be filled with the Holy Spirit inside his mother's womb. Gabriel told Zechariah his son would be great before the Lord, and would turn many in Israel to the Lord their God and make ready for Yeshua a people prepared.

"But Zechariah was skeptical and questioned Gabriel saying, 'How shall I know this? For I am an old man and my wife is advanced in years.' This did not make Gabriel happy, children. The angel answered him, 'I was sent to bring you this good news. But because you did not believe my words, you will be silent and unable to speak until the day that these things are fulfilled in their time.'

"When Zechariah came out of the temple, everyone realized he had seen a vision. He tried communicating to them but was unable to speak. At any rate, just as promised, Zechariah's wife Elizabeth conceived in Yahweh's perfect timing, and for five months kept herself hidden as if protecting a precious jewel from the rest of the world."

Like an excited child, Enoch shifted his weight and nearly knocked Grace over. "This is where Joseph and Mary enter into the history-changing story. In the sixth month of Elizabeth's pregnancy, the angel Gabriel was sent from God to Nazareth, to the virgin betrothed to Joseph, of the house of David.

"You can imagine, children, the surprise Mary must have felt when Gabriel appeared saying, 'Greetings, O favored one, the Lord is with you!' You can also imagine Joseph's shock when Mary tried explaining it to him later. But I'll come back to that. For now, let's focus on Mary. Scripture says she was greatly troubled as she tried to discern what sort of greeting this might be.

"As told in church tonight, the angel said to her, 'Do not be afraid, Mary, for you have found favor with God. And behold, you will conceive in your womb and bear a son, and you shall call his name Jesus. He will be great and will be called the Son of the Most High. And the Lord God will give to him the throne of his father David, and he will reign over the house of Jacob forever, and of his kingdom there will be no end.'

"Mary was quite confused and said to the angel, 'How will this be, since I am a virgin?' The angel answered her, 'The Holy Spirit will come upon you, and the power of the Most High will overshadow you; therefore the child to be born will be called holy—the Son of God. And behold, your relative Elizabeth in her old age has also conceived a son, and this is the sixth month with her who was called barren. For nothing will be impossible with God.'

"Instead of doubting all that she was told, Mary said, 'Behold, I am the servant of the Lord; let it be to me according to your word.' As quickly as the angel Gabriel appeared, he departed from her. Mary wasted no time going into the hill country, to a town in Judah, to the house of Zechariah and Elizabeth.

"When Mary greeted Elizabeth, the baby leaped in her womb. And at that precise moment, Elizabeth was filled with the Holy Spirit. With a loud cry she exclaimed to Mary, 'Blessed are you among women, and blessed is the fruit of your womb! For behold, when the sound of your greeting came to my ears, the baby in my womb leaped for joy. And blessed are you for believing what was spoken to you from the Lord.'"

Closing his eyes, Enoch went on, "And Mary rejoiced saying, 'My soul magnifies the Lord and my spirit rejoices in God my Savior, for he has looked on the humble estate of his servant. For behold, from now on all generations will call me blessed; for he who is mighty has done great things for me, and holy is his name. And his mercy is for those who fear him from generation to generation.'"

Enoch opened his eyes with a radiant expression on his face. This was a story he never grew weary of telling.

"The time came for Elizabeth to give birth, and she bore a son. And her neighbors and relatives heard that the Lord had shown great mercy to her, and they rejoiced with her. On the eighth day they came to circumcise the child.

"And they would have called him Zechariah after his father, but Elizabeth said, 'No; he shall be called John.' They replied saying to her, 'None of your relatives is called by this name.' They even made signs to Zechariah, inquiring as to what he wanted his son to be called. On a writing tablet he wrote, *His name is John.* And immediately Zechariah's mouth was opened and his tongue loosed, and he could speak again."

"Is this John the Baptist?" Matthew asked.

"Yes, Matthew," Enoch replied. "And just as prophesied the child grew and became strong in spirit, living in the wilderness until the day of his public appearance to Israel. Though only a handful of people knew what was happening at the time, this humble beginning would soon turn the religious establishment completely upside down, forever changing the world."

Looking down at Grace on his lap, Enoch said, "Which leads us to the birth of Yeshua..."

Save for the crackling of the fireplace and the soft Christmas music playing in the background, the Jensen household was completely silent.

Not a creature was stirring, not even Freeway or Alex!

29

IN A NEAR WHISPER, Enoch said, "Children, what if I told you Yeshua's life didn't begin in a manger?"

"Huh?" Matthew said, clearly puzzled, but still trying to look intelligent. "But isn't that what the Bible says?"

John and Lydia exchanged confused glances. Where was Enoch going with this? But they weren't at all concerned. If anyone was qualified to teach their children from God's Holy Word, it was him.

What they didn't know was that this part of the lesson was meant more for John than anyone else.

"Yes, it's true that our loving Savior was born in a manger in Bethlehem two thousand years ago," Enoch declared, as if he was an actual eyewitness to the birth of Christ, which, in fact, he was. "But the important thing to remember, children, is that long before Yeshua's birth in human form, He was with God in Heaven, even from the beginning of time."

Matthew nodded, realizing he already knew that.

"And this means Yeshua witnessed all things leading up to His own birth, including when Gabriel appeared to Mary, telling her what would soon take place. Imagine that..."

Matthew didn't answer. He was too busy piecing things together in his mind.

"Turn if you will to the Gospel of John, chapter one, verses one through four. Once everyone was there, Enoch closed his eyes and, from memory, recited it word for word. 'In the beginning was the Word, and the Word was with God, and the Word was God. He was with God in the beginning. Through him all things were made; without him nothing was made that has been made. In him was life, and that life was the light of all mankind.'"

Once again, the Jensens heard Enoch's words in the exact translation in which their Bibles were printed.

"Matthew, would you read verse fourteen to us?"

With his right pointer finger, Matthew scrolled down the page until he found it. "The Word became flesh and made his dwelling among us. We have seen his glory, the glory of the one and only Son, who came from the Father, full of grace and truth." Matthew looked up. "Jesus, right?"

"Yes," Enoch said, nodding approvingly. "Okay, now open if you will to the Book of Hebrews, chapter one. Once again we will read the first four verses."

John found it rather easily and inched closer to Lydia, causing her to raise an eyebrow. The married couple did their best to remain in the background, so the children could enjoy this special time with their remarkable house guest.

Once Grace was ready, Enoch closed his eyes and recited from memory, "'In the past God spoke to our ancestors through the prophets at many times and in various ways, but in these last days he has spoken to us by his Son, whom he appointed heir of all things, and through whom also he made the universe. The Son is the radiance of God's glory and the exact representation of his being, sustaining all things by his powerful word. After he had provided purification for sins, he sat down at the right hand of the Majesty in heaven. So he became as much superior to the angels as the name he has inherited is superior to theirs.'"

Once again, everyone heard it in the translation in which their Bibles were printed.

Enoch opened his eyes. "Only Yeshua can rightly be called the Word of God. No one else qualifies. Even when Messiah returns in the future, He will still bear that name. Turn if you will to Revelation chapter nineteen, verses eleven through sixteen."

Enoch waited until everyone was there, then closed his eyes and recited from memory. "'I saw heaven standing open and there before me was a white horse, whose rider is called Faithful and True. With justice he judges and wages war. His eyes are like blazing fire, and on his head are many crowns. He has a name written on him that no one knows but he himself. He is dressed in a robe dipped in blood, and his name is the *Word of God*," Enoch implied with emphasis.

"'The armies of heaven were following him, riding on white horses and dressed in fine linen, white and clean. Coming out of his mouth is a sharp sword with which to strike down the nations. 'He will rule them with an iron scepter.' He treads the winepress of the fury of the wrath of God Almighty. On his robe and on his thigh he has this name written: KING OF KINGS AND LORD OF LORDS.'"

The words, "Treads the winepress of the fury of the wrath of God Almighty," petrified John. It made him think about last night when Pedro explained how his good deeds were viewed by God as nothing more than filthy rags. He shivered at the thought.

"As you can see, children, when Yeshua returns to earth in the future, it will be quite different from when He was born in a lowly manger. For now, it's important to understand that while God used many prophets throughout the ages, everything they prophesied about was directed toward one Person, one Savior.

"Only Yeshua can rightly call Himself the Son of God. In the beginning when Yahweh created heaven and earth, He spoke in the singular sense, as recorded in Genesis, chapter one. But when it came to creating man, Yahweh said in verse twenty-six, '...let *us* make man in *our* image, in *our* likeness...'"

"What words stand out to you in that verse, John?"

"Us and our."

"Precisely. And, of course, the 'us' referred to here is Father Yahweh, Yeshua HaMashiach, and the Holy Spirit. If there's one thing you remember about this story it's that there never was a time when the Word—Yeshua—was not. Long before time, matter and space were ever measured and recorded, the Word was there. In that light, there never was a 'Before Christ', or a B.C., as the worldly calendar states. Yeshua was always there."

"Wow, Jesus really is the exact representation of God," John said softly to himself. He felt this deep stirring inside.

Lydia heard him and smiled.

Enoch heard it too and rejoiced but remained focused on the children. "Now that we've established that Yeshua was with God from the beginning of time and, in fact, is God incarnate Himself, did you know there are hundreds of prophecies found in the Old Testament pertaining to Messiah's life on Earth, from His birth in a manger to His death on the cross to His glorious resurrection three days later?"

"Prophecies?" Grace asked. She'd heard the word mentioned several times, but she was unsure of the actual meaning.

"Yes, Grace. God gave certain men visions of the future which wouldn't come to pass for hundreds or even thousands of years, all pertaining to the life of Yeshua. So, in that sense, Bible prophecy is history written in advance."

"Really?"

Enoch nodded yes. "What if you could trace your family roots back hundreds of years, only to find that one of your ancestors had foretold about your very life, including your name, the exact time and place of your birth, the names of your parents and even Matthew, and many other key moments that would happen to you in the future?"

"That would be cool," Matthew said, answering for his kid sister.

Enoch chuckled. "Well, that's precisely how it happened in the life of Yeshua. Since it's Christmas Eve, though December twenty-fifth wasn't the actual day of Messiah's birth, let's nevertheless focus for now on some prophecies pointing to His birth. Here's how we'll do it. One of you can read the actual prophecy in the Old Testament and the other can confirm it in the New Testament, okay?"

"Sure!" Grace was clearly enjoying this wonderful family moment.

"Who wants to read first?"

"I will," Matthew shouted.

"Very good then. Turn if you will to Isaiah, chapter seven, verse fourteen."

Matthew found it rather easily.

"Before you read it, Matthew, can I ask you, John," Enoch said, glancing over at the father of two, "to first read Second Peter one, verses twenty and twenty-one for us?"

"Okay." John flipped pages back and forth before finally finding it. "'Above all, you must understand that no prophecy of Scripture came about by the prophet's own interpretation of things. For prophecy never had its origin in the human will, but prophets, though human, spoke from God as they were carried along by the Holy Spirit.'"

"Thank you, John."

John didn't reply. This latest revelation rendered him speechless.

"Now that we know everything Matthew will be reading didn't come from the prophet's own interpretation, but from God Almighty Himself, as they were carried along by the Holy Spirit, would you now read Isaiah seven-fourteen to us?"

"'Therefore the Lord himself will give you a sign: The virgin will conceive and give birth to a son, and will call him Immanuel.'"

"Very good, Matthew."

"Grace, would you please read Luke chapter two, verses six and seven for us? They should sound familiar because they were read aloud in church earlier."

177

"'While they were there, the time came for the baby to be born, and she gave birth to her firstborn, a son. She wrapped him in cloths and placed him in a manger, because there was no guest room available for them.'"

"Sort of like connecting the dots, wouldn't you agree?" Enoch said, glancing quickly at John.

Grace nodded agreement.

John got the point.

"It's your turn again, Matthew. Please read to us Micah, chapter five, verse two."

Matthew flipped pages back and forth until he found it toward the end of the Old Testament. He read, "'But you, Bethlehem Ephrathah, though you are small among the clans of Judah, out of you will come for me one who will be ruler over Israel, whose origins are from of old, from ancient times.'"

Another wave of confirmation nearly knocked John over. It was as if he could feel God opening his spiritual eyes and ears. He liked the sensation.

"Okay, Grace, let's continue in the Book of Luke, chapter two, verses eleven and twelve."

"'Today in the town of David,'" the seven-year-old read aloud, "'a Savior has been born to you; he is the Messiah, the Lord. This will be a sign to you: You will find a baby wrapped in cloths and lying in a manger.'"

"Very good, Grace. For the record, the town of David is Bethlehem."

John and Lydia displayed the smile of two very proud parents.

"The reason Joseph and Mary were in Bethlehem in the first place was that Caesar Augustus had issued a decree that a census should be taken of the entire Roman world. Everyone went to their own town to register. Mary was pledged to be married to Joseph, who belonged to the house and line of David, so they went there together.

"Something else you heard at church tonight and even saw reenacted on stage were the shepherds living out in the fields keeping watch over their flocks. On the night Mary gave birth to Messiah, an angel of the Lord appeared to them, and the glory of the Lord shone around them, and they were terrified.

"But the angel said to them, 'Do not be afraid. I bring you good news that will cause great joy for all the people. Today in the town of David a Savior has been born to you; he is the Messiah, the Lord. This will be a sign to you: You will find a baby wrapped in cloths and lying in a manger.'"

Eyes shifting from one family member to the next, the angelic house guest said, "Once again, Yahweh chose humble and simple men to witness this monumental moment in history."

Yeah, men like you, John thought, keeping it to himself.

"Could you imagine being one of the shepherds that night?" Enoch said to Matthew. "Talk about a life-altering experience?! That one moment in time forever connected them to the birth of the Savior of the world. Imagine how they must have felt when suddenly a great company of the heavenly host appeared with the angel praising God and saying, 'Glory to God in the highest heaven, and on earth peace to those on whom his favor rests.'"

"Wow," Grace said, doing her best to envision the scene inside her head.

"When the angel left to go back to Heaven, the shepherds hurried off to Bethlehem and found Mary and Joseph exactly where the angel said they would be, with a baby lying in the manger. They wasted no time bowing down to the Child in worship," Enoch said, the words dripping from his tongue like sweet honey. "Do you like the story so far, children?"

"Yes."

"Would you agree it is better than the first one we read?"

"Much better."

"It's about to get even more gripping. Shall we?"

30

"THOUGH YESHUA'S BIRTH IN a manger sounds peaceful, as humanity slept under a bright shining star on that blessed silent night, the devil knew this was no ordinary Child, but a King leaving His throne for a lowly manger; a King emptying Himself of all glory in order to become a servant, meek and lowly in heart.

"As you can imagine, children, Satan was greatly panicked. If Yeshua fulfilled His mission on Planet Earth, it meant eternal doom for him and all who belonged to him. From day one, Yahweh's ultimate adversary was desperate to find a way to kill Messiah. He was about to throw the universe into complete turmoil.

"Matthew chapter two tells about the Magi—also known as the three wise men who were actually kings themselves. After seeing His star in the east, they went to Jerusalem asking to see the newly-born King of the Jews, so they could worship Him. When King Herod heard this, he was greatly disturbed. Not only that but all of Jerusalem with him. Under Satan's strong influence, the paranoid ruler called together his chief priests and teachers of the law asking where Messiah was to be born.

"'In Bethlehem in Judea,' they replied, quoting the same verse you read a short while ago, Matthew, 'for this is what the prophet has written: 'But you, Bethlehem, in the land of Judah, are by no means least among the rulers of Judah; for out of you will come a ruler who will shepherd my people Israel.'

"The fact that King Herod felt the need to consult his chief priests and teachers of the law proves that even though he wasn't a follower of Yahweh, he knew God's Holy Word was the infallible Book of Truth.

"His next actions proved it. He sent the Magi to Bethlehem saying, 'Go and search carefully for the child. As soon as you find him report to me, so that I too may go and worship him.' They went on their way. The star rose again and went ahead of them until it stopped over the place where the Child was. Could you imagine following a star for so many days until it suddenly stopped directly above the place where baby Yeshua was found lying in the manger?"

"That would be amazing!" Matthew exclaimed.

THE UNANNOUNCED CHRISTMAS VISITOR

"Amazing indeed. Now on coming to the house, they saw the Child with his mother Mary. Much like Satan, these three wise men were fully mindful of Isaiah chapter nine, verses six and seven. They knew Yeshua was no ordinary Child. How often will kings bow down to worship an infant? John, would you mind reading those two verses for us?"

"Sure." Opening his Bible to the Old Testament, he read in Isaiah, "'For to us a child is born, to us a son is given; and the government shall be upon his shoulders, and his name shall be called Wonderful Counselor, Mighty God, Everlasting Father, Prince of Peace.

"Of the increase of his government and of peace there will be no end, on the throne of David and over his kingdom, to establish it and to uphold it with justice and with righteousness from this time forth and forevermore. The zeal of the Lord of hosts will do this.'"

"Thank you, John. Those powerful verses make it easy to understand why the three wise men presented the Child with gifts of gold, frankincense and myrrh. And having been warned in a dream not to go back to Herod, they returned to their country by another route.

"An angel of the Lord also appeared to Joseph in a dream, telling him to get up and take the child and his mother and escape to Egypt, and stay there until told otherwise, for Herod was going to search for the child to kill him."

Letting that harsh part of history hang thick in the air a few moments, Enoch glanced over at Lydia, "Imagine the stress of nursing and caring for your child and recovering from the pain of childbirth, all the while fearing for your very life for simply giving birth?"

Lydia could only shake her head. It was impossible for her to comprehend how Mary must have felt at that time.

"So Joseph did as he was told and fled for Egypt in the middle of the night. When Herod realized he had been outwitted by the Magi, his fury aroused a murderous vengeance. Wanting to eliminate any threat to his sovereignty, the insecure ruler gave orders to slaughter all male children two years and under, in Bethlehem and its vicinity, in accordance with the time he had learned from the three wise men."

Seeing how sickened Grace looked, Enoch said, "No, Grace, he was not a nice king. But even this atrocious act fulfilled prophecy, as told by the prophet Jeremiah: 'A voice is heard in Ramah, weeping and great mourning, Rachel weeping for her children and refusing to be comforted, because they are no more.'"

181

"Wow! He really was an evil man," Matthew said, more to himself than anyone else.

"Yes, Matthew, he was. He was king of the Jews at that time, but certainly not ruler of the universe, like Yeshua was and is and will forever be. Even despite his best efforts, Herod was unsuccessful. That's because no human had the power to kill Messiah. His purpose for coming to earth was to freely give Himself up as a ransom for the sins of many.

"After the wicked king died, an angel of the Lord appeared in a dream to Joseph telling him to leave Egypt and take the child and his mother to the land of Israel, for those who were trying to take the child's life were dead. And so was fulfilled what the Lord had said through the prophet Hosea in the book bearing his name.

"Matthew, would you be kind enough to read to us from the Book of Hosea found in the Old Testament, chapter eleven, verse one?"

It took a while, but Matthew eventually found it. He read, "'When Israel was a child, I loved him, and out of Egypt I called my son.'"

"In order for Hosea eleven-one to be fulfilled, the three wise men had to infuriate King Herod by not reporting back to him, thus ordering the slaughter of all firstborn males under the age of two in the town of Bethlehem and its vicinity, thus causing Joseph to flee to Egypt with his family. Now, while en route to Israel, Joseph heard that Herod's son, Archelaus, was reigning in Judea in place of his father and was afraid to go there. Having been warned in another dream, Joseph withdrew to the district of Galilee, and he went and lived in a town called Nazareth. So was fulfilled that Yeshua would be called a Nazarene.

"In order for Micah five-two to be fulfilled, Joseph and Mary, who were both in Nazareth, needed to return to Bethlehem to register for the census decreed by Caesar Augustus. In order for Isaiah seven-fourteen to be fulfilled, Yahweh needed to supernaturally impregnate Mary, which He did, initially causing great grief to Joseph, until an angel of the Lord appeared in a dream telling him what was happening and why.

"These are just a few of the many prophecies that were fulfilled in the Person of Yeshua HaMashiach. In the thirty-three years He roamed Planet Earth, until He offered Himself up to be nailed to the cross for the sins of many, He fulfilled every prophecy that was written about Israel's Savior, save which are still to come. But He will fulfill all of those as well.

"As you can see children, those were extremely turbulent times on Planet Earth. Frightening as it was, it needed to happen exactly the way it unfolded, in order to be considered prophecy fulfilled.

"Even if you do not understand it all, every word in the Bible is there for a specific reason. The same is true in your own lives as well. When life seems unpredictable and not to your liking," Enoch said, his words intended more for their parents, "never forget that Yahweh works all things for good, even the bad things, to those who love Him and are called according to His purpose.

Enoch paused to draw in a deep breath. "To recap all we have read, since the fall of mankind, Yahweh, being holy and just, needed a ransom payment for the sin of mankind. Only then could fellowship that was broken between Himself and those He created ever be restored.

"Only one Person was capable of being that Ransom. And that was none other than Yahweh's only begotten Son, Christ Jesus. Only those who believe that Yeshua is the Son of God, the Christ, who was with God in the beginning, that through Him all things were made, are truly born of God.

"For if Messiah wasn't Divine, then He was no more than just a man. If He was no more than just a man, that would make Him a sinner. If He was a sinner, how could He possibly be Savior to anyone?"

Enoch grinned from ear to ear, "But Yeshua wasn't merely a man. Not by a long shot. On the complete authority of the Book I hold in my hand, I declare with absolute certainty that He is the Savior of the world and the exact representation of God's being, therefore making Him capable of saving any soul of God's choosing!"

Glancing at John he said, "Anyone!"

31

"PLEASE EXCUSE ME," JOHN said, rising from the sofa. He could no longer ignore the deep stirring in his soul that started late last night and hadn't stopped since. He knew it was the strong pull of the Holy Spirit tugging at his heartstrings.

It was time to take care of business. It could wait no longer.

Save for the soft background music, the Jensen household grew silent again, as the man of the house slowly trudged the stairs leading up to his bedroom.

Lydia wanted to follow her husband upstairs, but what she saw on Enoch's face told her to remain seated for now.

In the darkness of his own bedroom, John dropped to his knees and pressed his face into the mattress. He lost all strength and started sobbing hysterically. He wasn't just weeping; he was deeply grieved.

At times, his sobs were so loud, everyone downstairs heard him. This went on for several minutes before he fell into a deep sleep.

In his dream, John saw himself standing in a courtroom on trial. God was the Judge. A mountain of evidence was stacked so high against him, he couldn't see the top of it.

Knowing he was one-hundred percent guilty, John wanted to remain silent. But with no one there to defend him, he didn't have that option. He was forced to answer every-last charge that was brought against him.

John shrank further and further into fear as his Maker's firm hand—which he now knew was the only thing keeping him from falling straight into hell where he rightly belonged—loosened a little more with each new confession.

It was like hanging off a rocky cliff by a thread with no safety net, and seeing an endless lake of fire at the bottom. Its flames were ready to consume him the moment God let him fall.

John's heart nearly gave out on him, knowing there was nothing he could do to stop it from happening. He was doomed. He lowered his head in shame, terrified for his life.

Just before the Most High sentenced him to hell for all eternity, Jesus entered the courtroom, "Father, wait! Though You are right to banish him from Your presence for all eternity, I am willing to take all his sins as if they were My own."

The King of the ages looked straight into John's eyes and remained silent. The radiance on His face was unlike anything John had ever seen. Jesus' soul-penetrating gaze caused fear and trembling all throughout his body.

Now only a breath away from being swallowed up by the flames of hell, John had all the proof he needed that Jesus really was humanity's only Bridge to God. His former college professors were nowhere to be seen. Even if they were in the courtroom, how could their worldly intelligence possibly rescue him from God's righteous judgment?

The answer was glaringly obvious: nothing!

Enoch was right. Only Jesus could save him.

"Please save me, Jesus!" John shouted desperately, helplessly. His body quaked in terror.

Pausing to search his heart, Jesus nodded and the mountain of evidence against him instantly disappeared. John felt God's weakening grip slowly tighten again. It was the most comforting sensation. Nothing could compare to it.

John woke up in a cold sweat and realized it was only a dream. Even so, the feeling of God's secure grip protecting him from falling into everlasting destruction, was incredibly real. He felt eternally safe and secure in the hands of God and never wanted to be separated from his Maker again.

After a while, Lydia went upstairs to check on her husband. Enoch didn't protest. Pausing at the doorway of their bedroom, she found John on his knees with his arms lifted toward the ceiling in prayer.

She observed and listened in silence.

In between sniffles, John cried out in the darkness, "Father, in the name of Jesus, I come before You, with all my heart, confessing my need for You. Now that I've been given a small glimpse of just how big You really are, thanks to Enoch, I feel so unworthy being in Your presence for even a second.

"All I can do is humble myself before You, as the weak and helpless man I really am. Save me, Jesus, as only You can, from that dreadful place called hell. By faith and with all my heart I believe You really are the King of kings and Lord of lords. I also believe only You have the power to forgive my sins.

"Have mercy on me, Lord, and be my Savior. Cleanse me of my sins. Transform me by the power of Your Holy Spirit. If my friends at the park can accept Your Word as the highest authority over their lives, and if three kings bowed down to You in worship when You were just an infant, it's time for me to do the same.

"I also ask forgiveness for being a constant stumbling block to my wife and children all this time. Teach me to be more like You, Lord. Help me to pray more, share Your Gospel more, sacrifice more and weep more for that which breaks Your heart.

"Help me to be less self-centered and more in tune to the needs of others. Less judgmental and more compassionate. Less vengeful and more forgiving. Teach me to love *everyone* and not just some. These things I ask in Your mighty and precious name, dear Jesus, Amen."

"Amen," Lydia said, joyously.

John craned his neck back and saw his wife standing in the doorway wiping tears from her eyes.

Reaching deep for a breath, John rose to his feet. In the darkness, the newly converted child of God said, "I'm so sorry, Lydia. Can you find it in your heart to forgive me for all I've done?"

"Of course, I forgive you," she said, getting all choked up herself.

John cupped her face with both hands, tilted her head ever so gently, and kissed his wife firmly on the lips. Lydia let his affection wash over the dry wasteland of her heart like an overpowering river, healing and reviving her body everywhere it touched.

Gazing deep into her eyes, he said, "I'm sure it's crossed your mind as to whether or not there ever was another woman. I can assure you there never was. All that time I spent online was nothing more than me looking for ways to escape reality.

"Guess you could say I was locked up in the dark chambers of my own selfishness. Life became an endless cycle. I was dizzy and wanted to get off the hamster wheel for a while. But I'm ready to get back on again. With you."

John kissed her on the lips again. Then again. And again. He wanted her to know he still found her attractive.

Lydia rejoiced knowing something sweet had shifted inside her husband. It was the obvious result of Light breaking through the darkness of John's heart. Lydia bathed in it, as she silently praised God for this amazing day full of Christmas miracles.

After one more kiss, the newly restored couple descended the stairs hand in hand.

Freeway was lying at the base of the stairway and was the first to greet them. It was evident they both had been crying.

"Are you okay, Daddy?" Grace asked. Concern was splashed all over her face. But she couldn't ignore her father's facial features; they were softer, kinder, gentler and more peaceful, much like in the past. He even looked younger.

"I'm fine, sweetheart, just fine." John took his daughter in his arms for the first time in many months.

"Then why were you crying?" Grace squeezed her father for dear life, hoping to comfort him.

"Because I finally believe."

"Believe what?" Matthew asked.

"That Jesus is my Lord and Savior!" John declared, triumphantly.

"I thought you always believed that, Daddy?" Grace was clearly confused.

Looking his daughter in the eye, John explained, "So did I, sweetheart. Sorry to say that I was one of the many fake Christians in the world. I was quite the actor though, wasn't I?"

Grace looked shocked by her father's confession.

"I know, sweetheart. It took seeing Enoch's strong example as a true follower of Yeshua to force me to question my overall disbelief in God. After rededicating my life to Christ tonight, wait, strike that," John said, winking at Enoch, "I didn't rededicate anything. After finally surrendering my life to Jesus, I know what it feels like to be born again. I feel so rejuvenated."

John kneeled on the carpeted floor John gathered his two precious children in his arms. "Sorry for the way I acted the past few months. Daddy was simply lost and no longer knew how to act. I've already asked for your mother's forgiveness. Now I'm asking for yours. Can you please forgive me?"

Both nodded yes. They were too choked up to reply to their father.

John squeezed his two children, "Daddy loves you both so much."

"Love you too, Dad," Matthew replied softly, teary-eyed.

Air got stuck in John's throat when he saw a tear riding down his son's right cheek.

"I love you too, Daddy," Grace whispered in her father's ear.

187

"One gift you will not find under the tree tomorrow," John said to Lydia, "comes in the form of a promise from me to you. The three of you, in fact. From this moment forward, I promise to be a better husband and father in every way. Just like before, kids, only better.

"Now that my eyes have finally been opened, I'll never again overlook the precious family God has blessed me with."

Shifting his gaze to Enoch, John said, "Thanks to you, I plan to live the rest of my life alive. My new long-term goal is to hear Jesus say, 'Well done thou good and faithful servant.'"

"Glory to God," Enoch said, softly.

"And that, my dear family, is my main gift to you this Christmas."

Lydia threw herself into her husband's arms and wept joyously.

John stroked his wife's hair. "Oh, there's one more thing. How much did you spend yesterday, Matthew?"

"Seven-hundred and fifty dollars and thirty-seven cents, to be exact."

John reached into his back pants pocket for his wallet and retrieved a copy of his bonus check that had already been deposited into his bank electronically. "This will cover the seven-fifty..." The man of the house then pulled loose change from his front pocket. He counted thirty-seven cents. "This will cover the rest."

Then to Lydia: "When the credit card bill comes in next month, use my bonus check money to pay it in full."

Lydia gave her husband a sideways look. She felt a tight constriction in her throat. Worry filled her eyes. "Are you sure, honey? What about the other bills?"

"It's time for me to trust God in all things, not just some. Since my bonus check was one-tenth of last year's bonus check, consider it a tithe of sorts."

Lydia was taken aback by her husband's comment, "Yes, but ten percent of seven-fifty is only seventy-five dollars..."

John nodded agreement. "Hopefully God will apply the rest to the many times I short-changed Him over the years." He winked at Enoch.

The old man smiled and remained silent, not wanting to ruin this beautiful moment unfolding before him.

John steadied his gaze back onto his children. "I saw you at the park today."

"You did?" exclaimed Grace.

"It was one of the most beautiful sights these eyes have ever seen. I can't tell you how proud you made me."

Matthew said, "We were happy to do it, Daddy."

"I know. Everyone at the park knew it too. Do you plan on doing it again next Christmas?"

"We hadn't thought about it, but yeah, I guess so. Right, Grace?"

"Uh-huh."

"Would it be okay if I joined you next year? Who knows, perhaps the two of you have just started a new Jensen family Christmas tradition without even knowing it."

"Really?" Grace said. "Oh, Daddy, welcome back!" She kissed her father on the cheek.

To Lydia, John said, "Now that my mind's been renewed by the power of the Holy Spirit, when I go back to work next week, I plan on becoming a star employee again. But for totally different reasons than in the past."

"And what might they be?"

"First, so I can increase the amount we give at church without ever missing a single week. I also want to give ten percent of my earnings to you, as an offering, to help fund your upstart feeding ministry.

"Even if it becomes a struggle at times, we'll just have to learn to get by on eighty percent of what I bring home. But no more robbing God for me. I want to learn to rest in His future promises like our friends at the park do. And speaking of the park, I plan to volunteer all my free time and help you to the best of my ability."

"This is the best Christmas ever!" Grace shouted, seeing the sheer ecstasy in her mother's eyes, and she hadn't opened a single gift yet.

It was quite impressive for a seven-year-old.

The Jensens clung to each other on the living room floor. All pain from the past seven months dissipated as if it had never happened. It was replaced with a boundless joy that could only come from above.

Enoch remained silent. But hearing John say those words to his family, and seeing the expressions on their faces, satisfied him immensely. His joy filled the room so much, it nearly pressed against the panes of glass. His eyes shone like the brightest two stars in the universe.

And that's because this gift had nothing to do with the worldly, materialistic gifts Enoch feared most humans believed represented the true essence of Christmas, including the Jensens.

This gift didn't cost a cent, but it was more precious than any material item Lydia could ever receive, because it came straight from John's heart.

But the greatest and most important thing to happen to John Jensen went far beyond reconciling with his family. He finally knew what it meant to be a true child of God. This gave him the eternal sense of belonging he'd been searching for all his life without ever finding it.

Finally, he gets it, the old man thought, taking the final sip of his beverage.

Enoch also knew what that meant...

32

CHRISTMAS MORNING

"WAIT FOR MOMMY AND Daddy!" Lydia wiped sleep from her eyes. She sat up in bed and squinted at the clock: 8:13 a.m. *Didn't feel like six hours of rest*, she thought, lowering her feet onto the carpeted floor.

Just like in previous years, Matthew, Grace and Freeway were seated on the top step anxious to race down the stairway. They knew nothing under the tree could top the many priceless gifts already received, but with kids being kids, they were eager to see what was waiting for them.

John and Lydia emerged from the master bedroom wearing matching red robes. Both looked as if they hadn't slept in days.

Another hour of sleep would be the perfect gift now, Lydia thought, her mouth formed in a yawn.

Matthew and Grace rose to their feet. Both bubbled over with excitement.

"Not so fast, you too," Lydia said, "not until Daddy turns on all the lights and lights the fireplace."

"Okay..." Grace sat down on the top step again. Matthew followed.

John went to the kitchen and flicked the coffeemaker switch. As it brewed, he dashed through the house with an energy he hadn't felt in quite some time. He lit candles, turned on the Christmas tree lights and all other decorative lights.

Finally, he turned on Christmas music and struck a match to the kindling inside the fireplace. Satisfied that he hadn't forgotten to do something, he said, "Okay, kids, you can come down now."

Like a flash of lightning—two flashes—Matthew and Grace dashed down the steps straight to the Christmas tree.

Freeway was right behind them.

"Shh, don't wake Enoch!" Lydia ordered in a loud whisper, slowly descending the carpeted steps.

"Okay, Mommy," they replied softly, in unison.

John was mildly impressed that his children didn't flinch seeing the significantly-smaller piles of gifts beneath the tree. He was also relieved.

Even if Matthew and Grace didn't offer to sacrifice gifts, so they could give to others, they still would have found less under the tree this year.

Matthew wasted no time finding a package with his name on it.

Just as he was about to tear it open, John said, "Aren't you forgetting something, son?"

"Oops, sorry, Daddy..." Matthew carefully placed the gift back where he found it under the tree.

"Before we start, let me wake Enoch. I'm sure he'll want to pray with us before we open the gifts. Since it's Christmas morning, I'll bring him coffee."

"Okay, Mommy," Grace said.

Lydia went to the kitchen and poured coffee into three holiday-themed cups, then added the right amount of cream and sugar, leaving John's black. She poured milk into plastic cups for the kids and placed everything on a serving tray. Lydia carefully placed the tray on the living room coffee table, then grabbed the cup for Enoch.

"Be right back." Lydia climbed the stairs slowly to avoid spilling coffee on herself. A few moments later she returned downstairs, coffee cup in hand, totally bewildered. "He's gone."

"What do you mean he's gone, honey?" John asked.

"He isn't here. I knocked three times before opening the door. The bed was made and his new pajamas and outfit he wore to church last night were folded neatly on top of the blanket. And his slippers were beside the bed."

"Wonder where he went," Matthew said, feeling no need for concern. But what he saw on his mother's face told another story altogether.

John shrugged it off, "Perhaps he went to the park to wish everyone a Merry Christmas. I'm sure he'll be back soon enough."

"How would he get there?" Lydia replied. "And why is his coat still hanging on the rack by the front door?"

"Beats me." Now John, too, was perplexed.

Lydia stared out the front window. Call it woman's intuition, but the mother of two had a sinking feeling that Enoch was gone for good. *Where could he have possibly gone?*

"Let's pray," John said, hoping to redirect their focus. The family of four dropped to their knees and held hands. John began, "Lord Father God, as we celebrate the birth of our precious Savior this day, from the bottom of our hearts, we thank You for sending Enoch into our lives. Please protect and watch over our dear friend wherever he may be.

"Most of all, I want to thank You for restoring this family and for blessing me with the greatest Christmas Gift I could ever receive. Happy birthday, Jesus! Thanks for being my Savior and King. I will serve you all the days of my life, Amen!"

Much like Grace did at the park, Lydia started singing *Happy Birthday, Jesus.*

Happy birthday, Jesus,
I'm so glad it's Christmas,
All the tinsel and lights and the presents are nice
but the real Gift is You,
Happy birthday, Jesus,
I'm so glad it's Christmas,
all the carols and bells make the holiday swell
and it's all about You
Happy Birthday, Jesus,
Jesus, I love You.

The second time through everyone sang along. It was nice, but it couldn't compare to yesterday's rendition, with the assistance of the city park musicians.

Once they were finished singing, John said, "You know the rules, kids. One at a time, and Grace goes first."

"We know, we know," said Matthew.

Grace reached for a gift addressed to her. A smile curled onto her lips. It was the novel that was at the top of her list. She couldn't wait to start reading it. But beneath her smile was a sadness she couldn't hide, even despite her best efforts.

No one had to ask why. Grace wanted Enoch to be with them. It didn't feel complete without him.

More than anything, the seven-year-old wanted to see his reaction when he opened the "Best Friends Always" picture frame she got for him. Inside was a photograph her mother took of the two of them.

It was all Grace could think about before dozing off last night. Her shoulders slumped. She felt like crying.

Now his turn, Matthew tore off the shiny wrapping paper with reckless abandon, to find the sneakers he badly wanted stuffed inside the box. He wondered if his friends, Zach and Bryce, also got them. All three had asked for them for Christmas.

The smile on Matthew's face faded after he was seized with a thought: *Wonder how many people I could feed with these eighty-dollar sneakers?* Thanks to Enoch, his whole outlook on life was forever changed.

One by one they took turns opening packages. Grace unwrapped one of Freeway's gifts. Even though she wrapped the dog treats, she feigned surprise. She gave her a treat, "Merry Christmas, Freeway!"

Freeway practically inhaled it and begged and yelped for another.

"Okay. One more, but only because it's Christmas," Grace said, acquiescing to her pet's wishes. *Where are you, Enoch?*

With much less under the tree than in past years, it didn't take long to sort through all the gifts.

Lydia went to the kitchen to prepare breakfast. Despite the many miracles witnessed all this week, with Enoch gone, she couldn't help but feel melancholy.

The hardest part was that she never got to thank the man God had sent to restore her family. It was the least she could do after all he did for them.

With her family still in the living room, Lydia had a good cry...

33

AFTER BREAKFAST, MATTHEW REMOVED his and his kid sister's stockings that were hanging from the fireplace mantle. Handing Grace her stocking, they wasted no time emptying the contents onto the floor.

Lydia's phone vibrated. The message read: *Be there by 11.*

She replied, *OK. See you soon. Merry Christmas, Mom and Dad.*

John's parents were also out making the rounds, presently visiting John's brother and sister-in-law. From there they would visit John's recently divorced kid sister before dropping by at around 4 p.m.

Other than that, Lydia wasn't expecting anyone else. After the way Thanksgiving had gone, she decided weeks ago that she didn't want visitors this Christmas. Enoch changed everything.

Had he not miraculously appeared to save the day, so to speak, there's no telling how disastrous Christmas might have turned out this year at the Jensen household.

"Grandma and Grandpa will be here soon."

Matthew and Grace both smiled. Normally, Grace would be the first to shout, "Yippie", knowing it meant more gifts for her, but not now.

That's when Lydia noticed the cards. *Hmm, who put them there? They weren't there last night.*

Oblivious to the cards, Matthew and Grace both stuffed candy canes in their mouths.

"Did you place those cards in their stockings?" Lydia asked John in a near whisper.

"No."

"Who's the card from, sweetie?"

Without answering, Grace plucked the card from the envelope. On the front was a manger scene portraying the birth of Jesus. The caption read, "Today in the town of David a Savior has been born to you; he is the Messiah, the Lord" (Luke 2:11).

Grace smiled, after realizing it was the same verse she'd read to Enoch the night before. Opening it, her eyes were naturally drawn to the bottom of the card. Flicking long hair out of her face, her eyes widened.

With breathless wonder she exclaimed, "It's from Enoch!"

195

On the inside was another Bible inscription. This one was handwritten. Grace read it aloud for all to hear, *"For I was hungry and you gave me something to eat, I was thirsty and you gave me something to drink, I was a stranger and you invited me in..."* (Matthew 25:35).

Beneath that was handwritten, *You even combed my hair and gave me your favorite blanket in all the world to keep me warm at the park. The immense size of your heart can never be measured in terms of inches, dear Grace. Thanks for letting me sleep in your bed the past few nights. I never felt more at home.*

You made Yahweh smile so many times this week. By loving me and my fellow parkies so genuinely, you were also loving God. Merry Christmas, Grace. Love, your second-best friend, Enoch.

A teary-eyed Grace held the card closely to her chest and hugged it, as if receiving a priceless treasure.

John and Lydia exchanged sideways looks. Both were astonished and deeply touched by what their daughter had just read aloud to them.

Matthew removed his card from the envelope. On the front were the three wise men wandering in the desert on camels following the bright morning star. Matthew read the front of the card, *"Therefore the Lord himself will give you a sign: The virgin will conceive and give birth to a son, and will call him Immanuel"* (Isaiah 7:14).

Much like his kid sister, he, too, smiled realizing he'd read that very verse to Enoch the night before.

On the inside was another handwritten Bible inscription. Matthew read it aloud, *"Whoever is kind to the poor lends to the Lord, and he will reward them for what they have done"* (Proverbs 19:17).

Underneath that, in the same unique handwriting as on Grace's card was written, *Blessed are you, Matthew, for seeing beautiful things in humble places where others see nothing. I will never forget your first visit to the park when you insisted on serving lunch to me and my former fellow parkies.*

Well done good and faithful servant. You have the kind of heart that Yahweh will surely use for His glory. Keep lending to Him by being kind to the poor. Your reward in Heaven will be great. Merry Christmas. Love, Enoch.

Matthew lowered his head and wiped his moist eyes with his sleeves.

Lydia rose from the couch and removed hers and John's stockings from the fireplace mantle. Peeking inside, sure enough two cards were stuffed inside her stocking; one addressed to her and the other to Enoch's fellow parkies.

In John's stocking was a card with his name on it.

Lydia opened hers first. On the inside was written: *"Do not forget to show hospitality to strangers, for by so doing some people have shown hospitality to..."*

Lydia stopped reading. Her eyes grew wide. She was unable to mask her surprise. Her throat tightened, and she found herself unable to speak. She nearly collapsed onto John's lap.

"What's it say, Mommy?" Grace said, seeing her mother's mouth agape, unable to speak. The trembling mother leaned back onto the couch.

John grabbed the card from his wife and read it for himself. Clearing his throat, he then read it to the children, *"Do not forget to show hospitality to strangers,"* John said, his voice cracking, *"for by so doing some people have shown hospitality to angels without knowing it"* (Hebrews 13:2).

Grace's eyes grew wide like silver dollars. "Was Enoch an angel, Daddy?"

"It appears so, sweetheart, it appears so."

"Wow! A real, live angel!" Matthew exclaimed. "How cool is that!"

"There's more." *You see, Lydia, Yahweh was listening to your many cries for help all along. I'm just glad He sent me to do His will in the matter. Thanks for showing me and my former fellow parkies true Christian love when most others wouldn't. Thanks also for making me feel completely welcome in your home and for never making me feel homeless, even when I was.*

Regarding the generous gifts you gave me, kindly give them to our friends at the park. Where I am going, I no longer need them. See you on the other side someday. Merry Christmas, Lydia. Love, Enoch.

Instinctively, as if on cue, everyone looked out the window glancing skyward.

"I can't believe my second-best friend's an angel." It was impossible for Grace to comprehend the magnitude of it all.

No one replied to her outlandish comment. What could they possibly say?

John scratched his head, "That explains why I never heard the front door open or close this morning. He never used a door." *It also explains what happened at the park yesterday. He didn't walk or run with the stamina of a track star, he materialized then vanished only to materialize again as only an angel could!*

Lydia smiled through her tears. Not only had God answered her prayer—her plea—for a true Christmas miracle to occur, He sent one of His angels to hand-deliver it to her.

"What's your card say, Dad?" Matthew's curiosity was gnawing away on him.

John opened it. On the inside was handwritten, Genesis 5:24. Nothing more. John went to his study to retrieve his Bible. Stuffed between pages 4 and 5 he found a small piece of paper with handwriting on it. Before reading it, he found Genesis chapter 5, verse 24. Chills shot up and down his spine. John froze.

"What is it?" asked Lydia.

"What is it, Daddy?" Excitement coursed through Grace's body.

Matthew remained silent, waiting with bated breath.

Clearing his throat, the man of the house said, "'*Enoch walked faithfully with God; then he was no more, because God took him away.*'" John shook his head. "He left a note inside my Bible."

"What's it say?" all three said at the same time.

"I'm glad you were the one Yahweh chose as my Mission on Earth. Now that you have been rescued from the dominion of darkness and transformed by the renewing of your mind, never cease to fulfill the divine purpose for which you have been called. Let Matthew 6:33, which declares, 'But seek first the kingdom of God and his righteousness, and all these things will be added to you,' become your life verse.

Commit it to memory, child of God, as I believe it sums up the entire theme of the book of Ecclesiastes so beautifully. Let it guide every decision you make from here on out. Continue to be clay in Yahweh's hands, as He finishes what He started in you last night. Never stop dwelling in the Scriptures and living your life according to them.

I look forward to seeing you again at the time of our Maker's choosing, and hearing about the many good things you did for His glory from this day forward. Until then, always live your life vertically. Only then can you truly live life to the fullest.

Merry Christmas, John. Love, Enoch.

Once again, everyone gazed skyward out the front window. After the way everything had unfolded, it was only fitting that Enoch left them as mysteriously as he appeared in their lives, a few short weeks ago.

In the brief period he was among them, God used him to turn seven months of longsuffering in the Jensen household into joyful bliss.

Hearing Lydia's constant prayers being offered up on John's behalf, and out of love for his soul, God sent Enoch to Planet Earth just for him.

To John Jensen, it was a mind-numbing realization knowing that the man he openly mocked and ridiculed, at the outset, was no man at all but an angel; an angel John couldn't wait to see again someday.

Perhaps the reason God sent him in the first place was because John's heart was so hardened that no human could have possibly penetrated it. It took the work of an angel. *Go figure!*

Enoch was right all along. God really did work all things for good for those who loved Him and were called according to His purpose.

It was John's lack of productivity at work that had caused his boss to nearly fire him. What John received as tragic news at the time God ended up using for good, by giving him the necessary time with Enoch.

Had that not happened, there's no way the former severely-depressed man would have had the time nor the willingness to spend with Enoch. Nor would he have ever ventured to the city park that day. Yes, being temporarily laid off was part of God's Sovereign plan.

In the end, what looked dreadfully bleak when viewed through the scope of a human lens, God ultimately used for good, by giving John Jensen the best Gift he could ever receive this Christmas; the eternal privilege of being called a child of God.

Now that God had saved him for real, he was eager to see what his Maker had in store for him from this day forward...

34

LYDIA'S PARENTS LEFT JUST after 2:00 p.m. If there was one thing the seniors were grateful for, it's that the strange visitor to their daughter's house—a man they never got to meet in person—was finally gone.

Even if they were never in danger for a single moment, as Lydia had constantly insisted, that didn't change the fact that no one knew a thing about him, including his place of origin.

Who willingly opened their door to a complete-stranger, especially with two young children living under the same roof? Only irresponsible parents, Lydia's parents had both concluded.

Aside from being brainwashed by their freeloading house guest, what other explanation could there be? Granted, at Enoch's age, they weren't overly concerned that he would harm their offspring physically. But what about emotionally? Psychologically?

Normally seeing stacks of gifts with their names written on them would throw any child into a frenzy. But not this year.

If anything, Matthew and Grace were more interested in telling stories about their life-changing experiences at the city park than anything else. The glazed-over expressions on their faces caused even more alarm bells to go off and red flags to go up in their minds.

No, this wasn't normal behavior on any level. Now they proclaimed Enoch was an angel sent from Heaven?! How convenient that he suddenly upped and vanished on the day they were to meet him.

Good thing he was gone. If not, the only gift the concerned grandparents had for him was chastisement, for preying on their loved ones the way he had.

Lydia understood how it all sounded; she appreciated her parents' concern, she really did, but they never met Enoch and, therefore, were in no position to objectively assess the situation.

She watched out the front window until her parent's car was out of sight, leaving the Jensens a two-hour window before John's parents arrived.

Who knew how they would react to the shocking news? Time would tell. But one thing was certain: everyone at the city park would be riveted by this mind-blowing revelation.

With the energy of a high school teenager, as the rest of the family changed out of their pajamas, Lydia placed Enoch's gifts from under the tree into a large Hefty bag.

She then placed the pajamas Enoch wore, his fuzzy slippers, the outfit he wore to church, the coat hanging on the coat rack by the front door, and the green blanket he slept on at the park, into a separate bag.

Lastly, she stuffed the Christmas card inside that Enoch had left for his former parkies.

The only thing left out was the picture frame Grace had gotten for him. Surely, her daughter would want to keep it as a memento of sorts.

At that, the Jensens, including Freeway Jensen, piled into the minivan and drove off, bursting at the seams to share Enoch's true-identity with everyone.

Grace, especially, felt like the most blessed person in all the world. How often did one receive a handwritten greeting card from a real live angel?

Just knowing her second-best friend was mentioned in the Old Testament gave the youngster a deeper thirst to read the Bible all the way through, beginning in Genesis. The novel she was eager to start reading would have to wait.

They arrived at the city park a few minutes later.

The Christmas spirit that had flooded the hearts of each Jensen family member earlier was nowhere to be found at this place. It looked like just another ordinary winter day.

But to Freeway it was paradise. The eleven-year-old canine sprinted forward with all her might, eager to take in her new surroundings, until the leash pulled her back. Even restrained, this was a special treat for her.

"Merry Christmas guys," Tiwanna shouted, spotting them. "Didn't expect to see y'all today."

"Merry Christmas, Tiwanna," came the reply in unison.

Noticing the bags, the homeless woman said, "More gifts for us?"

"Sort of, yes. They were intended for Enoch."

"Why not give them to him then?"

"We can't. He's gone," Matthew said.

"What do you mean he's gone?" *As in dead*, Tiwanna thought. After all, he was quite old. Her lower lip started quivering.

"When we woke this morning, he was gone," Lydia said.

Grace said, "But don't worry, Tiwanna, he's safe. Very safe, in fact."

"Where'd he go then?"

"Once you read the cards he left for us, you'll understand."

"Cards?"

"Christmas cards. He left one for you, too."

"Me?" Tiwanna was getting all excited.

"All of you, actually."

"What's it say?"

"Don't know. We didn't open it."

"Listen up y'all," Tiwanna yelled, "we got a card from Enoch." Her voice was so loud it roused Troy, Dillon and Rocky from their sleep.

The three grunge rockers sat straight up, eager to hear what Enoch had to say to them.

John pulled the green blanket from the bag and spread it on the frozen surface for his family to sit on. As Grace read her card aloud, snow flurries started falling from the silvery-gray winter sky. Everyone listened with great interest, eager to learn the whereabouts of their dear friend.

When Grace read, *You even combed my hair and gave me your favorite blanket in all the world to keep me warm at the park,* the youngest member of the Jensen family got all choked up.

It was one thing to read it aloud at home, but altogether different at the city park in front of so many others.

Matthew was next. When he read, *Keep lending to Yahweh by being kind to the poor. Your reward in Heaven will be great,* he, too, got all choked up. The fact that he was surrounded by those who were the "objects of his lending" only added to it all. But Matthew knew they were richer than most other people on the planet.

The moment Lydia read Hebrews 13:2 aloud, there were a few gasps, followed by complete silence for the longest time, as everyone did their best to wrap their minds around what they'd just heard.

"Whoa! An angel!" Dillon shouted. The palms of his hands cupped the top of his hooded head.

"I'm freaking out here!" Troy said, unable to contain his bewilderment.

Rocky was too blown away to utter a response.

"I always knew he was an angel. But a real live angel?" Tiwanna was unable to keep from smiling. The inside of her mouth resembled a white picket fence with some of its pickets missing.

Leroy rose to his feet and paced back and forth on the frozen surface. "An angel? Ha!" He shook his head and started laughing. "Can't say I'm surprised!"

"Can't say I'm surprised, either," Pedro said. "I mean, look at us! Who else could accomplish what he did in so little time? Only someone under the complete control of the Holy Spirit. Without a penny to his name or place to call home, Enoch gave us all so much. Because of him we're forever changed. How could he be anything *but* an angel!"

Wanda looked skyward and whispered, "Thank you, Jesus!"

After a few moments of silence, Lydia said, "Who wants to read the card Enoch left for you?"

Suzie raised her hand like a child seeking the attention of her teacher, "May I read it?"

When no one objected, Lydia handed the card to her.

Suzie removed a folded sheet of paper from inside the card and held it in her hand. On the inside of the card was handwritten, *Now if we are children, then we are heirs—heirs of God and co-heirs with Christ, if indeed we share in his sufferings in order that we may also share in his glory. I consider that our present sufferings are not worth comparing with the glory that will be revealed in us (Romans 8:17-18).*

A few "Amen's" were uttered.

Suzie unfolded the piece of paper and read it aloud for all to hear. *Greetings fellow parkies! I'm sure by now you know my true identity. Surprise! Always know in your hearts that I enjoyed every day spent at the park and each night camped under the stars with you all.*

Now that I am gone, let nothing sidetrack the positive growth that took place in the short time we spent together.

Wanda, you have become quite wise in the ways of the Lord these past few months. It's time to break out of your shell, daughter of the Most High, and share the Good News with everyone in your path.

Let nothing, most of all your shy personality, stop your voice from being heard for Yeshua. From this day forward, never fail to acknowledge Him to anyone. For by so doing, He will acknowledge you to His Father in Heaven.

Tiwanna, I will surely miss your fiery spirit and endearing smile. It was my distinct honor to watch you come so far in so little time. You are a kind and generous soul. Keep giving yourself fully to the work of the Lord. Press on daily knowing that your labor will never be in vain.

If and when others treat you badly, always counter by being Yahweh's living love letter, knowing the problem is with them and not you.

Tiwanna closed her moist eyes, trying to comprehend that she'd just been mentioned by name, by a real live angel.

Seeing that her name was next, Suzie braced herself. *To my dear Suzie, I truly enjoyed watching Yahweh slowly but surely transform you from the inside out, these past few weeks. Never lose sight that even despite your present handicap, your eternal dwelling place is so magnificent, so wondrous, the human mind cannot begin to describe it.*

Not only will you walk again, you will also fly just like me! Your wheelchair is not welcome here, my dear precious child of God, only you are. But until that day arrives, keep dwelling in the Scriptures and living the sober life. I look forward to seeing you again someday...

Like a projectile, a tear shot out of Suzie's eye, splashing the card and the new pink gloves she received from Grace.

The "temporarily" handicapped woman closed her eyes and broke into joyous sobbing. Tears eased out from under her eyelids, one after the next, and slowly trickled down her frosty, chapped face.

Seeing she was unable to continue, Tiwanna took the card from Suzie.

Glancing at Pedro, she read, *Pedro, the things I have come to admire most about you are your true repentant heart, your unending hunger for the ways of God, and your deep yearning for the lost. Never let the comfort of four walls and a roof over your head extinguish this burden Yahweh has placed deep inside your heart. Keep fighting the Good fight down there. Fulfill the Mission for which you were called, and keep redeeming the time until Yahweh restores what the locusts have eaten away in your life.*

Leroy, words cannot properly express the joy I felt watching you go from one life extreme to the other. The moment Yahweh rescued your soul from perdition, I knew you would be the one chosen to replace me one day.

Our Maker made a wonderful choice! Kindly see that my personal belongings are distributed accordingly, with one exception: the green blanket. Since there is no official torch to pass along, as the new city park spiritual leader, please accept it as a small token in memory of me.

The leadership Yahweh blessed you with at birth is desperately needed at the city park! So keep pressing on, mighty warrior, and always be a Mission waiting to happen. Your reward will be great!

Normally the talkative one, Leroy was rendered speechless. He lowered his head and brushed tears from his moist eyes.

Tiwanna finished, *I look forward to seeing many of you again at the time of Yahweh's appointed choosing. Hopefully Troy, Dillon and Rocky will be among them. But that much is up to the three of you.*

Until we meet again, I challenge each of you to cherish this brief but blessed opportunity Yahweh chose for you to be alive at this precise moment in history, playing a small role in His eternal plan.

Merry Christmas, my dear fellow parkies. I love you all so dearly.

Tiwanna folded the sheet of paper and handed it back to Suzie.

Pedro said, "Now I understand why he never told us where he came from. How can someone properly explain Heaven to us lowly humans?"

Tiwanna removed a glove to wipe tears from her eyes. "I can't wait to see him again someday."

"Me too," John said. There was this ever-present glow on his face that wasn't there last time they met.

Tiwanna's eyes widened. "No, really?"

"Yup, I officially became a true child of God last night!"

"Praise God!" Tiwanna embraced her new brother in Christ.

"Welcome to God's family, John!" Pedro said.

"So, you were Enoch's Mission after all, huh?"

John paused to consider Leroy's comment, "I think it's safe to assume Enoch was answered prayer for all of us. So, in that sense, we all were his Mission. Because Enoch truly was who he said he was, his actions provided the perfect example for all of us to follow."

"True that," said Tiwanna.

"If Enoch can do it, why can't we, right?"

"Right, John," Suzie declared, raising her hands skyward. She looked like Sylvester Stallone in the movie, *Rocky*, only in a wheelchair wearing beggar's garments.

John handed the green blanket to Leroy. "I think this belongs to you."

Leroy clung to this most prized possession wondering, *How can I possibly replace a real live angel?*

"You can't replace him, Leroy," John said, knowing what his friend was thinking, "but you can rest assured knowing that you're off to a very good start as the new city park spiritual leader. I mean, look at me. The impact you made the other night was nothing short of life-changing."

The two men embraced.

"I look forward to seeing you at the next feeding, brother."

"Me too, John. Me too."

205

JOHN'S PARENT'S LEFT AROUND 8 p.m. that night, with the same level of concern and disdain Lydia's parents had shown toward Enoch.

John's mother kept looking at her son as if he had lost his cotton-picking mind, for allowing a stranger to live in their house.

His father was more of the happy-go-lucky type. Now that the old man he refused to call an angel was gone, concern was replaced with peace. "All's well that ends well," he had said, leaving it at that.

But John was now convinced that his father's statement was only true for those who belonged to God. Now that he was counted among His children, he looked forward to one day sharing in the magnificent eternal liberty everyone in Heaven gets to experience.

John's prayer from this day forward would be that his parents and in-laws would all come to faith in Christ Jesus. Only then could they, too, experience the greatest miracle that could ever happen to a person, the soul-saving miracle of receiving God's salvation.

Before going to sleep, for the second time this day, the Jensens dropped to their knees on the living room floor and prayed together, as a family. Soon after they were bedded down for the night, they were confronted with yet another shocking revelation.

Grace couldn't stop thinking about Enoch. After a while, she quietly got out of bed and tiptoed down the stairs in complete darkness.

Plucking the still-wrapped gift she got for Enoch from under the Christmas tree, she dashed back up to her room and turned on the light. This way, whenever she missed her second-best friend, all she had to do was look at the picture frame.

To her great surprise, when she unwrapped the package, Enoch's image was no longer displayed in the photograph.

Only hers was there.

Grace burst into her parent's room, "Look!" she yelled.

As her startled parents slowly adjusted their blurred vision onto the picture frame, Grace stormed Matthew's room and practically dragged her still-sleepy brother into their parent's bedroom.

Lydia turned on her tablet, and frantically waited for her Facebook page to open. Sure enough, all photographs and videos taken of Enoch were gone. Everyone else was still there, only he wasn't.

Grace started weeping.

Gathering his little girl into his arms, John felt like weeping too.

He kissed Grace's right cheek and said, "Only his image is gone, sweetheart. Nothing can ever remove Enoch from your heart and mind. Whenever you find yourself missing him, you have the power to recall the many wonderful memories you have of him. And never forget that you will see him again someday..."

Grace smiled. It felt good to take comfort in her father's words again.

John stared at his family sitting on the bed with him. A smile broke across his face. After seven long difficult months, he felt incredibly blessed again to have such a wonderful family.

He silently vowed to never take them for granted ever again.

Grace was right. This really is the best Christmas ever! Hallelujah!

Epilogue

THE GREATEST THING TO happen as a result of Enoch's letter being read aloud at the city park was that it finally caused Troy, Dillon and Rocky to examine their own lives, and the dangerous direction in which the three were headed.

The fact that the coolest old man they ever met was no man at all, but a real live angel, gave them a supernatural high that no drug or alcoholic beverage could possibly duplicate.

Confused by what Enoch meant when he said he was hopeful of seeing them again, but that much was up to them, gave Leroy and Gang the perfect opportunity to explain the Gospel to them while they were still sober-minded.

After sitting under Leroy's tutelage all week and hearing God's clear-cut plan of salvation, the trio became convinced that God really did love them. Even though He foresaw their every fault and every sin, His heart remained fixed on them despite it all.

To prove it, God sent His own Son to die in their places.

With their spiritual eyes and ears opened, the three-former wannabe grunge rockers finally saw Calvary for what it was: God's supreme demonstration of Divine love. With great joy, they became the city park's newest members of God's eternal Family.

When the Jensens arrived for the last feeding of the year, on New Year's Eve, they rejoiced upon hearing the wonderful news.

While eating their lunches, Rocky pulled Lydia aside and, speaking on behalf of the three of them, asked her to hold their government-issued cards that were set to reload electronically the following day.

For the first time in the four years they were homeless, they wanted to be drug and alcohol free.

"Instead of using the funds for drugs and alcohol," Troy had said, "we want it to go toward food, clothing and grooming products so we can look more presentable when we go looking for jobs after the new year. Having the cards in our possession will only cause temptation for us."

Lydia happily agreed to their wishes, and even offered to take her three brothers in Christ shopping whenever she was needed.

A few days later Troy, Dillon and Rocky found work. Two weeks after that, they were no longer homeless.

To start, they rented a cheap hotel room not too far from the city park, until they found a small two-bedroom apartment to share.

At the next feeding, all three gave their testimonies, explaining how God had saved their souls. In a hopeful attempt to encourage his former parkies, Dillon ended by saying, "They say most people living in homes are only a few weeks away from being homeless. Let this day serve to remind you all that the same is true with homeless people, only in reverse. We did it. By the grace of God, you can too!"

Everyone clapped their hands. It was a touching moment for all.

Before leaving the park that day, to everyone's great surprise, Wanda, the quiet and shy one, insisted on closing out the session in prayer.

Tiwanna was the most shocked of them all. As she listened to her best friend praying, she shed many tears of joy.

Troy, Dillon and Rocky became members of John's and Lydia's church the following Sunday, and even got to put their musical talent on display, on occasion, with the church band. They went from having too much time on their hands at the city park, wasting their lives away, to leading busy and productive lives in the service of their Maker.

They never missed church on Sunday. Nor did they ever miss a Wednesday night small group Bible study John Jensen had started at his residence shortly after the new year, or a Celebrate Recovery meeting at their church. And they certainly never missed a feeding at the city park.

These four things quickly became the pillars upon which God was rebuilding their new lives in Christ Jesus.

As the Jensens, and their growing army of volunteers, fed the homeless each Saturday afternoon—to include local businessmen and women, churchgoers, college students, teenagers and even toddlers—Troy, Dillon and Rocky provided all the worship music.

Their music style didn't change all that much. What changed was instead of singing songs about things that had totally consumed them for so many years—sex, drugs and rock and roll—now stone in love with Jesus, all songs glorified the One who rescued them from the pits of hell not too long ago, and completely delivered them from drugs and alcohol along the way.

A couple of weeks into the new year, Pastor Flores, encouraged by what he kept hearing from others, joined them at the city park to share the Word of God with the homeless before serving them meals.

A dozen or so members from church joined him that day, including Ann Chen. Ann was forever changed by the experience and came to love her new friends at the city park. Whenever she saw any of them in church, she practically begged them to sit with her.

Many other pastors in the community followed in Pastor Flores footsteps, by volunteering their time as well.

Regardless of who preached on Saturday, Wanda closed each session in prayer. It was her special way of openly acknowledging her Maker to everyone within the sound of her steadily rising voice.

Wanda looked forward to telling Enoch all about it someday...

THREE MONTHS LATER, EVERYONE'S joy knew no bounds when Pedro came to feed one Saturday afternoon. What made this day particularly unusual was that he wasn't alone this time. And there was a certain bounce in his step that none of them had ever seen before.

The reason was the young girl walking beside him, hand in hand. She looked taller and a little older than in the photograph Pedro always clung to in his days living at the park, but it was undoubtedly his daughter, Erica.

The eleven-year-old felt awkward at first being showered with hugs by a bunch of homeless people. But after being introduced to Matthew, Grace and Matthew's best friend, Bryce—who now came each week—Erica was able to find comfort in the company of those in her age range.

The smile on Pedro's face as his daughter fed the homeless was so wide, a small bird could have easily flown inside his mouth.

After just one feeding, Erica was hooked and promised to come back whenever she was in her father's care.

THANKS TO JOHN JENSEN, Tiwanna, Wanda and Suzie also found places to live; one place, rather. The mother of one of John's coworkers had a four-bedroom house she'd lived in for 53 years with her husband, until he died leaving the grieving widow incredibly lonely and all alone.

Her children had tried on several occasions to persuade their mother to sell the house and move to an adult community, where she would receive constant monitoring. The 73-year-old mother of five, and grandmother to twelve, stubbornly refused each time.

Her most common reply was, "Your father spent his last night on earth in this house. I plan on doing the same thing!"

The only solution to curing her loneliness was to find Christ-centered females to move in with her. On John's word that Tiwanna, Wanda and

Suzie were dedicated Christ followers and that all three were completely clean and sober—and on John's guarantee to make things right if the need ever arose—the women were invited to stay rent-free, the first six months.

In lieu of cash, the three women were expected to maintain the house and property. Suzie kept herself busy throughout the day folding laundry, ironing clothes, sewing, loading and emptying the dishwasher, and dusting the furniture, while Tiwanna and Wanda did the things Suzie couldn't do.

After just one month, the house and grounds never looked better. Grateful for having a roof over their heads, it was the least they could do, for the woman who lovingly took them in.

The elderly woman grew quite comfortable having the three women living in her house. What she looked forward to most were the 7 p.m. Bible studies they had each night, followed by rigorous prayer.

It was like having church each day without ever leaving the house. The old woman came to love Tiwanna, Wanda and Suzie like her own family.

IN MID-MARCH LYDIA celebrated her fortieth birthday. She ended up having two parties; one at home and a surprise party at the park. One day after the feeding, those who were the object of her kindness the past few months, formed a circle around Lydia and surprised her with a cake they'd purchased themselves.

Led by Troy, Dillon and Rocky, the *City Park Choir* sang Happy Birthday to the woman everyone had come to deeply love and respect, then presented her with a framed gift, Lydia hung on the wall above the front door when she arrived home. It read:

"Do not forget to show hospitality to strangers, for by so doing some people have shown hospitality to angels without knowing it"
(Hebrews 13:2).

TRUE TO HIS WORD, Leroy remained homeless knowing it was where God wanted him for now. But with one stipulation: after every Saturday feeding, the new city park spiritual leader gathered all dirty laundry from his fellow parkies and took it over to the Jensen residence, where he slept each Saturday night.

After taking his weekly hot shower, Lydia and Grace helped him with the mountain of laundry that needed washing.

After church service, as John drove Tiwanna, Wanda and Suzie home, Lydia and the children dropped Leroy back at the park with several bags full of clean laundry. Then another sermon was preached for all who were interested.

Sitting on his tattered green blanket, the City Park Preacher ministered to the steady flow of new homeless people to his domain.

Most were troubled souls battling various debilitating addictions. But just as God had loved him at his darkest, Leroy was committed to loving his fellow parkies through their darkest times as well, by extending the same measure of grace he was given, not too long ago.

The Jensens constantly reminded Leroy that he was always welcome to stay with them full time. He politely refused each time, saying he was a "Mission waiting to happen" at the city park, just like someone had once been for him.

JOHN JENSEN MADE GOOD on his promise to become a star employee again. He started traveling and reconnecting with old clients, and even brought new ones in house.

When asked by his boss what had gotten into him, John unhesitatingly said his life was supernaturally transformed by the Most High God of the universe. His boss looked at him rather strangely, but let it go. He was just happy that John had finally come back to his senses.

Another promise John kept was that he never failed to designate the first 20 percent of his paycheck to God; the first 10 percent to his church; the second to his wife's steadily growing feeding mission and laundry service. And whenever he was in town, he never missed a feeding.

Compared to the small fortune he spent at college seeking higher learning, the $1,000 he spent on the homeless last Christmas was quite small. As it turned out, it was the best investment John Jensen had ever made in his life. Especially since it was a four-for-one deal!

In just a few short weeks, the Jensens received a top-notch education on what mattered most in life, in such a way that no professor at any university could ever teach it.

Biologically speaking, the Jensens hadn't grown all that much over the past few months. But from a spiritual and wisdom standpoint they grew by leaps and bounds, having received an education at the very highest level from one of God's own representatives, even if they didn't know it at the time.

Honoring John's obedience, his Maker reciprocated by meeting all his needs and the needs of his family. God also restored and greatly increased his undying passion for life, filling him with a sustained peace, joy and contentment that only children of the Most High God got to experience.

In short: John Jensen had never felt better...Framed and hung on the wall where his college diploma once hung was:

"But seek first the kingdom of God and his righteousness, and all these things will be added to you" (Matthew 6:33).

Wise men still seek Him...

For Your Consideration...

This story is a work of fiction that was inspired by Hebrews 13:2: *"Do not forget to show hospitality to strangers, for by so doing some people have shown hospitality to angels without knowing it".*

Please keep in mind that this book is a work of fiction. A few embellishments were made on the author's behalf—regarding the above Scripture—that would never find their way into a non-fiction book.

But make no mistake: even though the story line is purely fictional, the Gospel message weaved throughout its pages is very real. Eternally real.

With that in mind, it is the author's hope that all who read this book will be impacted more by the Gospel message than by the story itself.

Though this story is not an exact representation
of what takes place each week with
Jesus Loves You, Love Him Back
feeding ministry, if you search
https://www.facebook.com/lovehim.back
you will clearly see many parallels.
To donate to Jesus Loves You Love Him Back feeding ministry,

www.JesusLovesYouLoveHimBack.org

To purchase Michael Higgins' new book titled,
Jesus Loves You Love Him Back:

www.lovehimbackbooks.com

Also available on Amazon

To do our part, *For His Glory Production Company* is proud to give a portion of the proceeds on each copy sold in paperback form to *Jesus Loves You Love Him Back.* This offer has no expiration date.

May God continue to richly bless all they do for the least of these...

About the Author

Patrick Higgins is the author of *The Pelican Trees, Coffee in Manila, The Unannounced Christmas Visitor* (Winner of the 2018 Readers' Favorite Gold Medal in Christian fiction), and the award-winning prophetic end-times series, *Chaos in the Blink of an Eye.* While the stories he writes all have different themes and take place in different settings, the one thread that links them all together is his heart for Jesus and his yearning for the lost.

With that in mind, it is his wish that the message his stories convey will greatly impact each reader, by challenging you not only to contemplate life on this side of the grave, but on the other side as well. After all, each of us will spend eternity at one of two places, based solely upon a single decision which must be made this side of the grave. That decision will be made crystal clear to each reader of his books.

Higgins is currently writing many other books, both fiction and non-fiction, including a sequel to *Coffee in Manila,* which will shine a bright, sobering light on the diabolical human trafficking industry.

Be sure to read Higgins' latest release, an award-winning prophetic series titled
Chaos In The Blink Of An Eye.
The first six installments are now available.

To contact author: patrick12272003@gmail.com
Like on Facebook: https://www.facebook.com/patrick12272003
https://www.facebook.com/TheUnannouncedChristmasVisitor
Twitter: https://twitter.com/patrick12272003
Instagram: https://www.instagram.com/patrick12272003
Amazon: https://www.amazon.com/Patrick-Higgins/e/B005ANHSU2
Goodreads: https://www.goodreads.com/author/show/10796904.Patrick_Higgins

What some readers are saying...

I didn't expect to like this book. Let's say I was concerned that it wouldn't live up to my hopes. Instead, I found a book that was well written, refreshing, and Christ-like. While some may see it as a bit preachy, sometimes we need reminders like that. I'm very glad I read this story, and I'd recommend it as important reading – Long Time AC – Vine Voice Reader onAmazon.

As an avid reader, I have read many stories in my 50 years. Through many genres and writing styles, I have loved the written word. In reading this story I know that the Word is the most important reading one can do in life. I thank the Creator that He is the supreme author!! This story truly touched my heart! I would and do recommend it to all who long for knowledge that God does indeed love us despite our many faults! On that, He will never waver!! Proof of that love is His risen Son!! I strongly encourage all who read this story to read the One story that truly matters! Read it, and let God's love and Grace move all to change the world for His glory! = Medina Jones - Amazon

Amazing read. It's not your typical Christmas story. This book really made me stop, think, question, and reflect. So much to think about. I thoroughly enjoyed the book. I am looking forward to see if Patrick Higgins' other books are all this good. – Suzy – Amazon.

Oh my gosh ! Do I have anything to say about this book? It was like the Holy Spirit was penning the words of this book Himself! So much revelation, and in a work of fiction at that! It felt like I was reading a Christian book about God rather than a Christian fiction! May God bless the author richly and use him for His glory! It made me question my Christianity... Praise God, I am a mission waiting to happen! – Kindle Customer on Amazon.

This is an amazing look at the redemption given by God! The characters in this book are incredibly well developed. There is so much variety that just about any person you will come across in real life is represented by one of them. The problems that they face are extremely believable and understandable. Some of them have deep seated doubts about God and life itself. Others are standing on the firm foundation of belief in Jesus Christ. I was captivated by all of the different interactions.
 The amount of scripture that is gone over is fantastic. I thoroughly enjoyed the in-depth look at the Bible itself and the truth that is found in it. There is a lot of soul searching and growth. It gave me a lot to think about as I sought God about my own life too. – Bookworm Debbie – Barnes and Noble.

A most incredible fiction book that required me to consider my relationship with God in a whole new way! 'Secular man boasts that his intellect alone is enough to provide the necessary means to eventually create a near-perfect world without the need for God.' The Jensen family found out that this statement is far from true.

This was a very well written story that uses many Bible verses to teach the promises of God and how these promises foretold His birth, death and ultimate plan for the salvation of man. Learning to give without expecting anything in return is a lesson we all can benefit from. In all, this book caused a great deal of thought about my own life and my willingness to live the way that God wants – BMACE – Barnes and Noble.

I have read the Chaos series, and love the way this author can draw me in to the story. This book about an unexpected visitor and his impact on a family in need of God's guidance, was a great read and rang true. We all need an unannounced visitor to remind us of God's love for us and our obligation to serve him joyfully and with our whole heart. I just know this is one book I will read over and over. – Csitzlar – Goodreads.

The Unannounced Christmas Visitor" by Patrick Higgins is without a doubt my favorite best fictional book about Christmas and the power of God's love that I have read this year. – Debbie – Goodreads.

WOW! WOW! WOW! This book is one of the top 10 for all time books I have read. When I walk away from a fiction book a better person then I know it will be a book I will be reading over and over again. I not only read this book but I highlighted parts of the e-book and it also got me to read Ecclesiastes (book in the Bible) and really sit down and really read it, like the people in the book did.

I recommend this book highly and to be it's not just a Christmas book but it can be read anytime during the year. We need to remember to be there for others all year long – Anne – Goodreads

A must read for all who seek deeper understanding of God's word. A riveting read, wanting to see how God will set up the circumstances that will transform this family and serve to glorify a growing ministry that helps to prompt all readers to join in and do their small part for all in their communities. – Sharon M. Guthrie – Goodreads

A book that keeps you guessing what is next. A fantastic novel that takes you on a Christmas adventure that is unbelievable with so much joy. A lesson of Christmas and God's love for all of us. A book that warms you all over and you will love reading – Virgie – Amazon.

217

A life-changing book! Mr Higgins, I was in great depression when I was reading your book. I lost God. You know, how you lose your cell phone, and panic starts to set in. You retrace your steps but to no avail. I felt like that when I lost God! Thank you for helping me find Him again – topgrog – Amazon.

An excellent book for those seeking an intellectual explanation of what being a Christian truly entails, or to the meaning of life as John in this novel was searching for. Also good insights into the life of homeless people – Lynn T – Amazon.

This is a great story backed with incredible biblical knowledge. Great read at Christmas or any time!! Loved it - great reminder of what's really important in life – Sullymom – Amazon.

A must read for all who seek deeper understand of God's Word! A riveting read, wanting to see how God will set up the circumstances that will transform this family and serve to glorify a growing ministry that helps to prompt all readers to join in and do their small part for all in their communities – Mummycat – Amazon.

A very touching book. It was a very good book. One of those books you want to keep and read every Christmas. It gives a whole new meaning to entertaining angels – Kelly I – Amazon.

Very insightful. If only we could all have an "unannounced Christmas visitor " to stir our weary souls when we need it most. Even though it's fiction, the scriptures speak loud and clear – Sheila Amazon.

A wonderful visitation! Outstanding & inspiring. The perfect reminder that calling oneself a Christian is not enough. One must perform acts of charity and love without concern for oneself in order to truly love and know Jesus – Katie – Amazon.

Indescribable! Wow. That's all I can say. If you're seeking, if you are feeling down and unworthy. If you want to find meaning for your life. Read this book – L O'C – Amazon.

There are so many answers packed in amid the entertainment of watching the family drama unfold. Light enough to make you feel happy, heavy enough to make you think – Amazon Customer.

Wow! This is by far the best novel I have read all year!!! I will not give the story away and will leave you with this....my heart has been changed forever! It made me laugh, made me cry, touched me in ways I cannot explain. It may be a novel, a fictional story but it is very much filled with The Truth – Kari B – Amazon.

59538881R00126

Made in the USA
Middletown, DE
11 August 2019